The School
at Thrush Green

The School
at Thrush Green

by Miss Read

ILLUSTRATIONS BY
John S. Goodall

HOUGHTON MIFFLIN COMPANY

BOSTON

1988

First American Edition 1988

Copyright © 1987 by Miss Read
All rights reserved.

For information about permission to reproduce selections from
this book, write to Permissions, Houghton Mifflin Company,
2 Park Street, Boston, Massachusetts 02108.

Library of Congress Cataloging-in-Publication Data

Read, Miss.
The school at Thrush Green.

I. Title.
PR6069.A42S36 1988 823'.914 88-9329
ISBN 0-395-46108-1

Printed in the United States of America

P 10 9 8 7 6 5 4 3 2 1

To
Betty and Vic
With Love

For personal reasons, John Goodall was unable to provide the illustrations for this book – apart from the jacket, from which the frontispiece is taken, and the drawings of the cat. Rather than publish the book without illustrations, the author and publishers – with John Goodall's agreement – have selected a number of illustrations from earlier *Thrush Green* novels all of which have been illustrated by John Goodall. It is hoped that the reader will appreciate the reasons for this, and we look forward to having John Goodall's illustrations in future Miss Read books.

Contents

Part One

Time To Go

1 Rough Weather

'JANUARY,' said Miss Watson, 'gives me the jim-jams!'

She jerked the sitting-room curtains together, shutting out the view of Thrush Green.

Firelight danced on the walls of the snug room, and shone upon the face of her friend Agnes Fogerty as she placed a log carefully at the top of the blazing coals.

The two ladies had lived in the school house at Thrush Green for several years, and had been colleagues for even longer. It was a happy relationship, for each middle-aged teacher felt respect and affection for the other.

In most matters Dorothy Watson, as headmistress, took command. She was a forthright and outspoken woman whose energy and enthusiasm had enriched the standing of Thrush Green school. As mistress of the school house she also took precedence over her companion when it came to any domestic decisions, and Agnes Fogerty was content that it should be so.

It was not that she always agreed with her headmistress's actions. Beneath her mouse-like appearance and timid ways, Agnes held strong views, but at this moment, with Dorothy's opinion of January, she entirely agreed.

'At its worst today,' she said. 'And the children are always so restless in a strong wind.'

A violent gust threw a spattering of rain against the

window at this point, and Miss Watson sat down in her armchair.

'Must blow itself out before morning,' she said, taking up her knitting.

All day Thrush Green had been buffeted by a howling gale and lashing rain. Rivulets rushed along the gutters and cascaded down the steep hill that led to the nearby town of Lulling. The windows of the stone Cotswold houses shuddered in the onslaught. Doors were wrenched from people's grasp, umbrellas blew inside out, and the chestnut trees along one side of the green groaned and tossed their dripping branches in this wild weather.

It had made life particularly exhausting for the two schoolteachers. Every time the classroom door opened, a score of papers fluttered to the floor pursued by delighted children. A vase of chestnut twigs which little Miss Fogerty was nurturing in order to show her children one day the fan-shaped young leaves and the interesting horseshoe-shaped scars where the old leaves had once been, was capsised by a sturdy infant intent on rescuing his drawing.

The ensuing chaos included a broken vase, a miniature Niagara down the front of the stationery cupboard, a sodden copy of *The Tale of Squirrel Nutkin* from Agnes's own library, and a great deal of unnecessary mayhem which was difficult to suppress.

Through the streaming windows the two teachers, in their respective classrooms, had watched the inhabitants of Thrush Green struggling to go about their daily affairs.

Mr Jones, landlord of The Two Pheasants hard by, had lost his hat when he was staggering outside with a heavy crate of beer cans. He pursued it, with a surprising turn of speed, across the grass, where it came to rest against the plinth of Nathaniel Patten's statue.

Molly Curdle, who lived in a cottage in the garden of the

finest house on Thrush Green, home of the Youngs, wheeled out her bicycle, and little Miss Fogerty was anxious on her behalf as she wobbled away townwards. Surely it was highly dangerous to cycle in such wicked weather! But then Agnes remembered that she had heard that Molly's father, Albert Piggott, the surly sexton who lived only yards from the school, was in bed with bronchitis and perhaps Molly was off to get him some medicine. No doubt his wife Nelly could have fetched it, but perhaps she too was ailing? With such conjectures are village folk made happy.

It was certainly a relief to be in the comfort of the school house at the end of such an exhausting day, and the fire was burning comfortingly.

Agnes opened a crack in a large piece of coal with an exploratory poker. A splendid yellow flame leapt out and she surveyed it with pleasure.

'I often think,' she mused aloud, 'that it must be trapped sunshine.'

'What is?' enquired Dorothy, lowering her knitting.

'Flames from the coal. After all, coal comes from very ancient forests, and it stands to reason that the trees must have seen sunshine. And when, after all these millions of years, we crack the coal – why, there it is!'

Dorothy, who was not given to such flights of fancy, considered Agnes's theory for some minutes. It might not be scientifically feasible, but it was really rather poetic.

She smiled indulgently upon her friend. 'It's a nice idea, dear. Now what about scrambled eggs for supper?'

Molly Curdle, tacking along Lulling High Street in the teeth of the gale, was indeed going to fetch some medicine for her father.

What a problem he was, thought Molly! Every winter now, it seemed, he had these spells of bronchial coughing.

His second wife Nelly could not be said to neglect him. Her cooking was as splendid as ever. Albert was offered luscious soups, casseroles, roasts, pies and puddings in abundance.

Nevertheless, thought Molly, swerving to dodge a roving Sealyham, it was a pity she was not at home more often. Nelly was now a partner in The Fuchsia Bush, a flourishing café in Lulling High Street, and her duties took her out from the house soon after eight in the morning, and her arrival home varied from five to seven o'clock.

Not that you could blame Nelly, Molly commented to herself. She could never really take to this step-mother, far too fat and vulgar for Molly's taste, but at least she took good care of Albert and not many would do that for someone as pig-headed as her father. This job at The Fuchsia Bush gave her some respite from Albert's constant moaning, and her salary was now the mainstay of the Piggott household.

By now she had reached the chemist's shop, and tried to lodge her bicycle against the kerb, but the wind made it impossible. She wheeled it across the pavement and leant it against the shop window.

'Not against the glass, please,' said a young woman peremptorily, and Molly pushed it wearily a few paces along to a brick pillar.

The chemist's assistant, resplendent in a white coat, watched smugly from the shelter of the door. When she caught sight of Molly, whose face was almost hidden in a sodden headscarf, her mood changed.

'Why, Moll, I never knew it was you! Come on in. You're fair soaked.'

Molly recognised a schoolfellow, Gertie, who had shared her desk at one time at Thrush Green school.

'I've come to get Dad's cough mixture. Doctor Lovell's given me a chit.'

She followed the snowy coat towards the back of the shop. It was marvellous to get out of the raging wind, and she was glad to sit down on a high stool by the counter.

'I'd have thought your ma could have come in for this,' observed the girl. 'She's only a few doors down the street.'

'She has to be at The Fuchsia Bush dead early. Long before Doctor Lovell's surgery opens. Anyway, he's my old dad. I don't really mind.'

The girl handed the prescription through a hatch behind her, and settled down for a few minutes' gossip.

'And how's Thrush Green then? I'm in one of them new houses behind the vicarage here. Don't get up your way often.'

'Much the same. The Two Pheasants is doing well. My Ben likes his job, Anne, my youngest, goes to play school, and our George is doing well with Miss Fogerty.'

'She still there? I heard as she and Miss Watson were thinking of retiring.'

'Well, that's been on the cards for some time, but they're both still at the school.'

'Proper bossy-boots that Miss Watson,' said Gertie, blowing some dust from a row of first-aid tins.

The hatch opened behind her, and a disembodied hairy hand passed out a large bottle. Gertie took it, the hatch slammed shut, and Molly looked in her purse for money.

'Hope it does the trick,' said Gertie. 'I'm not saying it will cheer him up, Moll. We all know him too well for that, don't we?'

Molly smiled. As a loyal daughter she had no intention of agreeing with this barbed remark, but nevertheless she knew it had the ring of truth.

People in Lulling and Thrush Green knew each other too well to be deceived, and there could be no hidden secrets in such a small community.

Whether this was a good thing or not, Molly could not

say, but she pondered on the problem as she set out again through the twig-littered street to her home at Thrush Green.

Meanwhile, Albert Piggott looked gloomily about his bedroom. Beside him on a small table stood a glass of water, a medicine bottle containing the last dose of cough mixture, a tin of cough lozenges, so strong that even Albert's beer-pickled tongue rebelled at their potency, and an egg-cup containing his wife's cure-all for ailing throats and chests, butter, sugar and lemon juice mixed together. At least, thought Albert grudgingly, Nelly's stuff tasted better than the rest.

He could hear the familiar sounds of pub activity going on beyond the window. The clattering of crates, Bob Jones's hearty voice and the occasional crash of the bar door made themselves heard above the roaring of the wind in the trees surrounding the churchyard opposite his cottage.

If only he were that much fitter he would darn well get out of this bed, and have a pint with the rest of them! But what was the use? Any minute now Molly would be in to fuss over him, and that dratted doctor had said he'd call. Trust him to come if he ever tried to go next door! He'd read the riot act if he even found his patient out of bed, let alone abroad!

Albert remembered his old mother had always maintained that doctors waited around the corner until a hot meal was dished up, and then they knocked at the door to create the maximum confusion within.

It was a hard life, sighed Albert. Here he was, for at least another week, living on slops, and not the right sort either. And then, he supposed gloomily, he would not be fit for cleaning the church or tidying the churchyard for weeks after that.

It was a good thing Nelly brought home a decent pay packet at the end of each week. His own earnings had halved over the last year, and if he felt as wobbly as he did now, what hopes of work in the future?

He pondered on his wife. True, she was no oil-painting, and had a temper like old Nick himself at times, but she still cooked a good meal, and brought in the money.

And heaven alone knew how important that was these days, with the price of a pint going up so alarmingly.

Doctor Lovell finished his surgery stint, and battled his way to his car, case in hand.

January was always a beast of a month, he mused, setting the windscreen wipers going, but this year it seemed more detestable than ever.

He decided to visit a family at Nidden before coping with the Thrush Green round. Chicken-pox was rife, and he was concerned about the year-old baby of the house who had seemed unusually listless when he had called the day before.

He planned to get back about midday to see Albert Piggott and one of his patients in the recently built old people's home, known as Rectory Cottages, on Thrush Green. With any luck he should be in time to have lunch at home with Ruth his wife.

The lane to Nidden was awash. Sheets of water flowed across its surface, and the ditches each side of the road were full. Heaven help us if it freezes, thought John Lovell.

The gale had brought down scores of small branches, and one large one which lay more than half-way across the road. It could cause an accident, and the good doctor drew into the side of the road, and emerged into the howling wind.

The branch was sodden and heavy. His gloves were soon soaked and covered with slime, and it was hard work

lugging the awkward object to a safer place on the grass
verge. By the time it had been dragged out of everyone's
path, John was thoroughly out of breath, and glad to
return to the shelter of his car.

'Too much flab,' he said aloud, fastening his seat belt
across the offending flesh. He would have to cut down
on the helpings of delectable puddings Ruth made so
well.

The hamlet of Nidden seemed to have suffered even
more severely than Thrush Green. A chicken house lay on
its side in one of the gardens. A bird-table was askew in
another, and a plastic bucket rolled about in the road.
Somebody's tea towel was fluttering in a hedge, and the
wind screamed alarmingly in the trees above.

He wondered if the mother of his patients would hear
his knocking above the bedlam around him, but she must
have seen him arrive for the door soon opened, admitting a
swirl of dead leaves into the hall.

'Come in, doctor. I'll be glad to see the back of January,
I can tell you!'

'Won't we all,' responded John Lovell.

It was later than he had hoped when at last he returned to
look in on Albert Piggott.

Molly had just taken up a tray with a bowl of soup, a
slice of bread, and some stewed apple for her father when
they heard the doctor's tread on the stairs.

'Just like my old ma always said,' grumbled Albert,
putting the tray to one side. 'Waits till the grub's ready,
then the blighters come.'

'And how's the patient today?' asked John entering.

'None the better for seeing you,' replied Albert. 'I was
just goin' to have me bit of dinner.'

'Well, I shan't keep you two minutes,' said the doctor.
'Just want to listen to those wheezy tubes again.'

'I'll go and keep the soup hot,' said Molly, vanishing with the bowl.

Albert bared his chest reluctantly.

'You're a lucky chap to have two good women looking after you,' said John, adjusting his stethoscope.

'No more'n they should do,' growled Albert. 'I've done enough for them in me time.'

The doctor applied his instrument to Albert's skinny chest.

'Cor! That's perishing cold!' gasped his patient. 'Enough to give a chap the pneumonics.'

The doctor smiled, as he went about his business. How long now, he wondered, since he first encountered this most irascible of his patients? A fair number of years, before he had married Ruth and settled so happily at Thrush Green.

'You'll do,' he said at length, buttoning the old man's pyjama jacket. 'You could do with a shawl or cardigan round your shoulders. There's a fine old draught from that window when the wind's in that quarter.'

'Can I get up then?'

'Not for a day or two. Tell me where to find you a woolly.'

He made his way towards a chest of drawers.

'I'll tell Molly to look one out. Don't want you scrabbling through my stuff.'

The doctor laughed. 'I'll tell her myself on the way down. Now you can stay there, take your medicine, drink plenty of warm liquid — *and not any alcohol* — and don't make a darn nuisance of yourself, or I'll put you in hospital.'

He was pleased to see that this awful threat seemed to subdue his recalcitrant patient and he made his way downstairs.

Molly was standing by the stove watching the soup. He

mentioned the shawl, and then added, 'You and Nelly do a fine job between you, and I know you get little thanks for it. He's coming along all right. We'll let him out when the weather changes.'

'If it ever does,' responded Molly, letting him out into the elements.

Some of the newest inhabitants of Thrush Green were the oldest, for recently a block of old people's homes, designed by the doctor's architect brother-in-law Edward Young, had been built on the site of a former rectory.

Here, seven little houses and their inhabitants were looked after by Jane and Bill Cartwright, the wardens, who lived in the last house of the eight.

Jane had been brought up in Thrush Green, had been a nurse at Lulling Cottage Hospital and then a sister at a Yorkshire hospital where she had met and married Bill. They were both pleased to be appointed to the post at Thrush Green and were doing a fine job among their charges.

While Doctor Lovell was speeding home to a late lunch, Jane Cartwright was sitting with one of the old people. Miss Muriel Fuller had been a headmistress at the little school at Nidden for many years, and was now thoroughly enjoying her retirement in this small house.

Unfortunately, a septic throat was causing her acute pain and loss of voice, which is why Jane, although a trained nurse, had thought it wise to get the doctor's opinion.

'I was sure I saw his car outside the Piggotts' house,' whispered Miss Fuller. 'I can't think why he didn't come over here. Perhaps he's forgotten.' She looked alarmed.

'I'm sure he hasn't,' said Jane sturdily. 'Perhaps he had an urgent call. An accident, you know. Something that couldn't wait.'

How all these professional people hang together, thought

Miss Fuller wearily! 'The point is,' she whispered, 'I'm due to take my remedial class tomorrow morning at the school, and I ought to let Miss Watson know.'

'Now don't you worry about that,' replied Jane, patting the patient's hand. 'As soon as the doctor's been I shall telephone Miss Watson. In any case, they won't be home until four at the earliest, and I'm sure he will have called long before that.'

Miss Fuller nodded, and reached for a very nasty throat lozenge. The more unpleasant the taste, the more good it does, she remembered her grandmother saying. But then her grandmother had always been one of the fire-and-brimstone school, and thoroughly enjoyed being miserable.

Jane rose to go. 'I'm just going to see the others, and I'll come along as soon as Doctor Lovell arrives.'

Miss Fuller nodded. What with her throat and the lozenge, speech was quite impossible.

'Now who can that be!' exclaimed Dorothy Watson when the telephone rang.

She heaved herself from the armchair and made her way to the hall. A freezing draught blew in as she opened the sitting-room door, and sparks flew up the chimney from a burning log.

Agnes closed the door quietly and hoped that the call would not be a lengthy one. She would have liked to spare dear Dorothy the bother of answering the call, but as headmistress and the true householder it was only right that she should take precedence.

Within a few minutes her friend returned, and held out her hands to the blaze.

'That hall is like an ice-well,' she shuddered. 'Of course, the wind is full on the front porch, and fairly whistling under the door. I fear that this house is getting too old for comfort.'

'Anything important?' queried Agnes. It was so like Dorothy to omit to tell one the main message.

'Only Jane Cartwright. Muriel Fuller has laryngitis and won't be able to come along tomorrow.'

'Poor Miss Fuller!' cried Agnes. 'It can be so painful! Has the doctor been?'

'So I gather. Anyway, it need not make much difference to the timetable. After all, Muriel's visits are very much a fringe benefit.' She picked up her knitting and began to count the stitches.

Agnes considered this last remark. It seemed rather callous, she thought. Her own soft heart was much perturbed at the thought of Miss Fuller's suffering, but Dorothy, of course, had to think of the school's affairs first, and it was only natural that she saw things from the practical point of view.

'Eighty-four!' pronounced Miss Watson, and gazed into the fire. 'You know, Agnes,' she said at length, 'I really think it is time we retired.'

'To bed, do you mean? It's surely much too early!'

'No, no, Agnes!' tutted Dorothy. 'I mean retired properly. We've been talking of it for years now, and the office knows full well that we have only stayed on to oblige the folk there.'

'But we've nowhere to go,' exclaimed Agnes. 'It was one of the reasons we gave for staying on.'

'Yes, yes, I know we couldn't get what we wanted at Barton-on-Sea, but I think we should redouble our efforts. I really don't think I could stand another winter at Thrush Green. Sitting in the hall just now brought it home to me.'

'So what should we do?'

'First of all, I shall write to those estate agents, Better and Better, at Barton, and chivvy them up. They know perfectly well that we want a two-bedroomed bungalow with a small garden, handy for the church and post office and shops. Why they keep sending particulars of top floor flats and converted lighthouses heaven alone knows, but they will have to pull their socks up.'

'Yes, I'm sure that's the first step,' agreed Agnes. 'I will write if it's any help.'

'You'd be much too kind,' said her headmistress. 'I think I could manage something sharper.'

'You may be right,' murmured Agnes. 'But when should we give in our notice?'

'The sooner the better,' said Dorothy firmly. 'We'll arrange to go at the end of the summer term. That gives everyone plenty of time to make new appointments.'

'We shall miss Thrush Green,' said Agnes.

'We shall miss it even more if we succumb to pneumonia in this house,' replied Dorothy tartly. 'We can always visit here from Barton. We shall have all the time in the world, and there is an excellent coach service in the summer.'

She caught sight of her friend's woebegone face. 'Cheer up, Agnes! It will be something to look forward to while we endure this winter weather. What about a warming drink?'

'I'll go and heat some milk,' said Agnes. 'Or would you like coffee?'

'I think a glass of something apiece would do the trick,' replied Dorothy, 'and then we shan't have to leave the fire.'

She rose herself and went to fetch their comfort from a corner cupboard.

2 Dorothy Watson Takes Steps

THE rumbustious January weather continued for the rest of the week, and the inhabitants of Lulling and Thrush Green were as tired of its buffeting as the rest of the Cotswold villages were.

But on Saturday morning the wind had dropped, and a wintry sun occasionally cast a gleam upon a thankful world.

Miss Watson and Miss Fogerty agreed that the weekly wash would benefit from a spell in the fresh air, and Agnes was busy pegging out petticoats, night-gowns and other garments, when she was hailed by a well-known voice on the other side of the hedge. It was her old friend Isobel, wife of Harold Shoosmith, who lived next door.

When Agnes had heard that her old college friend of many years was going to be her neighbour, her joy was unbounded. The two students had soon discovered that they both hailed from the Cotswolds, and this drew them together.

Isobel's father was a bank manager at Stow-on-the-Wold, and Agnes's a shoemaker in Lulling. It meant that they could visit each other during the holidays, and the friendship grew stronger over the years.

Marriage took Isobel to Sussex so that family affairs prevented her from visiting Thrush Green as often as she would have liked. But on the death of her husband she had renewed her close association with Agnes and her other Cotswold friends and, now that her children were out in the world, she had decided to find a small house in the neighbourhood.

But marriage to Harold Shoosmith, who had retired to Thrush Green some years earlier, had provided a home and a great deal of mutual contentment, and everyone agreed that the Shoosmiths were an asset to any community.

'Isn't it wonderful to have no wretched wind?' called Isobel, advancing to a gap in the hedge, the better to see her neighbour. 'How are you both?'

'Very well. And you?'

'Fed up with being stuck indoors. Harold has battled out now and again, but I really couldn't face it. One thing though, I've caught up with no end of letters, so I suppose that's a bonus.'

Agnes wondered whether she should say anything about their proposed retirement but, cautious as ever, decided that dear Dorothy might not approve at this early stage of the project. She remained silent on this point, but joined her friend by the gap.

'Not snowdrops already?' she cried with pleasure. 'Now isn't that cheering!'

'And aconites too at the end of the garden,' Isobel told her. 'And my indoor hyacinths are at their best. Come round, Agnes, when you have a minute and see them.'

Agnes promised to do so, and the two ladies chatted for five minutes, glad to see each other again after their enforced incarceration.

'Well, I must go and see about lunch,' said Isobel at length.

'And I must finish my pegging out,' agreed Agnes, and the two women parted company.

What a warming thing friendship was, thought Agnes, fastening two pairs of respectable Vedonis knickers on the line. Even such a brief glimpse of dear Isobel enlivened the day. She would miss her sorely when the time came to move to Barton.

✵   ✵   ✵

While little Miss Fogerty was busy with the washing, Nelly Piggott was in The Fuchsia Bush's kitchen in Lulling High Street.

Here she was engaged in supervising the decoration of two large slabs of sponge cake ready to be cut into neat squares for the afternoon teas for which The Fuchsia Bush was renowned.

The new recruit was a nervous sixteen-year-old whose hand shook as she spread coffee-flavoured water icing over the first of the sponges.

Lord love old Ireland, thought Nelly! Would the girl never learn? She had come with a glowing report from her school's domestic science teacher, and another, equally fulsome, from her last post. Glad to see the back of her no doubt, thought Nelly grimly.

'If you dip your knife into the warm water more often,' said Nelly, striving to be patient, 'it won't drag the icing.'

The girl flopped the palette knife into the jug and transferred a small rivulet of water on to her handiwork.

Unable to bear it any longer, Nelly took over and began to create order out of chaos. To give her her due she bit back the caustic remarks trembling on her tongue.

'You fetch the walnut halves,' she commanded, 'and I'll leave you to space them out when this has begun to set.'

The girl fled, and at that moment Nelly's employer and partner at The Fuchsia Bush entered the kitchen from the restaurant.

'Can you leave that a moment? Bertha Lovelock is in the shop and wants to know if we can send in lunch – an *inexpensive* lunch – for three today.'

Nelly gave a snort, drew one final steady blade across her masterpiece, and followed Mrs Peters.

The Misses Lovelock were three ancient spinsters who lived next door to The Fuchsia Bush in a splendid Georgian house in which all three had been born and which they had inhabited all their lives.

Although quite comfortably off, and the possessors of many valuable antiques, the sisters were renowned for their parsimony. No one knew this better than Nelly Piggott, who had 'helped out' for a time before finding permanent work next door.

Nelly still remembered, with a shudder, the appalling meals she had been expected to cook from inferior scraps which she would not have offered to a starving cat. The memory too of a tablespoonful of metal polish, intended for a score of brass and copper articles, still rankled, and the meagre dab of furniture polish with which the dining-room table and chairs were meant to be brought to mirror-like condition.

Nowadays, she rejoiced in catering and cooking amidst the plenty of The Fuchsia Bush. She had grown confident in the knowledge that her work was appreciated and that, as a partner, she was enjoying the fruits of her expertise.

She approached her former old employer secure in the knowledge that here she had the upper hand.

'Good morning, Miss Lovelock. Lunch for three, I gather? You'll take it here, I imagine, so I'll book a table, shall I?'

Nelly felt pretty sure that this was not what Miss Bertha really wanted. For a time, when the three old ladies had been quite seriously ill, the doctor had suggested that their midday meal might be sent in from next door.

It had not been easy to find someone free at exactly the right moment to take in a hot meal, but Nelly and Mrs Peters had felt sorry for the Lovelocks and had been obliging.

They were glad though when the arrangement ended. The Lovelock sisters, anxious to stop the expense, had cancelled the lunches as soon as possible, to the relief of all.

But now, it seemed, the Misses Lovelock were attempting to use the staff of The Fuchsia Bush as if it were their own, and Nelly was determined to nip this plan in the bud.

'No, Nelly, that is not quite what I meant. Miss Violet is in bed with her chest – '

Not that she would be in bed without it, thought Nelly reasonably.

'And neither Miss Ada nor I really feel up to coping with the cooking and shopping,' continued Miss Bertha. 'It would be a great help if you could send in a hot meal each day as you did before.'

Nelly assumed an expression of doubt and regret. 'It can't be done, Miss Lovelock,' she said. 'We haven't enough staff to make a regular arrangement like that. As you know, we're run off our feet here at lunch time.'

'But you did it before!'

'That was an emergency. We did it to oblige the doctor as well as you, but it couldn't be a permanent arrangement.'

'Well, that's very provoking,' said Miss Bertha, turning pink. The Lovelock sisters almost always got their own way.

'If I might suggest,' said Nelly, 'that you was to advertise for a cook-general in the paper, you might get suited quite quickly. Or the Labour might help.'

'The Labour?' echoed the old lady, looking mystified.

'Exchange,' added Nelly.

'Exchange?' echoed Miss Bertha.

'Job Centre like,' amplified Nelly. 'Up near the Corn Exchange.'

Miss Bertha picked up her gloves from the counter and began to put them on with extreme care, smoothing each finger. Her mouth was trembling and Nelly's kind heart was moved.

'Tell you what,' she said. 'You let me know if you'd like

me to look out for someone when you've had a talk with Miss Ada and Miss Violet.'

'Thank you, Nelly,' said Miss Bertha. 'Most kind. We shouldn't want a great deal of cooking done. Just something light.'

'I know that,' said Nelly, with feeling, as she opened the door for her.

It was dark when Nelly toiled up the hill to Thrush Green, but it was a relief to find the air so still and the stars already twinkling from a clear sky.

Albert, still in his dressing gown and slippers, was sitting by the fire, but he had put on the kettle Nelly noted with approval.

'Well, and how have you been getting on today?' she enquired, sitting down heavily on a kitchen chair.

'Had a look at the paper. Took me medicine. Took a dekko out of the winder. This sunshine's brought 'em all

out. Even old Tom Hardy, over at the Home, took out Polly for a walk on the green.'

'That dog must be on its last legs,' commented Nelly. 'Nearly as shaky as old Tom.'

The kettle set up a piercing whistle, and she rose to attend to it.

'I near enough went next door for a drink,' said Albert, 'but our Molly came in and put a stop to it.'

'So I should hope! What'll I say to the doctor if you catch your death?'

'Won't matter much what you say,' rejoined Albert morosely, 'if I'm a corpse, will it? Molly says he's coming on Monday, and may let me get out again, if I don't go too far.'

'Well, next door's about as far as you'll want to go anyway,' replied Nelly, stirring the teapot vigorously.

'There was a car stopped over by Mrs Bailey's,' observed Albert changing the subject. 'Some young chap got out.'

'Meter man, most like.'

'No. I knows him. Looked like that nephew of hers, Richard.'

'He'll be about as welcome as a sick headache,' pronounced Nelly. 'What's he come badgering his poor aunt for, I wonder?'

It would not be long before Nelly, Albert and the rest of Thrush Green knew the purpose of Richard's visit to Dr Bailey's widow. Meanwhile, there could only be the pleasurable conjecture of diverse opinions on the subject.

That weekend, there was considerable literary activity at the school house as Dorothy Watson took up her pen to write to the estate agents at Barton-on-Sea, who had the honour to be dealing with her affairs. She had chosen them from many in the area as she thought their name, Better and Better, sounded hopeful.

Agnes was busy sewing together the pieces of a baby's matinée jacket, in between bobbing in and out of the kitchen to keep an eye on a cake in the oven.

As she stitched she listened, in some alarm, to Dorothy's occasional snort as her pen hurried over the paper. She did so hope that the letter was *courteous*. After all, civility cost nothing, as her old father had so often said, and really one did not want to antagonise the estate agents at Barton on whom they were relying for their future comfort. Dear Dorothy could be so *downright* at times, and not everyone realised how kind her heart really was.

She was about to rise and go into the kitchen to stab the cake with a skewer, when Dorothy threw down her pen, leant back and said proudly, 'Now listen to this, Agnes.'

I write on behalf of my friend Miss Agnes Fogerty and myself. For some time now we have had our names on your books, and, to be frank, have had very poor service.

Although all the particulars of our needs are with you, let me repeat them. We need a two-bedroomed bungalow, on a level site, with a small garden. It must be within walking distance, i.e. no further than half a mile from shops, post office and church (C of E).

It must be in a good state of repair, as we hope to move in this summer, preferably in July.

Please do not waste your time and ours by sending particulars of outrageously useless properties such as the converted windmill, the granary with outside staircase and the underground flat made from a wine cellar, which were enclosed in your last communication.

I expect to hear from you by return.

Yours sincerely.

She turned to smile at Agnes. 'How's that? Can you think of anything else, Agnes dear?'

Agnes looked hunted. Her hands were shaking with agitation as she put the baby's coat aside.

'Well, I do think it was wise to repeat what we need, Dorothy, but I just wonder if that last paragraph isn't the tiniest bit – er – '

'Strong? That's what I wanted! It's about time they were jerked up.'

'Yes, I know, dear, but we don't want them to think us *unreasonable.*'

'Unreasonable? They're the ones that are unreasonable! Fancy sending two middle-aged ladies those absurd properties! We told them about my hip and that we are retiring. We're not a couple of mountain goats to go skipping up an outside staircase in a howling gale, and *with no handrail*, as far as one could see from that inadequate photograph. Or to go burrowing down a flight of steps into the black hole of Calcutta like that idiotic wine cellar!'

Dorothy's neck was becoming red, a sure sign of danger, and little Miss Fogerty knew from experience that it was time to prevaricate.

'My cake!' she exclaimed, hurrying out.

She busied herself for some minutes with her creation, allowing Dorothy to calm down before returning to the sitting-room. A delicious scent of almond cake followed her into the room.

'Something smells good,' said Dorothy smiling. 'Well, Agnes dear, let's go through the last paragraph and perhaps temper it a little before I make a fair copy.'

She picked up the letter and began to read. Agnes resumed her sewing, trying to hide her agitation.

It was not until the next day that she realised that she had sewn in the sleeves inside out, and would have to face a good deal of tedious unpicking.

But at least, she told herself, it was really a small price to pay in the face of making enemies of a reputable estate agent.

The young man, whom Albert Piggott and various other observers had noticed calling on Winnie Bailey, was indeed her nephew Richard, and his visit occasioned her some alarm.

She discussed this with Doctor Lovell the next day when he paid his customary morning visit after surgery next door.

Winnie's husband Donald Bailey had been the much-loved doctor at Thrush Green for many years, and John Lovell had become his junior partner when the older man's health began to fail.

It had been a happy relationship, and John deeply appreciated his partner's wife's kindness. When Donald died, he kept on the same surgery which the two men had shared and made sure that he did all he could for Donald's widow.

He knew a good deal about Richard. He was a brilliant young scientist and mathematician, completely selfish and inclined to batten on Winnie whenever he was in difficulties. His marriage had collapsed a year or two previously, and his young child was with his wife Fenella and her current paramour Roger. John Lovell, who liked a tidy life himself, had little time for Richard's vagaries, but he knew that Winnie loved her nephew, despite his gross selfishness.

'You see,' Winnie told him, 'he is absolutely set on buying a little house here or in Lulling. In some ways I can see that it would be a good thing. He really needs a base to keep his things and to prepare his lectures and so on. And of course, I should enjoy seeing him now and again, but – '

'But?' prompted John.

'Well, he wants to stay here until he finds something, and I simply can't have him here for any length of time. Jenny and I have all we can do to cope with our own little chores, and Richard would be in and out at all hours, needing meals and so on.'

'Surely you told him that? He knows well enough how you are placed.'

'Of course I told him, but you know Richard. He doesn't want to hear. I said I'd see if I could find lodgings somewhere handy, and would let him know.'

'Give me his number,' said John, 'and I'll ring him myself today. He can hear your doctor's honest opinion that neither you nor Jenny is fit enough to cope with him.'

Winnie looked perturbed. 'Oh, John! I don't know if I should let you. After all, he is my nephew, and it seems so awful to turn the poor boy away from my doorstep.'

'He can easily find another doorstep,' replied John firmly. 'He's rolling in money. What's wrong with a hotel room? Leave this to me, Winnie. I promise to be quite civil to him, but you need some support over this little problem.'

'It's at times like this,' confessed Winnie, 'that I miss Donald.'

'You're not the only one,' the young doctor assured her, setting off on his rounds.

3   News Travels Fast

NELLY Piggott did not forget her promise to Bertha Lovelock, made in a weak moment and much regretted.

It soon became apparent, however, that there would be no ugly rush for the proposed post of cook-general at the Lovelocks' establishment.

'No fear!' said the first woman approached by Nelly.

'Not Pygmalion likely!' said the second.

Nelly put her problem to her friend Mrs Jenner, as they walked to bingo one evening. Mrs Jenner was the mother of Jane Cartwright, warden of the old people's homes, and a much respected character locally.

Unlike Nelly, she had known Lulling, Nidden and Thrush Green all her life, and the doings of the Misses Lovelock were old history to her.

'My dear,' she told Nelly, 'don't waste your time and energy. No one is going to take on a job like that these days. Those old things are still living in the past when they could get some poor little fourteen-year-old to skivvy for them for five shillings a week. You know yourself how mean they are, and the rest of Lulling knows too.'

'That's true enough,' agreed Nelly.

'They'll just have to face facts,' went on Mrs Jenner. 'After all, they're lucky enough to live next door to The Fuchsia Bush, and have enough money to eat there daily without breaking the bank. And if things get really tough for them they will have to apply for a home help.'

'Well, I just felt I should make an attempt, as I'd promised,' said Nelly.

'And so you have,' replied Mrs Jenner. 'Now let them do their own worrying. From what I know of those old dears they really don't deserve a great deal of sympathy.'

The two friends entered the bingo hall in Lulling High Street, content to shelve the problem in the face of an evening's pleasure.

Doctor Lovell too had been keeping a promise, and had rung Winnie Bailey's nephew.

It had not been easy to get hold of Richard, but he tracked him down one evening.

Richard sounded suspicious and uncommonly haughty.

'I'm not sure why you are telling me this,' he exclaimed, when John began his tale. 'After all, she is my aunt, and I know how she's placed quite as well as you do. If I may say so, I find your interference somewhat offensive.'

Doctor Lovell, no coward, was firm in his reply.

'I don't think you do know as much as I do. Winnie is now in her seventies, and Jenny not much younger. They are neither of them in the best of health and they have quite enough to do coping with everyday living. A visit, no matter how short, would be too much for them.'

There was a snort from the other end of the line. 'What rubbish! She said she would be delighted to have me there for a few days.'

'Naturally, she would. She is fond of you and would do all she could to fall in with your requests. My point is that you should not make any. She is my patient, and so is Jenny. I won't see their health put at risk.'

There was another snort.

'If you must stay in the area,' went on John remorselessly, 'I'm sure you could get a room at The Fleece. I can give you the telephone number.'

'I *know* the telephone number, thank you very much,' replied Richard stuffily, and rang off.

'Well, I hope that's choked him off,' said John, replacing the receiver. 'And if it hasn't, I'll have the greatest pleasure in knocking his block off.'

News of Richard's visit and his intention to find somewhere to live locally was soon common knowledge at Thrush Green. How this came about was the usual mystery, for Winnie had only mentioned the matter to Jenny and her old friend and neighbour Ella Bembridge, and John Lovell had said nothing, not even to Ruth, his wife.

Nevertheless, speculation was rife, and sympathy for Winnie Bailey's predicament was general.

Betty Bell, who kept the school clean and rushed round the Shoosmiths' house next door twice a week, told Isobel all about it as she wound the vacuum cleaner cord into the tight figure-of-eight which Harold so detested.

'Too soft by half Mrs Bailey is,' she pronounced. 'That nephew of hers gets away with murder over there.'

'Oh come!' protested Isobel.

'Well, near enough,' conceded Betty, crashing the vacuum cleaner into a cupboard and capsising two tins of polish, a basket full of clothes pegs and half a dozen bottling jars. 'Luckily, Doctor Lovell's given him a piece of his mind, so maybe he'll stop bothering his poor auntie.'

She sat back on her haunches and began to repair the damage. 'And anyway,' she continued, 'what's he want coming to live here? He's all over the place, from what I hear. America, China, Bristol, Oxford, lecturing or something. Waste of money, I'd say, to have a home.'

'He needs somewhere to keep his things,' Isobel pointed out.

'But why here? It's all coming and going, isn't it? You heard as they're giving up next door?'

Isobel felt shocked. 'Are you sure?'

'Positive. Miss Watson said so. In the summer, she said.'

Isobel could not help wondering if this were true. Surely, Agnes would have told her if this were so.

'Awful lot of clobber you keep in here,' commented Betty, rising from her task. 'You really want it all?'

'It has to go somewhere, Betty,' said her employer. 'Like Richard, you know.'

The house was remarkably peaceful after Betty Bell had departed on her bicycle and Isobel, still a little perturbed by her news, went in search of Harold.

She found him in his study with his old friend Charles Henstock, rector of Thrush Green and vicar of Lulling.

'What a nice surprise! Is Dimity around?'

'No, she's busy shopping in the town and calling at the Lovelocks.'

'Not for lunch, I hope,' said Harold.

Charles laughed. 'No, no. Nothing like that. I have to be home at twelve-thirty for lunch, Dimity told me.'

Harold glanced at his watch. 'Well, far be it from me to speed a parting guest, particularly such a welcome one as you, Charles, but it's nearly ten to one now.'

'Good heavens!' exclaimed the vicar, much flustered. 'I must run for it. Can I leave the upkeep account with you then?'

'Of course you can, and don't worry about it. I'm sure there's some simple explanation about the discrepancy.'

Charles was busy collecting his gloves, scarf, hat and a brown paper bag bulging dangerously with over-ripe bananas.

'Well, thank you, thank you, my dear fellow. I don't know how I'd get on without you.'

He hastened to the door, and made for his car. Isobel and Harold waved him off.

'What's worrying the dear old boy?' asked Isobel.

'He has just over fifty pounds in the tobacco tin he keeps the Thrush Green Church upkeep money in, and his accounts say he should have just over five hundred.'

'That's worrying!'

'Not with Charles's arithmetic. He never has been any good with noughts. I'll soon sort it out.'

Over lunch, Isobel told him about Betty's disclosure.

'It seems so odd. Not that I've seen a great deal of Agnes and Dorothy, but I did have a natter over the hedge recently and I'm sure Agnes would have told me.'

'Probably forgot,' said Harold equably. 'You'll know soon enough.'

It seemed that almost everyone knew about the ladies' retirement plans, other than Isobel.

Not that Agnes had told anyone, for she still felt obliged to keep silent about things until Dorothy deemed otherwise.

It was some shock to her, therefore, when three of her young charges, four mothers, Betty Bell, the milkman and Mr Jones the publican mentioned the subject all in the course of one day.

She mentioned the matter to Dorothy that evening.

'Oh yes!' said that lady carelessly. 'I did tell the office, of course, and I believe I mentioned it to Betty Bell a day or two ago. No harm done, is there?'

'Well, no, I suppose not,' said Agnes doubtfully, 'but I have been particularly careful to say nothing. Not even to Isobel,' she added.

It was plain that she was upset, and Dorothy was quick to apologise.

'It was thoughtless of me, and I should have realised how the news goes through this place like a bush fire. I really am deeply sorry, Agnes dear. I had no idea that it was putting you into an awkward position. Anyway, it's now common knowledge that we are retiring in the summer, so we can be quite open about it.'

Agnes smiled her forgiveness. 'I will have a word with Isobel when I see her,' she said. 'I shouldn't like her to hear our news from somebody else first.'

'Why not telephone now?' suggested her friend. 'The sooner the better. After all, she may well be told by someone else very soon.'

If not already, she said to herself, watching Agnes roll up her knitting before going to the telephone.

Really, it was exasperating! Was *anything* private in a village? And would Barton-on-Sea be equally enthralled by its neighbours' affairs?

Time alone would tell.

Luckily for Charles Henstock, Dimity too had been delayed, so that he was not late for his meal.

'And how are the Lovelock girls?' he enquired, using the usual Lulling euphemism for the three ancient sisters.

'Worried about help in the house,' answered Dimity. 'Well, perhaps not so much *the help* as having to pay for it.'

'Have they advertised?'

'No, I don't think so. But they've asked Nelly Piggott and they are wondering if The Fuchsia Bush would put a postcard in the window.'

Charles, who could not help thinking that both these aids would cost nothing, dismissed the thought as unworthy and uncharitable, and forbore to comment.

'They told me, by the way,' went on his wife, 'that Miss Watson and Miss Fogerty are retiring at the end of the school year.'

'Then we must start thinking about some little celebration to mark the occasion. I mean,' he added, feeling that this could have been better expressed, 'they have both been so much respected and admired all these years, that I'm sure Thrush Green will want to honour them in some way.'

'A sort of bunfight and presentation of a clock?'

'Well, something like that,' agreed Charles, feeling that perhaps dear Dimity had over-simplified the matter to the point of banality. 'We shall have to consult various people and come up with something suitable.'

'I should ask them what they would like,' said Dimity, always practical. 'You know how difficult it is to find houseroom for some of those presents you've been given over the years. I mean, who wants a silver inkstand with cut-glass inkwells these days? And that black marble clock like the Parthenon has to be kept in the spare bedroom. And as for those silver-plated fish servers the Scouts gave you, well, I don't think they've been used more than twice in twenty years. No, Charles, I should see that Agnes and Dorothy get something they really need. Like money, say.'

'I'll bear it in mind,' the rector assured her.

February, everyone agreed, was much more cheerful than January at Thrush Green. It was true that the first few days had been dark and foggy, but the relief from the battering winds of the first month of the year had made even the gloomy days quite welcome.

But by St Valentine's day there were a few signs of spring. Clumps of brave snowdrops, first espied by Agnes across the Shoosmiths' hedge, were to be seen in many cottage gardens. Aconites, their golden faces circled with green ruffs, responded to the sunlight and good gardeners were already making plans to put in new potatoes, broad beans and peas as soon as the ground was warm enough.

Winnie Bailey thought how hopeful everything seemed as she had one of her first walks of the year.

She set off up the road to Nidden, noting the activity of the little birds, chaffinches, sparrows, starlings and an

occasional robin, darting from hedge to hedge or pecking busily at the grit on the edge of the road. Soon there would be nests and young birds, butterflies and bees to add to all the joys of early summer. Winnie felt a surge of happiness at the thought.

It had been a long hard winter and the older she grew the more she dreaded the bitter cold of the Cotswolds in winter. She half-envied the two schoolteachers planning to move to the south coast, but she knew that she would never emulate them. Her whole married life had been spent at Thrush Green. The house held many memories and every mile around her home was crowded with remembered incidents. The cottages she passed were the homes of old friends. The shepherd, to whom she waved across the field on her right, had brought Donald from his bed one snowy night. It was a breech birth and Mrs Jenner, the midwife, had sent an urgent message for help. That waving figure, knee-deep in his flock, must now be forty years old.

She turned along a bridle-path on her left. It was very quiet between the trees. The small leaves of the honey-suckle were a vivid green. The buds on the pewter-grey ash twigs were black as jet. A few celandines had opened on a sunny bank.

Before long she was skirting Lulling Woods and beginning to feel tired. There was no doubt about it, she could not walk the distances she once had done. She resolved to call on her old and eccentric friend, Dotty Harmer, whose cottage was now in sight. She had much to talk about, and she might even mention this worrying business of Richard's move. Sometimes Dotty was uncommonly shrewd, despite her odd ways.

The door was opened by Connie, Dotty's niece. Her husband, Kit Armitage, stood beside her.

'What a lovely surprise!'

'I'm having the first stroll of the year,' said Winnie. 'How's Dotty?'

'Waiting for her coffee,' said Connie. 'Go into the sitting-room and I'll bring it in.'

Dotty was sitting on the sofa looking remarkably like the scarecrow Winnie had just passed in a neighbouring field, but her eyes were bright and her voice welcoming.

'Winnie! I've just been talking about you and dear Donald.'

For one dreadful moment Winnie wondered if Dotty still thought that Donald was alive. She had these lapses of memory which could be most disconcerting for those trying to carry on a conversation. This time, luckily, all was well.

'I remember how good he was to old Mrs Curdle. Is her grandson still with the Youngs?'

This was splendid, thought Winnie relaxing. Dotty was definitely on the ball this morning. She accepted the cup of coffee which Connie offered and sat back to enjoy it.

'We hear Agnes and Dorothy are off,' said Kit. 'They'll be missed.'

'Betty Bell told us,' added Dotty. She moved some crochet work from her lap and stuck the hook behind her ear like a pencil. It gave her an even more rakish appearance than usual.

'What's more to the point,' she said, 'how is Albert Piggott? I've got all sorts of jobs waiting here for him to do, and I suppose he's still ill, as we don't see him.'

Winnie said that as far as she knew Doctor Lovell was still attending him.

'A nice boy,' conceded Dotty, pulling up her skirt and exposing stick-like legs festooned in wrinkled stockings.

She scrabbled in the leg of her knickers, which at a cursory glance appeared to be constructed of whipcord, and produced a man's khaki handkerchief.

'But not a patch on your Donald, of course.' She blew her nose with a loud trumpeting sound, replaced the handkerchief and covered her legs again.

'Kit's made a lovely little pond for the ducks, Winnie. You must see it. I want Albert to put in some irises and other water plants.'

'You know I can do that,' said Kit. 'No bother.'

'No, I want Albert to do it. He's good with such things and I want the angle right when the sun's overhead. Ducks like shade, you know. Albert understands their needs.'

Kit smiled at Winnie and shook his head. How patient he and Connie were, thought Winnie, with this lovable but infuriating old aunt.

'Now, I want to hear all about Richard's new house. Where is it?'

'Nowhere, as far as I know,' replied Winnie. 'Obviously you know that he hopes to find something in these parts. He asked me to put him up while he looked around.'

'And is he going to do that?' asked Connie.

'No. I don't think so. John was rather firm about it and, to tell the truth, I can't face Richard for an indefinite time, fond of him as I am. But I should like to see him settled somewhere near by, so if you hear of anything do tell me.'

'I hear Nod Hall is on the market,' said Dotty, picking up her crochet again and looking about wildly for the hook. Connie rose without a word, removed it from her aunt's hair and handed it to her.

'But surely,' said Kit, 'that's got about twelve bedrooms, a lake and eighty acres!'

'He could always marry again,' said Dotty, 'and have a large family. I think it's such a pity that people don't have

more children these days. Leave it too late, I suppose. I
mean, gals got married at eighteen or so when I was young
and had about six by the time they were thirty. Much
healthier, I'm sure.'

'Nowadays, Dotty, the girls have to go out to work
before they can make a home. And large families need large
incomes.'

'Perhaps we could have him here,' said Dotty brightly.
'As a lodger.'

'No!' said Kit and Connie in unison. 'He wouldn't want
that!'

'And neither should we,' Kit added. 'But we'll keep our
ears open, Winnie, in case we hear of anything. Now come
and see the pond.'

Farewells were made, and Winnie followed her friend
into the garden, much refreshed by her rest, the coffee and
the encounter with the resilient Dotty.

The mild weather meant that the children of Thrush Green
school could play outside, much to the relief of the staff.

Miss Watson and Miss Fogerty paced the playground
together, smiling indulgently upon their charges.

'I had a brainwave in bed last night, Agnes. I think I shall
take driving lessons.'

Agnes could not believe that she had heard aright, which
was more than possible as two little boys were being
Harrier jets and making almost as much noise as the real
thing, not three yards from her.

'I'm sorry, I didn't catch what you said.'

'*Driving lessons!*' shouted Dorothy fortissimo. 'It would
be so useful to have a little car at Barton. We could have
trips here and there.'

She broke off and bent to face one of the Harrier jets.
'Go away!' she bellowed. Looking pained, the child
shuffled off with his fellow.

'But don't you have to have a test?' queried Agnes. She felt some alarm at this idea of Dorothy's.

'I shan't,' said her friend, with some satisfaction. 'I learnt, you know, when I first started teaching, and have kept up my licence luckily.'

She looked at her watch and raised a whistle to her lips. At the first blast the children stood still, with a few exceptions. Two of them were the disgruntled Harrier jets, but a quelling glance from their headmistress soon brought them to a standstill.

The second blast sent them all running to lines and the third set them walking into school. Really, thought Agnes, watching these manoeuvres, Dorothy is a wonderful organiser! Of course, one was bound to get one or two naughty little things, like John Todd who *pushed*, but on the whole Thrush Green children were very well disciplined. How she would miss them!

She shelved the troublesome problem of Dorothy's latest brainwave, and followed her class indoors.

4 Spring Plans

IF little Miss Fogerty had hoped that Dorothy's wild idea of taking driving lessons would pass, then she was to be disappointed.

Her headmistress brought up the subject again with great enthusiasm that evening.

'I could brush up my driving skills while we are still here, you see, and get some advice about the most suitable car to buy.'

'But won't that cost a great deal of money? And there is the insurance and licensing and so on.' Agnes was becoming agitated.

'I've thought of all that. I have quite a nice little nest egg, and an insurance policy that matured last Christmas. And then think of the money we should save in fares!'

Agnes nodded doubtfully.

'We could actually drive down to Barton to look at properties,' went on Dorothy. 'Every weekend, if need be. And it would mean that we have more scope in choosing a place down there, if we don't have to rely completely on buses or our two feet. Don't you like the idea, Agnes?' She spoke kindly, knowing her old friend's timid ways and her dislike of anything new.

'If you are quite happy about it, Dorothy,' she said slowly. 'But I was thinking not only of the *expense*, and of course I should like to pay my share, but whether you would feel up to facing all the dreadful traffic about these days. After all, it was some thirty years ago that you started to drive. Things were much more peaceful.'

'Now, Agnes, just listen to me! This car will be *mine*,

and I can well afford to run it, so don't worry about that side of things. As for the traffic, well, one sees plenty of people driving who are far older than we are. I'm quite sure that I can cope with *that*.'

Agnes remembered, with a shudder, seeing Dotty Harmer tacking to and fro across the hill from Lulling, when that lady owned a car for a mercifully short time. And Dorothy's own brother, Ray, had spent some time in hospital as the result of a car accident.

But there it was. If Dorothy was set upon having a car then who was she to try and stop her? And surely she would have guidance and advice from whoever would be teaching her?

'Who would you ask to give you lessons?' she enquired.

'Well, I know Reg Bull has taught a number of people, and of course he knows a great deal about cars as a garage owner, but I'm not too sure about him.'

'He is getting rather old,' agreed Agnes. 'And sometimes the worse for liquor, I hear.'

'Quite. Also he might try to sell us a car that is not quite suitable. One that he has had in stock for some time, say, and can't get rid of. We have to face the fact, Agnes dear, that some men are inclined to take advantage of ladies if they think that they are gullible.'

Agnes nodded her agreement.

'Would it be a good idea to have a word with the rector?'

Dorothy gave one of her famous snorts.

'Charles Henstock is a living saint, my dear, and if I had any spiritual doubts he would be the first person I should turn to. But he doesn't know a carburettor from a sparking plug, and I doubt if he has even *looked* under the bonnet of his car.'

'What about Harold?'

'Ah now!' said Dorothy speculatively. 'That's a different kettle of fish altogether! Harold really knows about cars, and what's more, he may know of someone really reliable to give driving lessons. What a brilliant idea of yours, Agnes!'

Little Miss Fogerty basked in her friend's approbation. Now that she was getting used to this novel idea, she realised how much dear Dorothy was looking forward to owning a car again.

In any case, there was nothing that she could do to stop her. Far better to agree with good grace. And Harold Shoosmith, she felt sure, would be a tower of strength and wisdom in this new adventure.

While the two schoolteachers were considering the question of driving lessons, the three Miss Lovelocks at Lulling were making a momentous decision.

This was really the result of Dimity Henstock's morning visit. The sisters had told her of their domestic problems and Dimity had been unusually forthright in giving her advice.

'For a start,' she said, 'book a table regularly for lunch next door.'

'What! Every day?' exclaimed Miss Ada.

'The *expense*!' echoed Miss Bertha.

'Not every day,' conceded Dimity. 'Say once or twice a week. And then shut up the attics here and the bedrooms that are not in use. That will save fuel and cleaning.'

She looked about the vast chilly drawing-room, littered with occasional tables, unnecessary chairs and a never-used grand piano.

'I'd be inclined to close this too,' she said decisively. 'Your kitchen and dining-room are much the pleasantest places in the house.'

'But one can't live in the *kitchen*!' protested Ada.

'And we should miss the view of the street,' added Bertha.

Miss Violet spoke at last. She was the youngest of the three, and less hidebound in her ways. 'I think Dimity's ideas are right. We ought to use The Fuchsia Bush more. After all, we aren't exactly short of money.'

Miss Ada drew in her breath sharply. 'You know mother always said that it was vulgar to mention *money*, Violet. In any case, there is such a thing as *thrift*, though one doesn't hear a great deal about it these days.'

She inclined herself towards Dimity. 'Thank you, my dear, for your advice. We will consider it most carefully.'

'Yes, indeed,' echoed Bertha.

Violet gave a conspiratorial smile, as she showed Dimity to the door.

Later, the matter had been discussed with great earnestness.

'I think,' said Ada, 'that we might go to The Fuchsia Bush on Wednesdays – and perhaps Thursdays – for our luncheon. The Sunday roast usually lasts through Monday and Tuesday.'

The Sunday roast at the Lovelocks' establishment was never anything so splendid as a round of beef or leg of lamb. Often it was breast of lamb stuffed and rolled or, as a treat, half a shoulder of that animal. Occasionally in the summer, a small piece of forehock of bacon was eaten cold with an uninspiring salad from the garden. How any of these meagre joints afforded meals for three days for the three sisters was one of the wonders of Lulling.

'What about Fridays and Saturdays?' queried Bertha.

'We can do as we normally do,' responded Ada. 'Something on toast, such as a poached egg. And the herrings are looking very good at the moment. To think we once called them "penny herrings", girls!'

The three sisters nodded sadly, mentally visualising the dear dead days of long ago.

'Then shall we settle for Wednesday and Thursday?' said

Violet briskly, the first to return to the present day. 'I will go to see Mrs Peters tomorrow morning, if you agree, and give a standing order.'

Her two sisters nodded.

'But I certainly shan't dream of doing as Dimity suggested about shutting up the drawing-room! The very idea! There's no room to sit in the dining-room, and in any case all our best pieces are in the drawing-room.'

'And the window looking over the street,' said Bertha. 'One must keep in touch with what's afoot.'

'Absolutely!' said Violet. 'But I think shutting the attics and the second spare bedroom is a good idea.'

'Well,' replied Ada doubtfully, 'we must bear it in mind. I'm sure Dimity's suggestions were made with the highest motives. But one doesn't want to *rush* things.'

'Perhaps,' said Violet, beginning to wonder if matters were not slipping back into general apathy, 'it would be a good idea to bob into The Fuchsia Bush now before Mrs Peters closes.'

'Very well,' said Ada. 'But make it quite clear that we shall need only a *light luncheon*. Our digestions won't stand a great deal.'

'Nor our purses,' added Bertha, as Violet made her way into the hall to fetch her coat, hat and gloves.

Tho Fuchsia Bush might only be next door, but a lady did not walk in the High Street at Lulling improperly dressed.

Albert Piggott's first venture outside after his illness did not involve a long journey. He simply took a few paces northward from his own front door to the shelter of The Two Pheasants.

Mr Jones, a kindly man, greeted him cheerfully. 'Well, this is more like it, Albert! How are you then? And what can I get you?'

'I'm pickin' up,' growled Albert. 'Slowly, mind you. I bin real bad this time.'

'Well, we're none of us getting any younger. Takes us longer to get back on an even keel. Half a pint?'

'Make it a pint. I needs buildin' up, Doctor says.'

'Well, your Nelly'll do that for you,' said the landlord heartily, setting a foaming glass mug before his visitor. 'I hear she's doing wonders down at Lulling.'

'That ain't here though, is it?' responded Albert nastily. He wiped the froth from his mouth with the back of his hand, and then transferred it to the side of his trousers.

'You going to get back to work?' enquired Mr Jones, changing the subject diplomatically.

'Not yet. Still under the doctor, see. Young Cooke can pull his weight for a bit. Won't hurt him.'

At that moment Percy Hodge entered and Mr Jones was glad to have another customer to lighten the gloom.

'Wotcher, Albie! You better then?' said Percy.

'No,' said Albert.

'Don't look too bad, do he?' said Percy, appealing to the landlord.

'Ah!' said he non-committally. If he agreed it would only give Albert a chance to refute such an outrageous suggestion, and maybe lead to the disclosure of various symptoms of his illness, some downright revolting, and all distasteful.

On the other hand, if he appeared sympathetic to Albert claiming that he still looked peaky and should take great care during his convalescence, the results might still be the same, and Albert's descriptions of his ills were not the sort of thing one wished to hear about in a public place.

Mr Jones, used to this kind of situation, betook himself to the other end of the room, dusted a few high shelves and listened to his two clients.

Percy Hodge had a small farm along the road to Nidden. He was related to Mrs Jenner, but had nowhere near the resourcefulness and energy of that worthy lady.

His first wife Gertie had died some years earlier. For a time he had attempted to court Jenny, at Winnie Bailey's, but was repulsed. He then married again, but his second wife had left him. Since then, he had been paying attention to one of the Cooke family, sister to the young Cooke who looked after the church at Thrush Green and its churchyard.

'Still on your own?' asked Albert, dying to know how Percy's amorous affairs were progressing.

'That's right,' said Percy. 'And better off, I reckon. Women are kittle-cattle.'

From this, Albert surmised that the Cooke girl was not being co-operative.

'Here I am,' went on Percy morosely, 'sound in wind and limb. Got a nice house, and a good bit of land, and a tidy bit in Lulling Building Society. You'd think any girl'd jump at the chance.'

'Girls want more than that,' Albert told him.

'How d'you mean?'

'They want more fussing like. Take her some flowers.'

'I've took her some flowers.'

'Chocolates then.'

'I've took her chocolates.'

'Well, I don't know,' said Albert, sounding flummoxed. 'Something out of the garden, say.'

'I've took her onions, turnips, leeks and a ridge cucumber last summer. Didn't do a ha'p'orth of good.'

'Maybe you're not *loving* enough. Girls read about such stuff in books. Gives 'em silly ideas. Makes them want looking after. They wants attention. They wants – '

He broke off searching for the right word.

'*Wooing!*' shouted Mr Jones, who could bear it no longer.

'Ah! That's right! *Wooing*, Perce.'

Percy looked scandalised. 'I'm not acting *soppy* for any girl and that's flat. If they turns down flowers and chocolates and all the rest, then I don't reckon they're worth bothering about. If they don't like me, they can leave me!'

'That's just what they are doing,' pointed out Albert. 'I take it you're still hanging around that Cooke piece as is no better'n she should be.'

Percy's face turned from scarlet to puce.

'You mind your own business!' he bellowed, slamming down his mug and making for the door.

'There was no call for that,' said Mr Jones reproachfully, when the glasses had stopped quivering from the slammed door.

'I likes to stir things up a bit, now and again,' said Albert smugly. 'I'll have a half to top up.'

The mild spell of weather which had brought out the first spring flowers and those people, like Albert, recovering from their winter ills, now changed to a bitter session of hard frosts and a wicked east wind.

The good folk of Thrush Green pointed out to each other that after all, it was still February, a long way to go before counting the winter over, and February and March were often the worst months of the winter.

It was cold comfort, and Jane Cartwright took extra care of the old people in her charge. The health of old Tom Hardy, in particular, caused her some concern.

She mentioned her worries to Charles Henstock one afternoon when he paid a visit to his old friends at the home.

'It isn't anything I can pin down,' she said. 'His chest is no worse. He eats very little, but then he always did. He goes for a walk every day with Polly, but something's worrying him. See if you can get it out of him. He'll tell you more than he will me.'

The rector promised to do his best, and made his way to Tom's little house, bending against the vicious wind which whipped his chubby cheeks.

He found the old man sitting by a cheerful fire, fondling the head of his much-loved dog.

To Charles's eye old Tom seemed much as usual as he greeted his visitor warmly.

'Come you in, sir, out of this wind. I took Poll out this morning, just across the green, but I reckon that's going to be enough for today.'

'Very wise, Tom. And how are you keeping?'

'Pretty fair, pretty fair. I never cease to be thankful as I'm here, and not down at the old cottage. Jane Cartwright looks after us all a treat.'

Polly came to the rector and put her head trustingly upon his knee. The rector stroked her gently. She was an old friend, and had stayed at Lulling vicarage when her master had a spell in hospital.

Charles wondered whether to mention Jane's concern, and decided that it could do no harm.

'She's a marvellous woman. I think she worries rather too much about you all. She certainly said just now that she hoped that everything was right for you.'

Tom did not reply.

'She said you seemed pretty healthy, which was good news, but she had the feeling that something was troubling you. Is it anything I can help with?'

Tom sighed. 'It's Polly. I frets about her.'

'But let's get the vet then.'

'It's not that. It's nought as the vet can do. She's got the same trouble as I have, sir. We be too old.'

'We're all getting old,' replied Charles, 'and have to face going some time. But what's wrong otherwise with Polly?'

He looked at the dog's bright eyes, and felt her tail tap against his legs as she responded to her name.

'It's what happens to her when she goes,' said Tom earnestly. 'All the dogs I've had has been buried by me in my garden. There's two graves now down at my old place by the river.'

'So what's the difficulty?'

'There's no place here to bury poor old Poll when her time comes. It grieves me.'

The old man's eyes were full of tears, much to Charles's distress.

'Then you can stop grieving straightaway,' he said robustly, leaning across Polly to pat his old friend's knee. 'If it makes you happier, let Polly be buried in the vicarage garden at Lulling. There are several pets buried there and Polly was well content when she stayed with us.'

Tom's face lit up. 'That's right good of you, sir. It'd be a weight off my mind.'

'And if you go ahead of her, Tom,' said the rector smiling, 'she can come to the vicarage anyway and be among friends. So now stop fretting.'

Tom drew in his breath gustily.

'I wish I could do something to repay you,' he said.

'You can, Tom. What about a cup of tea?'

He watched the old man go with a spring in his step to fill the kettle. He was humming to himself as he went about setting a tray.

If only all his parishioners' troubles could be settled so simply, thought Charles!

As Agnes Fogerty had guessed, Harold Shoosmith was proving most helpful on the subject of Dorothy's driving tuition and the buying of a small car.

The two ladies had been invited next door for a drink to discuss matters and Harold was waxing enthusiastic.

It was strange, thought Agnes, how animated most men became when discussing machinery. Her dear father, she recalled, could read a book without any sort of reaction to its contents. It was the same with a play or a concert. He was quite unmoved by these products of the arts, but his joy in his old tricycle, upon which he rode when delivering the shoes he repaired, was immense.

Later, he had taken to driving a three-wheeled Morgan and the same fanatical light had gleamed in his eyes. To

Agnes any form of locomotion was simply the means of getting from one place to another and she looked upon this male fever as just one more incomprehensible facet of man's nature.

'I've thought a good deal about driving lessons,' Harold was saying. 'I shouldn't get Reg Bull if I were you. I'd offer myself, but I don't know that friends make the best instructors. Worse still are spouses, of course, but you are spared those.'

'I certainly shouldn't have allowed you to teach me,' said Isobel. 'As it is, you gasp whenever I let in the clutch.'

'Do I? I never realised that!'

'Well, you do. And very trying it is,' said his wife briskly. 'But go on. Tell Dorothy your bright idea.'

'It occurred to us both, that perhaps Ben Curdle would be willing to give you lessons. He's a marvellous driver, very steady and calm. I'm sure he'd be first-class. If he's willing, of course, to let you learn on his Ford. It's a good gearbox. You could do worse than buy a little Ford when the time comes.'

'Ben Curdle would be just the man,' agreed Miss Watson. 'But would he do it? He doesn't seem to have much spare time.'

'If you like, I will have a word with him and let you know the result. One thing I do know – he would be glad to earn some money in his spare time.'

'That would be very kind of you. I have the greatest respect for Ben, so like his dear grandmother. If he will take me on, I shall be delighted.'

'And, of course,' added Harold, 'I can take you out occasionally for a run in my car, just to get the hang of things.'

'How lovely! I should appreciate that. And I hope you will advise me when it comes to buying a car.'

Harold's eyes sparkled at the prospect. 'What was the car you drove earlier?' he enquired.

Dorothy frowned with concentration. 'Now, what was it? I know it was a red one, with rather pretty upholstery, but I can't think what make it was.'

Harold looked flabbergasted.

'I'm sure the name will come back to you when you are not thinking about it,' said Isobel soothingly. 'Like throwing out the newspaper and knowing immediately what ten down was in the crossword. Harold, Agnes's glass is empty.'

Recalled to his duties as host, Harold crossed to the side-table, but he still appeared numb with shock at the abysmal ignorance of the female mind.

5   Personal Problems

'I'VE just had a letter,' said Miss Watson at breakfast one morning, 'from Better and Better.'

'From who?'

'From whom,' corrected Dorothy automatically. 'From Better and Better, dear. The estate agents. My sharp note to them seems to have done some good. They've sent particulars of two bungalows and a ground-floor flat. Mind you, I suspect that the ground-floor flat is really the *basement*, but at least it's an improvement on that converted oast house with five bedrooms, and that attic flat in some terrible old castle, which they sent last time.'

Agnes Fogerty nodded, looking bewildered. She was perusing the Appointments pages of that week's *Times Educational Supplement*.

'Our advertisement's in,' she said. 'But no house.'

Dorothy put down her letter. 'Not a *house*, Agnes. Two bungalows and a flat.'

'I know, Dorothy, about the Barton properties. I'm talking about *our* house, this one.'

'What about it?'

'Well, last time our posts were advertised, it said something about a school house. It doesn't this time.'

Miss Watson held out an imperious hand. 'Here, let me look!'

Agnes handed over the paper meekly, noticing, with a wince, that one corner had been dragged across the marmalade on Dorothy's toast.

'Well, how extraordinary!' said that lady. 'What can it mean? Perhaps they just forgot to mention it.'

'Or perhaps the printers made a muddle of it,' suggested Agnes.

'I shall be ringing the office this morning,' replied her friend, 'and I'll see if I can find out about this. Not that I shall learn much if that fiddle-faddling secretary fellow answers.'

'What's wrong with him?'

'Terrified of his own shadow! Never gives a straight-forward answer to any question,' said Dorothy trenchantly. 'I asked him only the other day about those desks which have been ordered for two years, and he gets flustered and waffles on about things being *at the committee stage*, whatever that means, and he has no power to tell me.'

Secretly, Agnes felt rather sorry for the man. Dorothy, at her most demanding, could instil great terror.

'Still, never fear, Agnes! I shall do my best to see what lies behind this omission.'

She handed back the paper, catching another corner on the marmalade in transit, and poured herself a second cup of tea.

The bitter east wind did not show any signs of abating, and the old people at Rectory Cottages were once more house-bound, and particularly glad of Jane and Bill Cartwright's daily visits.

Tom Hardy seemed much more cheerful after the rector had called. Jane had not had an opportunity of finding out the reason for this improvement, but was glad when the old man volunteered the information.

'Mr Henstock says he'll have my old Polly in his garden.'

Jane was somewhat bewildered. 'Which day is this to be?'

'Why, for ever!'

'You mean that you are letting him have Polly? Can you bear to part with her, Tom?'

'No, no, no!' exclaimed the old man testily. 'Why should I want to give Poll away?'

Jane waited for enlightenment.

'When she's dead,' continued Tom. 'I've been fretting about what would happen to her when she's gone. No decent garden here to bury her, see? All my other dogs was buried proper. Dug their graves myself, and wrapped their poor bodies in their own dog blanket for comfort like.'

Jane was touched by the old man's concern. 'I'm sure we could have found a corner for her somewhere, Tom.'

'Well, now there's no need,' said Tom, with great dignity. 'She'll be comfortable in the vicarage garden, when the time comes.'

Jane looked from the frail old fellow to his equally aged pet lying at his feet.

As if reading her thoughts, Tom spoke again. 'And if I goes first, then Mr Henstock's having Poll,' he said. 'A good man is the rector, and a fine gentleman.'

And with that Jane heartily agreed.

At Winnie Bailey's, Jenny had just come in from the garden where she had been hanging out the tea towels.

'My goodness!' she gasped, crashing the kitchen door behind her. 'Don't you go out today, Mrs Bailey. Enough to catch your death in this wind. I shan't be surprised to find the tea towels in Mrs Hurst's garden when we go to fetch them.'

'I've nothing to go out for, I'm thankful to say,' said Winnie. 'Ella's coming along later, probably early afternoon.'

'Will she stay to tea?' asked Jenny hopefully. She loved an excuse to make scones or hot buttered toast.

'No, Jenny. She's only dropping in the magazines. She won't stop.'

At that moment the telephone rang. It was her nephew Richard.

'Aunt Win, can I pop in?'

'Of course. When?'

'About twelve?'

'Fine. We'll put another two sausages in the oven.'

'Splendid! And another thing!'

'Yes?'

'I'll have Timothy with me. In fact, I wondered if you could have him for an hour or two, while I go along to Cirencester to pick up some books waiting there.'

'Of course. I haven't met Timothy yet. I shall look forward to it.'

'Good!' said Richard, sounding much relieved. 'See you soon then.'

Winnie conveyed the news to Jenny.

'How old is this Timothy?' she enquired.

'Four, I think.'

'Well, if he doesn't like sausages he can have an egg,' replied Jenny decisively. 'And don't let him wear you out. Didn't we hear he was a bit of a handful?'

'Good heavens! We surely can cope with a four-year-old for an hour or so!'

'Let's hope so,' said Jenny, 'but children today aren't what they were in our young days.'

'They never were,' responded Winnie.

The arrival of Richard's car was first noted by Albert Piggott who was standing at his kitchen window.

He had just returned from a visit to The Two Pheasants, and was watching the dead leaves eddying round and round in the church porch opposite his cottage.

The wind seemed more formidable than ever. The

branches of the chestnut trees outside the Youngs' house were tossing vigorously. The grass on the green flattened in its path, and no one seemed to be stirring at Rectory Cottages.

The advent of a car outside Winnie Bailey's was a welcome diversion in the waste of Thrush Green. Albert recognised Richard and was intrigued to see a small boy being helped from the car. The child appeared to be reluctant to get out, but at last the two figures set off for the front door.

Albert watched avidly. Jenny opened the door, and Richard and the boy vanished inside.

'Now, whose can that be?' pondered Albert. 'One of Richard's by-blows maybe?'

But he did Winnie's nephew a disservice. Timothy, had he known it, was the child of an earlier marriage of Fenella, his wife, so that Richard was the boy's stepfather.

To all appearances, he seemed to be taking his responsibilities seriously.

'Must ask Nelly about this,' said Albert to his cat. 'Women always knows about such things.'

The cat, who was engrossed in washing his face, ignored his master's remarks.

'So this is Timothy,' smiled Winnie, surveying the newcomer.

The child was dark-haired and skinny. He looked sulky, and tugged at Richard's hand.

'Say "How do you do",' prompted his stepfather.

'No,' said the child. 'Let's go home.'

The two grown-ups sensibly ignored this, and Winnie served some refreshments. Timothy sidled to the chair where Richard sat and hoisted himself on the arm.

Winnie noticed that his knees were dirty, and his jersey stained with food droppings of some antiquity. Why, she wondered, was Richard taking charge of the child? The last she had heard about the marriage was that there was talk of a divorce. Obviously, Richard had a responsibility towards his own child of the marriage, but Timothy really had little claim on him.

As if reading her thoughts, Richard spoke. 'Fenella suddenly remembered, when she woke this morning, that she had to take Imogen to the clinic for an injection. Timmy always screams the place down, so I said I'd keep him out of the way.'

Winnie noticed that the child gave a satisfied smirk at hearing of his behaviour at the clinic, and wished that Richard would have more sense than to mention such things before the boy.

'And what time will Fenella be home again?'

'Well, you know what these places are,' Richard replied, shifting in his chair so that Timothy could squash down beside him. 'Every one there wants to be done first, and there seems to be a lot of muddle one way and another. I don't suppose she'll be back until the afternoon.'

'I want my mummy,' whined Timothy.

Luckily, Jenny put her head round the door and summoned them to lunch.

'You'd better wash his hands in the kitchen,' said Winnie.

'I *never* have my hands washed,' announced Timothy.

'You do here,' said Winnie, leading the way.

A lordly dish of sausages, bacon, eggs and tomatoes graced the kitchen table, and Timothy surveyed it as Richard tried to wash the child's hands.

'I don't like sausages,' he said.

'What a pity,' said Winnie, settling herself at the table.

'And I don't like eggs.'

'Oh dear!'

'Nor bacon, nor none of what's for dinner.'

'You will be hungry,' said Winnie matter-of-factly.

She began to serve out. Richard took his seat, and Timothy was hoisted by Jenny on to a cushion in the chair beside him.

Winnie served the three adults and then looked enquiringly at Timothy.

'Are you going to try any of this?'

'No.'

'Very well, we won't worry you.'

Conversation flowed while Richard enquired about his old friends at Thrush Green, and Winnie tried to find out discreetly about Richard's domestic plans. Was the marriage still on or not? What had happened about the proposed divorce? Was Fenella's paramour, Roger Something, still living at the art gallery which was her home? If so, where did Richard fit in? It was all rather bewildering, thought Winnie, who was used to a tidy life.

Timothy, who disliked being ignored, now began to kick the table leg and was restrained by Jenny.

'Would you like to get down?' said Winnie.

'No. I want something to eat.'

Winnie lifted the servers.

'Not that old stuff!'

Winnie replaced the servers.

'So tell me about Imogen,' she said politely to Richard. 'Any teeth yet?'

Timothy began to tug furiously at Richard's arm, and a piece of sausage fell to the floor.

'I hardly know,' said Richard. 'Should she have teeth by now? I don't see much of her.'

By the time the first course had been demolished, Timothy had sunk down in his chair and was sucking a thumb disconsolately.

Jenny cleared away and returned with a steaming dish of baked apples.

'Shan't eat that,' said Timothy.

'Then you may get down,' said Winnie, serving the three
adults imperturbably.

The child slid to the floor, and remained seated under the
table.

Winnie looked enquiringly at Richard.

'What does he have at home?' she asked in a low voice.

'Oh, he eats when he feels like it. Bananas or peanuts,
anything he fancies really. He doesn't have meals with us.
He fits in very well with Fenella's work, you see. She has to
be in the gallery quite a bit. We don't stop for regular meals
as you do.'

When the meal was over, Jenny offered to take the child
to play on the green, where there were some swings and a
slide. Amazingly enough, the boy went with her, smiling.

'Now Richard,' said Winnie, when they were settled
with their coffee, 'I want to know how things are with you.
Are you and Fenella making a fresh start? What's happened
to Roger? And are you still determined to find a home
down here?'

Richard stirred his coffee thoughtfully. 'Well, first of all, Roger's gone back to his wife, but I can't see it lasting long. That's partly why I want to get Fenella away. We might make a go of it, without Roger looming over us all the time.'

'Very sensible. So the divorce is off?'

'Oh yes. So far, at any rate. I think we should consider the children.'

Better and better, thought Winnie. Richard seemed to be growing up at last.

'Mind you,' continued Richard, 'it's not going to be easy to pry Fenella from the gallery. It's her whole life really. Besides, she hates the country.'

Not so good after all, thought Winnie.

'And, of course,' went on her nephew, 'we do live rent free there. We should have to find a pretty hefty amount for a house round here. It needs thinking about.'

'I should imagine it's worth it to save your marriage,' said Winnie. 'And surely, if Fenella sold the gallery it would fetch a substantial sum, in such a good part of London.'

'I suppose so,' said Richard, but he sounded doubtful.

'Well, you must work out your own salvation,' replied Winnie briskly. 'And now you will want to get along to Cirencester. We'll see you about five, I suppose? No doubt you will want to get Timothy home again for his bedtime.'

'Oh, he doesn't have a set time for going to bed. He just has a nap when he feels like it.'

He set off to his car, followed by Winnie. Across the green she could see Timothy on a swing, with the gallant Jenny pushing him lustily.

At least he was happy at the moment, thought Winnie, waving goodbye to Richard, and noticing that Ella was emerging from her gate.

As it happened, it was half-past eight when Richard returned, and by that time Timothy had eaten an apple, a banana sandwich, and had had two short naps on the hearth-rug.

He was in excellent spirits when he drove off with Richard, and looked fit for several hours of activity.

But Winnie and Jenny went to bed early, with an aspirin apiece.

Harold Shoosmith kept his word and spoke to Ben Curdle about driving lessons for Miss Watson.

That young man considered the suggestion for some minutes.

'Don't make up your mind now,' Harold urged him. 'Just let me know when you've talked it over with Molly. You may not feel like letting a learner-driver loose on your Fiesta.'

Ben smiled. 'I don't need to think it over,' he said at last. 'I think Miss Watson would be pretty steady, and she's driven before.'

'But donkey's years ago!'

'Never quite leaves you, you know. And I'd be glad to help.'

'Shall I let her know, or will you?'

'You have a word with her. She can come over to see me and the car any evening. I take it she's got a licence?'

'Yes, she was wise enough to keep it up. I'll tell her, Ben, and I'm sure she will be most grateful.'

The two men parted, and Harold returned to his gardening pondering on the remarkable fortitude of Ben Curdle. He himself would rather face a mad bull than give a woman driving lessons.

Still, he told himself, Dorothy Watson should prove less horrifying than Dotty Harmer at the wheel.

'By the way,' said Dorothy to Agnes that evening, 'I found out a little more about that advertisement.'

'Which one, dear?'

'About the posts, of course,' said Dorothy.

'The posts?'

'In the *Times Educational Supplement*,' said Dorothy impatiently, 'with no house.'

Agnes seemed to make sense of this garbled explanation and nodded.

'I understand that the present policy is to get rid of the school house when a new appointment is made.'

'But surely,' said Agnes, 'the new head teacher might want it.'

'Not according to the office. Their attitude is that nine out of ten heads want to live well away from the school, and as almost all of them now have cars they can live where they like.'

'Yes, I can see that,' agreed Agnes, 'but it was so nice to live close to the school. And after all, that was why the house was built – to go with the job.'

'Those days have gone, my dear, and you must admit that this house wants a lot doing to it. The education authority can make a nice little sum in selling off these old school houses for others to renovate. It seems to make sense.'

'So when will it be on the market? I don't like the idea of having to get out.'

'I gather that nothing will happen until later in the year. There is no need for us to hurry our plans, they told me.'

At that moment, Harold entered with the message from Ben.

'Well, well!' said Dorothy, her face alight with excitement. 'What marvellous news!'

She glanced at the clock.

'I think I may slip over now, Agnes, to see Ben and make arrangements. So very kind of you, Harold. Won't you sit down and have a little something with Agnes?'

Harold excused himself, and he and the would-be driver left Agnes alone, in a state of some agitation.

Their home to be sold! Driving lessons! Really, thought poor little Miss Fogerty, life sometimes seemed to go too fast for comfort!

6 What Shall We Give Them?

THE news of Agnes and Dorothy's retirement created a great deal of activity among such bodies as the Parent–Teacher association, St Andrew's church where the two ladies worshipped, the local Women's Institute, as well as individual friends.

Respect and affection for the two hard-working spinsters united all these bodies, and it was generally agreed that some appropriate tribute should be paid. Dimity's suggestion of 'a bunfight and a clock' rather summed up the general feeling but it was expressed more elegantly, and at much greater length, when the various committees gathered together to come to a decision.

Charles Henstock, as chairman of the school managers – or *governors*, as he tried to remember they were now designated – consulted his old friend Harold Shoosmith before approaching his fellow managers.

'Have you any ideas, Harold? Dimity suggests money – but somehow I feel that might not be acceptable. I rather favour a nice piece of silver. Perhaps a salver?'

'Does anyone ever use a salver?'

'I suppose not,' replied Charles doubtfully. 'And Dimity says silver would need cleaning.'

'What about a piece of glass?' suggested Isobel who was sitting in the window-seat, doing the crossword.

'Such as?'

'Well, a nice Waterford fruit bowl, or a decanter. Dorothy has a little tipple now and again, and Agnes says she "sometimes indulges", so it would be used.'

'I should see how much is contributed,' said Harold sensibly, 'and then decide. You might find that you get a hefty sum and then you could give a cheque as well. I take it that you are combining with the Parent–Teacher association in this?'

'That was the idea.'

'And the church members, I suppose, will give their own present?'

'That's what we thought. After all, a great many of the parents attend chapel or, sadly, no place of worship at all, so the church's offering will be separate. We thought that perhaps a book token, or something for their new garden, might be appropriate.'

'But they haven't got a house yet,' pointed out Isobel, 'let alone a garden.'

The rector sighed. 'It really is a problem. Of course we must fix our dates for the little parties and the presentations and that alone is fraught with difficulties in the summer months, what with bazaars, and garden parties, and fêtes. Every weekend in July and August seems to get booked up by February, if you follow me.'

'We do indeed,' said Harold.

'If need be,' went on Charles, looking distracted, 'we can have these occasions at Lulling Vicarage, but it's such a truly Thrush Green affair that I feel we should have things arranged here.'

'If you want a garden you are very welcome to this one,' said Harold. 'Otherwise, what's wrong with the school itself?'

'Thank you, my dear fellow. You have been a great help, and I feel that I can make a few suggestions to the managers – I mean, *governors* – when I meet them. We are having a private meeting next week at the vicarage to sort things out.'

Harold accompanied him down the path.

The rector looked at the village school next door. 'I wish they weren't going,' he lamented.

'Don't we all,' responded Harold.

A few days later, the committee of the Parent–Teacher association also met to pool ideas. This was held at a house belonging to the Gibbons along the road to Nod and Nidden.

Mr and Mrs Gibbons were newcomers to village life and, as they were anxious to play their part in Thrush Green affairs, they were heartily welcomed, and very soon found that they were chairmen, secretaries, treasurers and general servants to an alarming number of local activities.

Mrs Gibbons had been chief secretary to a firm of exporters in the City of London, and retained her drive, industry, and, to be frank, her formidable bossiness, in this her new place of abode. Half the residents of Thrush Green were afraid of her. The other half viewed her activities with amused tolerance, and wondered how soon she would tire of all the responsibilities so gladly heaped upon her by the lazier inhabitants of the village.

Her husband's business seemed shrouded in mystery, much to the chagrin of his neighbours. It took him from home early in the day, and often obliged him to spend the best part of the week away from Thrush Green.

Some said that he was one of the directors of that same firm of exporters for whom his wife had worked.

Others maintained that he had a top job – very hush-hush – in the Civil Service, the Army, the Admiralty or MI5.

A few knew, for a fact, that he was connected with Lloyd's, the Stock Exchange, the Treasury and the Ministry of Transport.

Whatever he did, it was universally agreed that it was something of enormous importance giving him power over a great number of people, so that Harold Shoosmith had been heard to dub him irreverently 'Gauleiter Gibbons', but not, of course, to his face.

The meeting of the PTA committee met in Mrs Gibbons' large upstairs room which she called her office. It was a strange apartment to find in Thrush Green, where local committee members usually found themselves sitting in chintz-covered armchairs in someone's sitting-room, balancing a cup of coffee and an unsullied notebook, whilst discussing the latest gossip.

Mrs Gibbons' office was decidedly functional. There was a large desk made of grey metal and upon it stood two telephones, one red and one blue. There were two matching grey filing cabinets and a shelf along one wall which bore a number of mysterious gadgets, rather like miniature television sets, which had rows of keys, buttons and switches attached.

On a side wall was a chart with red and green lines swooping spectacularly across it, reminding at least one committee member of her own fever chart when confined once to Lulling Cottage Hospital. On another wall was a map of Europe and beneath that, on a shelf of its own, was a splendid globe, lit from within, which rotated majestically and drew all eyes to its movements.

Mrs Gibbons seated herself at the desk and surveyed her companions sitting before her in a semi-circle on rather wispy bedroom chairs. There were, she noted severely, far too few committee members.

The PTA really had eight committee members, but this evening only four were present. Besides Mrs Gibbons there were Molly Curdle, whose son was at the school, unmarried Emily Cooke who also had a boy in the same class, and a quiet father who had three children at Thrush Green school. Mrs Gibbons herself had a boy and a girl there, both remarkably bright, as might be expected from such parentage, but also thoroughly modest and sociable.

'Such a pity so many of the committee members are absent,' commented Mrs Gibbons. 'Never mind, we constitute a quorum so we can go ahead.'

The three nodded resignedly.

'It's just about Miss Watson and Miss Fogerty's presents, isn't it?' asked Miss Cooke. 'Won't take long, I mean? I've left my Nigel with Mum and she's got to go to Bingo later on.'

'Oh dear me, no!' replied Mrs Gibbons briskly. She added a particularly sweet smile, for although she secretly felt it highly reprehensible of Emily Cooke to produce a child out of wedlock, she did not want to appear censorious or hidebound in any way, and after all it might have been a grievous mistake on a young girl's part years ago. But somehow she doubted it. One did not need to live in Thrush Green very long before becoming aware of the sad laxity of the Cooke family.

'Well, let's get down to business,' said Mrs Gibbons. At that moment, the red telephone rang, and she picked up the receiver.

'Indeed?' said Mrs Gibbons. 'You surprise me,' she added. 'Not at all,' she continued. 'I will ring you back.'

She replaced the receiver, and smiled brightly at her companions, who had found the interruption decidedly disappointing, and had been looking forward to seeing their chairman with the receiver tucked between chin and shoulder, whilst taking down notes in efficient shorthand, just as people did on the telly.

'Any ideas?' she enquired.

As one would expect, there was a heavy silence. A blackbird scolded outside. A motor cycle roared past.

'That'll be me brother,' volunteered Miss Cooke, and silence fell again.

'Well,' said Mrs Gibbons at last, 'shall I start the ball rolling? I thought it would be a good idea to present the ladies with something really *personal* connected with Thrush Green.'

'How d'you mean, personal?' asked Molly. 'Like something they could wear, say?'

'No, no! Nothing like that. I was thinking of something on historical lines. Perhaps a short account of all that had happened in Thrush Green during their time here.'

'A sort of *book*?' queried Miss Cooke, sounding shocked. If Mrs Gibbons had suggested a pair of corsets apiece for the ladies, the committee members could not have appeared more affronted.

'I shouldn't think they'd want a *book*,' volunteered the quiet father, who was called Frank Biddle. 'Unless of course, you have come across a contemporary account of Thrush Green which we haven't yet seen.'

'I envisaged *compiling* such a book,' said Mrs Gibbons. 'From people's memories and cuttings from the local paper. And photographs, of course.'

Silence fell again, as all present considered the magnitude of the task and the inadequacy of anyone, Mrs Gibbons included, to undertake it.

Frank Biddle rallied first. 'A nice idea if we had thought of it a year or two ago perhaps,' he began cautiously, 'but we'd never get it done in time.'

Molly Curdle and Emily Cooke hastened to agree.

'Right! Scrub out that one!' said Mrs Gibbons, wielding a large blue pencil and slashing across her notepad.

'Then what about something for their new home to which we all contribute? I thought a large rug – perhaps a runner for their hall – with a few stitches put in by every person in the parish.'

'It'd take a fair old time,' observed Molly.

'And we'd have to cart it about from one house to the

next,' pointed out Emily. 'Get it wet most likely, or find people out.'

'Yes, rather a *cumbersome* project,' agreed Frank Biddle.

Mrs Gibbons' blue pencil tapped impatiently on the desk top. 'Well, let's have your ideas,' she said shortly.

Silence fell again, broken only by the tapping of the pencil, and a distant squawk from one of Percy Hodge's chickens.

Molly Curdle was the first to pluck up her courage. 'What about some sort of *thing*? I mean, a nice vase, or set of glasses, or a wooden salad bowl, if you think breakables a bit silly.'

'Not silly at all,' said Frank, relieved to have someone beside him with ideas to offer.

Molly cast him a grateful look.

'I was thinking rather on the same lines,' said Frank, not entirely truthfully, as he had toyed with suggesting a lawn mower or some window-boxes for the new residence.

'Possible,' said Mrs Gibbons with a marked lack of enthusiasm.

Emily Cooke, anxious no doubt to return to Nigel, came out strongly in support of Molly. 'Far the best thing to go to a shop for something nice. See it all ready, I mean, and make a choice, like. A book or a rug, like what you said, Mrs Gibbons, would need no end of time and trouble, and there's plenty could make a muck of their bit and spoil it for the others.'

'That's very true,' agreed Frank Biddle. 'I suggest that we make a list of suggestions ready to forward to the rector.'

'Very well,' said Mrs Gibbons resignedly, 'if that is agreeable to you all.'

There was a murmur of assent.

'I must say,' went on their chairman, ripping off a clean sheet from the notepad, 'that I had envisaged something more *personal*, something more inspired, but there we are.'

She spoke more in sorrow than anger, as though her best students had failed Common Entrance through no fault of her own. Her three companions appeared relieved rather than rebuked, and smiled warmly at each other.

'Ideas again?' prompted Mrs Gibbons, pencil poised.

'Piece of glass. Vase or similar,' repeated Molly.

'Something for the garden,' said Frank, feeling that he should make some contribution as the only man present. 'Perhaps a garden seat?'

'Garden seat,' muttered Mrs Gibbons, pencil flying.

'Wooden salad bowl,' added Emily, conscious that it was really Molly's idea, but unable to think of anything of her own.

'And servers, if the money runs to it,' added Molly, smiling forgivingly at Emily.

'Very good,' said Mrs Gibbons sitting up from her task. 'And I think I shall add a picture of the school. Perhaps a water-colour or a *really good* photograph.'

'Now that *would* be nice,' exclaimed Emily who felt that they could now afford to be generous as the meeting was almost over and the list of suggestions was mainly their own effort.

'I agree,' said Molly. 'They'd treasure that, I'm sure.'

'A really bright idea,' said Frank, collecting his stick ready for departure. 'Thank you for managing things so splendidly, Mrs Gibbons.'

He gave her a polite bow and made for the door, soon followed by the two ladies.

'I don't know that I really approve of the suggestions,' said Mrs Gibbons to the Gauleiter later that evening, 'but they all seemed grateful for my guidance, so I suppose one must be content with that.'

At the school itself, young Miss Robinson who had

recently finished her probationary year and was beginning to settle nicely with the lower juniors, was contemplating the same problem. It was she who would have to collect contributions, amidst deadly secrecy, from all the children and then decide what form the present should take.

She confided her worries to the rector when he called one afternoon. As always, he was comforting.

'I should tell the children that we do not want them to give more than say ten pence. It is fairer to the less well-off, and in any case should bring in enough to buy a beautiful bouquet, or a box of chocolates, something welcome but unpretentious, don't you think?'

'And a big card with everyone's name on it, I thought,' said Miss Robinson.

'I'm sure that it would be deeply appreciated by both ladies,' agreed the rector, giving her the gentle smile which mollified even the most militant of his critics.

Later, at the insistence of her own class, she was obliged to outline this plan, stressing the fact that no money should be brought until sometime during the summer term.

However, this did not dissuade one conscientious child from arriving one March morning and offering her a hot tenpenny piece with the words:

'It's for the teachers' wreaths.'

It was in March that Miss Watson was given her first driving lesson by Ben Curdle.

He arrived at six o'clock. The Fiesta gleamed with much polishing and not a speck sullied the mats on the floor.

A few children who had been playing on the green came to watch the proceedings, as Miss Watson, pink with excitement, took her place beside Ben.

'I'll take you up the Nidden road,' said Ben, eyeing the interested spectators. 'Be more peaceful, like. Then we'll change places when I've shown you the controls.'

'A good idea,' said his pupil, much relieved.

She decided to ignore the children. If she smiled at them, they might be encouraged to familiarities she did not wish for at the moment. On the other hand, it would not be fair to scold them. After all, they had every right to play on the green. It was just annoying that they appeared so curious. Perhaps a word about *being inquisitive* at tomorrow's assembly? But then, that would be an aspersion on their parents, who were every bit as agog at others' affairs. How difficult life was, thought Dorothy, trying to attend to Ben's explanations.

They drew up a little way beyond Mrs Jenner's house, where there were only a few black and white Friesian cows watching from one of Percy Hodge's fields.

Dorothy and Ben changed places and, with the car stationary, Ben began his lesson.

'First thing is the seat belt. Get that fixed. Then look in both mirrors and see if you can see the road behind in the top one and a view along at an angle in the wing mirror.'

Dorothy nodded vigorously and did as she was told, finding some difficulty in slotting the belt to safety in her excitement.

'Now these three pedals,' went on Ben, pointing floorwards, 'I expect you remember is the clutch, the brake and the accelerator.'

It was some twenty minutes later that Dorothy was allowed to switch on, to put the car into low gear and to let in the clutch.

The cows, who had watched with deep interest, now backed away in alarm as the Fiesta jerked forward in kangaroo hops.

'You wants to take it a bit smoother,' said Ben kindly. 'Let's start again.'

Half an hour later, Dorothy Watson reappeared in Thrush Green, driving at approximately twenty miles an hour in second gear, and feeling triumphant but exhausted.

She drew up at the gate of the school house and sighed happily.

'I *did* enjoy that, Ben. Thank you for being so patient. How did I do? Be truthful now.'

'All right, miss,' said Ben warmly. 'You'll soon get the hang of it, and everyone muddles the brake and the accelerator to begin with.'

'Will you come in and have a cup of coffee?'

'That's nice of you, but I'd best get back. Molly's expecting me.'

'Then I'll see you on Thursday. And many thanks again.'

Ben smiled at her, and drove his hard-worked car homeward.

He could do with something stronger than coffee when he got in, he told himself.

Little Miss Fogerty was all of a twitter when Dorothy arrived.

'And how did it go? Were you nervous? Was Ben pleased with you? Would you like a drink, or are you too tired?'

Dorothy bore the spate of questions with composure. 'It went quite well, and I wasn't nervous. Ben said he was pleased with me, and yes, I should love a drink. Coffee would be perfect.'

The two ladies went into the kitchen. Dorothy set out two cups and saucers, and Agnes poured milk into a saucepan.

'And I've had some excitement too,' said Agnes, as they waited for the milk and the kettle to boil.

'And what was that, dear?'

'A little cat came to the back door – a tabby one. I think it must be a stray, as I'm sure I haven't seen it before.'

'Better not encourage it,' said Dorothy.

'Well, I did give it some milk,' confessed Agnes, 'it seemed so very hungry. And a few scraps of chicken skin from the meat dish.'

'It probably comes from one of those new houses off the Nidden road,' said Dorothy, snatching the milk saucepan from the stove where it was hissing dangerously.

'I do hope it has got a home,' replied Agnes wistfully. 'It had the sweetest little face.'

'I shouldn't think we'll see it again,' said Dorothy with satisfaction, lifting the tray.

Following her friend into the sitting-room, little Miss Fogerty hoped that Dorothy was mistaken. There was something so endearing about that tabby cat. It had backed away when she had attempted to stroke it, eyeing the plate anxiously, until Agnes had gone indoors. She watched it return and gulp down the food ravenously, and her tender heart was touched.

Dorothy waxed enthusiastic about her driving lesson, and explained to Agnes how difficult it is to let in the clutch *really smoothly*, and how pleasantly responsive the Fiesta was, and it might well be the right car for them, when the time came to buy.

Agnes smiled and nodded over her coffee cup, but she was not really attending.

Would that little cat have a warm bed tonight? She hoped so. Perhaps it would be possible to make a straw bed in the wood-shed? It would mean leaving the door ajar at night, and perhaps Dorothy would object.

'I shall turn in early tonight,' said Dorothy yawning. 'I must say, learning something new is very tiring. I must try and remember that when I'm teaching the children.'

Agnes nodded her agreement. She too was tired with hearing about the mysteries of the combustion engine, in which she had no interest.

Dorothy dreamt that she was driving a large and powerful car of Edwardian design across the grass of Thrush Green. Her right foot twitched in her sleep, as she did her best to distinguish between brake and accelerator.

But next door, Agnes dreamt of a tabby cat, warm and purring, asleep on her lap.

Part Two

Battling On

7 Spring at Thrush Green

THE long doleful winter seemed to be coming to an end when a welcome warmth crept across the land, the daffodils lengthened their stems, and lambs bleated in the fields near Thrush Green.

Hopeful gardeners itched to put out from their greenhouses the waiting trays of annuals. The vegetable plots were raked over in readiness for early potatoes, peas and runner beans. Older and wiser gardeners did their best to restrain these optimists, and took gloomy pleasure in pointing out the late snowfalls of yester-year and the innumerable frosts which April and May could bring with doom in their wake.

The ladies of Lulling and Thrush Green hastened to the two dress shops in the High Street to replenish their wardrobes with cotton frocks, only to be told, with considerable satisfaction on the part of the assistants, that all summer clothing should have been bought last October, and that now they were showing winter wear only.

'But surely that's rather silly,' commented Winnie Bailey, wondering if she would find a Viyella button-through frock a good investment, and deciding, on looking at the price ticket, that it might be wiser to invest in a few dozen gold bars instead.

'The Trade has always followed this traditional pattern,' said the assistant loftily.

Some rock music was blaring round them making conversation difficult.

'Do you think we could have that switched off?' asked Winnie.

The assistant looked shocked. 'Quite out of the question,' she replied. 'It's *Company Policy* to have background music. The customers like it.'

'Well, here's one who doesn't,' retorted Winnie with spirit, casting the Viyella frock across the counter.

She strode out into Lulling High Street, vowing never to darken the doors of that insufferable shop again, and noticed a fluttering of hands at the windows of the Lovelocks' house.

She responded vigorously, crossed the road, and was welcomed indoors by the three sisters.

'I don't know what's come over that shop,' commiserated Ada. 'Ever since that new woman came and called it "Suzilou" it has gone downhill.'

'We *always* bought our stays there,' volunteered Violet. 'Right from girlhood, but now they say they aren't stocking *foundation garments*! Would you believe it?'

'I believe it readily,' said Winnie. 'Also I am getting heartily tired of asking for a size sixteen or eighteen only to be told that those sizes are so popular that they have sold out.'

'Most trying,' agreed Bertha. 'If that is so, why don't the manufacturers make more of those sizes?'

All four ladies sighed and shook their heads.

'A cup of coffee, Winnie dear?'

'Or a glass of sherry?'

'Or we have some madeira somewhere, if you prefer it?'

'Nothing, thank you. Tell me, how are you faring at The Fuchsia Bush, and have you been able to get help in the house?'

Ada, as the eldest, took it upon herself to answer.

'On the whole,' she began judicially, 'we are being well served at The Fuchsia Bush. We go every Wednesday, and sometimes, when we feel we can afford it, on a Thursday as well.'

Winnie Bailey, who had known the sisters' parsimony for almost half a century, was not affected by the pathos of the Thursday decision.

'Of course, we always let Mrs Peters or Nelly know on the *Wednesday*, if we shall be requiring lunch on the *Thursday*,' explained Bertha.

'The food is excellent,' added Violet.

'But expensive,' reproved Ada.

'It's far dearer at The Fleece,' responded Violet, sounding militant. 'I looked at the menu outside when I was passing yesterday, and their set lunch is twice the price of Mrs Peters'.'

'We were not considering The Fleece,' retorted Ada. 'For one thing it is far too far to walk there, particularly if the weather is inclement. I can't think why you troubled to pry into their tariff at all.'

Winnie hastened to break into this family squabble. 'Well, I'm sure you are wise to go next door occasionally. They were so obliging to you when you were all ill. It's a good thing to repay their kindness, by giving them your custom.'

The ladies smiled.

'But to answer your other question,' went on Ada. 'No, we haven't found regular help yet. Nelly Piggott approached one or two people, but they were unable to come.'

'It isn't as though we are asking them to do too much, you know,' said Bertha. 'Just a hand with the silver cleaning.'

Winnie surveyed the occasional tables, laden with silver bric-à-brac, recalled the drawers full of heavy silver cutlery, and the vast tureens and sauce boats in the dining-room, and was not surprised that any cleaner's heart would plummet at the magnitude of the task.

'And scrubbing the kitchen floor, and the back places,' added Violet.

'And taking the gas stove to pieces for a monthly spring clean.'

'And, of course, the windows,' added Violet. 'We do seem to have rather a lot of windows. And Father always liked to see the steps whitened with hearth stone, and we like to keep that up.'

'We *did wonder*,' said Ada meditatively, 'if she would undertake some decorating as well, now and again. Just simple paper-hanging and gloss-painting for the wood-work. You don't know of anyone who would like a light job, I suppose?'

'Well, no,' said Winnie rising. 'But if I hear of any able-bodied person who might suit you, I will let you know.'

She made her farewells, and walked down the steps to the pavement.

'And an able-bodied person,' thought Winnie to herself, as she traversed the High Street in the warm sunlight, 'is what would be needed in that household.'

She approached the steep hill leading to Thrush Green.

'And would they be able-bodied for long?' she wondered aloud, much to the astonishment of a passing collie dog.

The warm spell jolted everyone into activity. The inhabitants of Lulling and Thrush Green, who had been hibernating as thoroughly as the hedgehogs, now stirred themselves to clean windows, wash curtains, throw rugs on to the clothes lines for thorough beating and generally welcome the spring with a spurt of domesticity.

Local telephone lines hummed with invitations to coffee,

lunch, tea, a drink, or even a full-blown formal evening dinner. People who could not be bothered to do more than fend for themselves during the bitter winter months, now remembered how much they wanted to see their friends again, particularly as the gardens were at their best, aglow with daffodils, aubrietia and golden alyssum, and mercifully free, so far, from the more noxious weeds which would be rampant in a month's time.

Harold Shoosmith's garden was particularly colourful. Yellow, blue and mauve crocuses like gas flames had burst through the soil beneath the flowering cherry trees and the golden forsythia bushes. His Thrush Green neighbours paused to admire the garden when they passed, and even Albert Piggott had to admit that it was 'a fair picture'.

Harold had kept his word and had taken Dorothy Watson for a trial spin in his own car. He confessed to Isobel, before he called for his pupil, that he was a bundle of nerves, but gained confidence after a mile or so, for Dorothy seemed to be making steady progress, and was careful when changing gear.

Harold's new car was an Audi which Dorothy handled very well, but she gave a sigh of relief when at last they drew up at the Shoosmiths' house.

'Lovely, Harold dear,' she said, 'but I think a *small* car would be more suitable for Agnes and me.'

Harold agreed that there was no need for the two ladies to own a car as large – or as expensive – as the Audi, and that parking would be a lot easier with a vehicle the size of Ben's Fiesta, or even smaller.

'When the time comes,' he offered, 'I should enjoy trying out any that you favour. That is, if you still propose to buy.'

'Yes, indeed. Ben seems to think that I am getting on quite well. I only hope he's right.'

'I'd trust Ben's judgement.'

By this time they were in Harold's house where Agnes and Isobel were comfortably ensconced.

'And what news of the house-hunting?' enquired Isobel.

'Very little news, I fear,' replied Dorothy. 'Except that the particulars from Better and Better have been more plentiful with spring on the way, and rather more realistic.'

'Dorothy wrote to them,' explained Agnes, 'about how silly it was to send us details of top floor flats or bits of castles. Such a waste of everyone's time.'

'Well, we've all been through it,' said Isobel. 'Harold always says that after forty-three viewings he simply settled for forty-four, which was this one, because he had cracked completely.'

'You were let off comparatively lightly,' Harold reminded her. 'Only a dozen or so, and then I persuaded her to marry me. I still don't know if I or the house was the real attraction.'

'Fifty–fifty,' his wife told him, with a smile.

'Well, we don't know any nice single men in Barton,' said Dorothy. 'And certainly not one who would offer us marriage. I think we shall simply have to rely on Better and Better.'

'I'm looking forward to visiting you there when you've settled in,' said Isobel. 'I visited it on a couple of occasions when I took my neighbour in Sussex to visit her aunt there. It was an awkward cross-country journey by train, so I ran her across. We had a splendid picnic on the way, I remember, which she insisted on preparing. Asparagus, strawberries and cream! Delicious!'

'Why don't we have grand picnics like that?' queried Harold.

'Because you prefer thick ham sandwiches, or a plough-man's in a pub,' said Isobel.

She rose and beckoned to the ladies. 'Now come and have a proper look at the garden. Harold's done wonders.'

And the party moved out to enjoy the last of that day's spring sunshine.

On the following Wednesday, Ada, Bertha and Violet Lovelock walked to The Fuchsia Bush. Nelly Piggott herself placed their lunch before the Misses Lovelock.

Miss Ada had ordered fillet of plaice, Miss Bertha lasagne and Miss Violet braised beef. As the youngest of the three sisters, she was well aware that she would have to face some criticism when she returned home. Braised beef was more expensive than plaice or lasagne. Miss Violet was content to face her sisters' strictures later. In any case, she was not only used to them, but would be fortified by good red meat.

'There you are then,' said Nelly encouragingly, 'and I hope you enjoy it.'

The ladies inclined their heads.

'Not got suited yet, I suppose?' went on Nelly.

'I'm afraid not,' murmured Ada.

'Marvellous, innit? All this unemployment they keep on about, and yet no one wants a day's work.'

'Quite,' said Bertha.

'Could we have some mustard?' asked Violet. 'English, please.'

'Well, I won't forget to look out for someone,' said Nelly, as she departed in search of home-produced mustard. 'But it'll be an uphill job, I warn you.'

Through the window of The Fuchsia Bush the life of Lulling High Street pursued its peaceful way. Young Mr Venables, retired solicitor of Lulling, and now in his seventies, was chatting to an equally venerable gentleman beneath the pollarded lime tree immediately outside the restaurant. Several dogs were trotting about on their daily affairs, and young mothers were gossiping over their prams.

On the other side of the road, the greengrocer had put out some boxes of early annuals on the pavement below the rich display of apples, oranges, forced rhubarb and melons.

Velvety pansies, glowing dwarf marigolds and multi-coloured polyanthus plants all tempted the passers-by, particularly those gardening optimists who were dying to get down to some positive work after the months of winter idleness.

Among them was Ella Bembridge, close friend of Dimity, Charles Henstock's wife, and an old friend of the Lovelock sisters.

She was stooping over the boxes, her tweed skirt immodestly high, and a plume of blue smoke from one of her untidy cigarettes wreathing above her head.

Violet, who was facing the window, noticed her first, and wondered idly if their old friend would also be lunching at The Fuchsia Bush.

She did not wonder for long. Ella straightened up and plunged across the road towards the restaurant. A startled motorist screeched to a halt, stuck his head out of the window, and presumably rebuked Ella.

Violet saw Ella give him a dismissive flick of her hand, as she gained the kerb. Her expression was contemptuous. The motorist, muttering darkly, drove on.

'Well, well! Hello, hello!' she shouted boisterously. 'Got room for one more at your board?'

The two older Misses Lovelock looked up in surprise, and Ada choked delicately on a bone which had no business to be in a fillet of plaice. It was left to Violet to do the honours.

'Of course, Ella dear. Just let me move the water jug and the ashtray. Oh no! You may need that, perhaps.'

'Not for a bit, thanks. How nice to see you here.'

She settled herself with a good deal of puffing and blowing, throwing off her jacket, tugging at her cardigan sleeves, dropping her gloves to the floor, and generally creating as much disturbance as a troop of cavalry.

'Nearly got run down by some fool car driver who wasn't looking where he was going,' she announced. 'Proper menace some of these chaps. I hear Dorothy Watson's learning to drive. Think she'd have more sense.'

Violet, handing the menu to the newcomer, considered this comment. Did Ella mean that she would imagine that Dorothy would have more sense than the male drivers who were menaces? Or did she think that Dorothy ought to have more sense than to have undertaken driving lessons and the probable future ownership of a car? Really, the English language was remarkably ambiguous.

Ella studied the menu briefly and then slapped it down on the table. The salt and pepper pots jumped together.

'What are you lot having?' she said, peering at their plates in turn.

'Don't care for fish in white sauce myself, and that

lasagne is no tastier than wet face flannel I always think.'

She studied Violet's half-finished portion. 'Looks good that!'

She caught sight of Nelly hovering by the kitchen door.

'Ah, Nelly!' she roared cheerfully. 'Bring me a plate of Miss Violet's stuff, will you? There's a good girl!'

She turned to her companions in the greatest good humour.

'What luck catching you here! I was just about to call to see if you would like to contribute to the Save The Children fund. Dimity asked me to help.'

Ada and Bertha exchanged looks of horror, speechless at the idea of parting with money.

Violet rose to the occasion.

'Of course, Ella dear. Such a good cause.'

She ignored the glances of her two sisters. If she were to get a wigging anyway for choosing braised beef, then she might just as well be hanged for a sheep as a lamb.

No one relished this amazingly warm spell as keenly as little Miss Fogerty. Her bird-like frame suffered severely in the bitter Cotswold winters despite sturdy underclothes and several hand-knitted garments protecting her shoulders and chest.

The sunshine woke her earlier now in the mornings, and it was a joy to come downstairs early to see that the breakfast table was in good order, and to greet whichever Willie was postman for the week.

Willie Bond, large and lethargic, came one week. He was a cousin of Betty Bell's who cleaned the school and also attended to Harold and Isobel Shoosmith's domestic affairs, and to Dotty Harmer's at Lulling Woods.

His counterpart was Willie Marchant, a lanky and morose individual. Nevertheless, he was always polite to

Agnes Fogerty, remembering an occasion when she had personally escorted a nephew of his to his home, when the child had been smitten with a severe bilious attack.

'Not many would've bothered,' he told people. 'She's a kind old party, even if she was behind the door when the looks was given out.'

Agnes enjoyed these few precious minutes of tranquillity before the rigours of the day.

There was another reason too for her pleasure in this early morning privacy, for more often than not these days the little tabby cat approached timidly, and sat by the dustbin waiting for his milk.

Agnes did not fail him. She also added a few scraps which she had garnered during the day before, and had taken to purloining any specially acceptable tit-bits from the school left-overs.

She put this largesse on the flagstones behind the dustbin. The cat always ran away, but she noticed with joy that he fled less far away as the days passed, and he returned to Agnes's bounty very quickly.

She stayed at the window as he ate, hoping that Dorothy would not appear before he had finished his meal.

It was not that she was *ashamed* of feeding the poor little thing, she told herself, but there was no reason to upset Dorothy who had seemed to be rather dismissive about their visitor when Agnes had mentioned it.

While she waited she admired the dewy garden. Already the birds were astir, and a pair of collared doves were fluttering by the hedge. A young rabbit sat motionless nearby, and Agnes thought how perfectly the pearl-grey of feathers and fur matched.

The cat licked the last delicious drops of milk from the saucer and made off quickly through the hedge. The doves whirred away, and the rabbit vanished.

Whose cat could it be, wondered Agnes? Although it

was thin, it seemed to be domesticated and certainly knew how to cope with provender on saucers.

She went out to collect his crockery, and washed it up as Willie Bond dropped the letters through the front door.

Perhaps the children would know about the cat, she thought suddenly, bending to collect the post. She must remember to enquire, but not, perhaps, in dear Dorothy's hearing.

8   Cat Trouble

AS one might expect in March, the fine spell was of short duration. After about eight days of heart-lifting sunshine, the clouds returned, the temperature dropped, and the winter garments, so joyously discarded for a brief time, were once more resumed.

One chilly morning when Miss Fogerty's infants were struggling with various arithmetical problems, designated Number on the timetable, and involving a great many aids such as coloured counters, rods of varying length, and a good deal of juvenile theft between the children, Agnes was surprised to see the tabby cat sitting on the wooden bench inside the playground shed, sheltering from the drizzle.

She clapped her hands, and the children looked up.

'Can anyone tell me,' she said, 'who owns that nice little cat out there?'

There was a surge of infant bodies towards the window, which Agnes quelled with consummate experience.

'We don't want to frighten it! Just look quietly.'

It was Nigel Cooke, son of Miss Cooke of the PTA committee, who spoke first, hand upraised in quivering excitement.

'Please, miss, it lives next door to us, miss.'

Agnes felt her heart sink. So it had a home after all!

'Well, it used to, sort of,' said another child. 'Them Allens left it behind when they done a moonlight flit.'

'They never paid the rent, see,' explained Nigel. 'They went one night. My dad saw 'em go, as he was on late shift.'

'Well, where does the cat live now?' enquired Miss Fogerty.

'He don't live nowhere like,' said one little girl. Agnes decided that this was not quite the time to point out the result of a double negative. She was too anxious to know the present position of the animal.

'He comes up ours sometimes,' said another Nidden child. 'My mum gives him bits, but he won't come in. My mum says the Allens should be persecuted, and was going to give the cruelty to animals man a ring, but my dad said she was to let well alone, so she never.'

Really, *men*! Agnes felt furious and impatient. Anything for a quiet life, she supposed, was their motto! No thought for the poor starving cat!

She hid her feelings, and spoke calmly. 'Who knows where it sleeps?'

Nigel was again the first to answer.

'If it's fine he sleeps on the step up against his back door.'

Agnes's eyes pricked at this poignant picture. 'And if it rains?'

Nigel looked blank. 'Up the farm sheds at Perce Hodge's, I reckon.'

Agnes determined to find out a little more, by discreet enquiries of Percy himself and any other reliable adult living along the Nidden road.

Meanwhile, work must be resumed.

'Back to your tables now. I want to see who can be first solving these problems.'

Comparative peace enfolded the class and Miss Fogerty, watching the cat washing its paws, made plans for the future.

It was about this time that Charles Henstock had an interesting telephone call from his great friend Anthony Bull.

Anthony had been Charles's predecessor at St John's of

Lulling. He was a tall handsome man with a splendid voice which he used to great effect in his rather dramatic sermons.

Despite a certain theatricality which a few of the males in his congregation deplored, Anthony Bull was deservedly popular, for he was a conscientious parish priest and a good friend to many.

The ladies adored him, and at Christmas a shower of presents descended upon the vicar, many hand-made, and creating a problem in their discreet disposal. Anthony's wife grew efficient in finding worthy homes for three-quarters of this bounty, all at some distance, so that the givers would not take umbrage. There had been one occasion, however, when one particularly devoted admirer of the vicar's had come across a piece of her handiwork at a cousin's bazaar in Devonshire. It had taken all Mrs Bull's ingenuity and church diplomacy to explain that unfortunate incident.

When Charles had first taken over the parish at Lulling and its environs, there had been some comparisons made by many of Anthony's more ardent followers. They found Charles's sermons far too simple and low key after Anthony's perorations from the pulpit. Charles, short and chubby, modest and unassuming, ran a poor second to his predecessor in looks and panache.

But gradually his congregation began to admire their new vicar's sincerity. They came to value his advice, to appreciate his unselfish efforts, to recognise the absolute goodness of the man.

The two men, so different in temperament, remained firm friends although they only met occasionally now that Anthony had a busy parish in Kensington.

The telephone call was greeted with joy by Charles, standing in his draughty hall and looking out into the windswept vicarage garden.

After the first greetings, Anthony came to the point. It appeared that he had been approached by a young woman who had been brought up in Lulling and was now in service in his London parish. She wanted to return to be near her mother. Did Charles know if it would be easy for her to get work?

'Domestic work do you mean?' asked Charles. 'Or something in a shop or office? Has she any particular qualifications? I know that Venables wants a typist, and there's a new supermarket opening soon, and there might be jobs there. I take it she will live with her mother?'

'Well, no! I think she wants cheap digs, or a living-in job. There's a snag. She has a little boy of three or thereabouts. No husband, of course, and I gather the fellow was a bad lot, but I've only heard one side of the affair, naturally. The mother, by the way, is Gladys Lilly. Chapel, I think.'

'I know her slightly. Yes, she does go to the chapel at the end of the town, I believe. A jolly sort of person.'

'Well, she wasn't too jolly about the baby, I gather, but she's willing to mind him while the daughter is at work, so that's a step in the right direction.'

'I'll have a word with Dimity,' promised Charles, 'and keep my ears open. As soon as I have any news I will ring. Now, when are you coming this way? The garden is looking very pretty despite the weather, and you know we'd love a visit.'

Anthony said he would do his best to get to Lulling again, and with mutual messages of affection the old friends rang off.

'Dimity!' called Charles, setting off towards the kitchen. 'We have a problem before us!'

The end of term was now in sight at Thrush Green school,

and all three teachers were looking forward to the Easter holidays.

Agnes and Dorothy admitted to being even more tired than usual.

'I suppose it's because we've had such a wretchedly long winter,' said Dorothy, who was standing at the sitting-room window, surveying the grey drizzle outside.

'Partly,' agreed Agnes, busy with her knitting. 'And then we've been doing a good deal of clearing up at school. And your driving lessons must be a strain.'

'I enjoy them,' said Dorothy shortly.

'Then, of course, we have the house business hanging over us,' continued Agnes. 'It would be nice to get that settled.'

'Not much point in buying at the moment with a whole term to get through,' commented Dorothy, 'although I suppose we'd need time to get anything we bought put into order.'

She sounded a little snappy, Agnes thought. Dear Dorothy had been somewhat on edge lately, and to be honest, she had felt irritable herself. Perhaps the approaching break after so many years at the school was beginning to take its toll.

'There's that cat!' exclaimed Dorothy suddenly. 'Do you

know, that's the second time I've seen him this week. I hope he's not coming regularly.'

Agnes made no answer. Dorothy turned round from the window.

'Agnes, are you *feeding* that cat?'

Little Miss Fogerty's hands trembled as she put down the knitting into her lap. She took a deep breath.

'Well, yes, Dorothy dear, I am!'

It was Dorothy's turn to breathe in deeply, and her neck began to flush. This was a bad sign, as Agnes knew very well, but now that the matter had arisen she was determined to stick to her guns.

'Well, really, Agnes,' protested her friend, with commendable restraint, 'you know I think it is wrong to encourage the animal. We can't possibly take on a cat now when we are off to Barton in a few months. And what will happen to it when we have gone?'

'I can't see the poor little thing go hungry,' answered Agnes. 'I've only put down milk, and a few scraps.'

'When, may I ask?'

'First thing in the morning, and as it gets dusk. I don't leave the saucers down in case mice or rats come to investigate.'

'I should hope not. In any case, the mere fact of putting food out in the first place is enough to encourage vermin.'

'It's a very *clean* little cat,' said Agnes, becoming agitated.

'I daresay. Most cats are. But I think you have been very silly, and short-sighted too, to have started this nonsense. It's cruel to encourage the poor animal to expect food when we know we shall not be here to provide for it before long.'

'It would be far more cruel to let it starve to death,' retorted Agnes with spirit.

Dorothy rarely saw her friend in such a militant mood, and resolved to deal gently with her.

'Of course it would, Agnes dear. I'm simply pointing out that we must look to the future. If it becomes dependent upon us it is going to be doubly hard on the animal when it finds we have gone.'

She noticed, with alarm, that Agnes was shaking.

'Perhaps we could find a home for it if it is really a stray,' she continued. 'So often cats go from one house to another for anything they can cadge, when they have a perfectly good home of their own.'

'This one hasn't,' snapped Agnes.

'And how do you know?'

Agnes explained about the Allens' departure, and abandonment of the cat, and its present plight. By now her face was pink, her eyes filled with tears, and her whole body was quivering.

'Then we must certainly try and find a home for it,' said Dorothy. 'Perhaps the RSPCA could help.'

'I don't see why we shouldn't take it on ourselves,' protested Agnes. 'It is getting tamer every day, and *whatever* you say, Dorothy, I intend to go on feeding it. I am very fond of the little thing, and I think – I'm sure – it is fond of me.'

Dorothy gave one of her famous snorts. '*Cupboard love!*' she boomed.

At this the tears began to roll down little Miss Fogerty's papery old cheeks, and splashed upon her knitting.

Dorothy, curbing her impatience with heroic efforts, tried to speak gently. 'Well, carry on as you are, dear, if you think it right. You know my own feelings on the subject.'

Agnes blew her nose, and mopped her eyes. She was too overwrought to speak.

'I think,' said her headmistress, 'that we could both do with an early bed tonight.'

And early to bed both ladies went, much perturbed. Civil goodnights were exchanged on the landing as usual, but both were relieved to enter the peaceful surroundings of their respective bedrooms.

Little Miss Fogerty washed her face and hands, cleaned her teeth and brushed her hair. Normally, she did a few exercises to help her arthritis, as directed by John Lovell, but tonight she was too exhausted to bother.

The night was bright. A full moon was hanging in the branches of the Shoosmiths' plum tree next door. Standing in her sensible night-gown, long-sleeved and high-necked, she noticed the cat's saucer behind the dustbin. She had forgotten to retrieve it in the worry of the evening.

In a strange way the sight calmed her. Well, now Dorothy knew. What was more, Dorothy had accepted the fact that the cat was going to be fed. There was now no need for subterfuge. It was quite a relief to have things out in the open. Tomorrow, she thought rebelliously, she would buy a few tins of cat food and discover the cat's preferences. The tins could be stored on the scullery shelf, and she would buy a new tin-opener to be kept specially for the cat's provender.

These modest plans gave her some comfort. She crept between the sheets and lay watching the shadows of the branches move across the ceiling in the moonlight.

She was truly sorry to have upset dear Dorothy, and she would apologise for that before breakfast. But she was not going to apologise for feeding the cat. It was the right thing to do – the *Christian* thing. The hungry should be fed, and she was determined to do it.

As the warmth of the bedclothes crept around her, Agnes's eyes closed. Yes, an apology first, then a saucer of milk for the cat, and perhaps a little of the minced lamb she had prepared for a shepherd's pie, and then . . .

But that was the last waking thought of little Miss Fogerty before she dropped into the sleep of the utterly exhausted.

Next door, Dorothy was more wakeful. She too regretted the evening's upset. Perhaps she had been too sharp with Agnes. She had not quite realised how deeply Agnes was involved with the little animal. It was extraordinary that she had never noticed that the cat was being fed regularly. Agnes must have been putting the food out in a well-hidden place. It was pathetic really.

She began to feel deeply sorry for her friend. She had always recognised her devotion to animals. It was akin to the strong affection she had for her young children and all defenceless things, and Dorothy heartily approved of such compassion. She supposed that some psychiatrists would dismiss it as 'thwarted motherhood', but Dorothy knew it was far more than that. It was a respect for life in all its forms, and a right-minded desire to protect and cherish it.

Maybe, thought Dorothy with a guilty pang, it was simply that she herself was worried about the extra responsibility of an animal about the place, when there were so many things to consider at this time. Would she normally have been so thoughtless to dear Agnes? Would she have been willing to welcome that cat into the household if they had been staying at Thrush Green indefinitely?

She tossed restlessly in the bed. Really, the moonlight was almost too bright, and yet it would be unpleasant with the curtains drawn.

On impulse she threw off the bedclothes and went to look out of the window. Thrush Green was deserted and beautiful. The bare branches threw black lacy shadows on the dewy grass, and Nathaniel Patten's statue gleamed in the moonlight.

What a world of utter tranquillity, thought Dorothy! Yet here she was, at its very centre, aquiver with self-torment and unhappiness.

Well, she must make amends tomorrow, she told herself, clambering back into the bed. Probably they were both over-tired with all this wretched end-of-term worry, and the added tension of the final break ahead.

She would tell Agnes, first thing, that she was truly sorry

to have upset her, and she would try and say no more about the cat. With any luck, it would adopt someone else well before the move to Barton.

The chief thing was to be reconciled with dear Agnes. She was not going to let a mere cat come between old friends!

At half-past three, as the moon dipped behind Lulling Woods, she fell into a troubled sleep.

Albert Piggott's first real outing was down the footpath at the side of his cottage to visit Dotty Harmer.

He had, of course, visited The Two Pheasants daily, and during the brief spell of warm weather, had shared a seat on the green with Tom Hardy and Polly one bright morning.

But this was his first proper walk, and he sniffed the air appreciatively as he made his way towards Dotty's cottage some quarter of a mile away.

It was good to be out and about again after his enforced sojourn indoors. Some young dandelion leaves caught his eye, and he pulled a few as a present for Dotty's rabbits.

Bending down caught his breath, and he had to stand still for a while in case a fit of coughing followed, but all was well.

He watched a coral-breasted chaffinch hopping up the stairs of the hawthorn hedge where it had its home. A rook floated down across the field on its black satin wings, and in the distance he could hear the metallic croak of a pheasant, now safe from man's guns.

Albert felt almost happy. He liked being alone. He liked all the country sounds and smells. They reminded him of his boyhood in these parts, when he had run across this same meadow at buttercup time, and gilded his broken boots with their pollen.

He looked forward to seeing Dotty after so long. The two strange people had much in common. Neither cared a

button about appearances or other people's opinions of
them. Both loved the earth and all that could be grown in
it. Both had a way with animals, preferring them to their
own kind, and each respected the other.

Dotty waved towards a small, freshly constructed pond,
She was well wrapped up in a man's old duffel coat girded
at the waist with orange binder twine. She wore a balaclava
helmet, knitted in airforce-blue wool, which was obviously
a relic from the days of war.

Wellington boots, much muddied, hid her skinny legs,
but her hands were bare and as muddy as her boots.

Her face lit up as Albert approached.

'My dear Albert! This is a lovely surprise. Come and sit
on the garden seat, and tell me how you are.'

'Not too bad, considering,' replied Albert, secretly much
touched by the warmth of her welcome. 'You better
now?'

'Never had anything wrong,' asserted Dotty roundly.
'But you know what families are.'

'I do that,' agreed Albert. 'Everlastin' worryin'.'

Dotty waved towards a small, freshly constructed pond,
around which half a dozen Muscovy ducks were sliding
happily.

'You haven't seen that, have you, Albert? Kit dug it out
and lined it. So clever. The only thing is, I want your advice
about shady plants.'

Albert considered the problem. The ducks were slithering
about on the muddy edge of Kit's creation, and it was
obvious that nothing much would grow there while the
birds disturbed the surroundings.

'If I was you,' he said, 'I'd put some sort of stone edging
round it.'

'But it would look *horrible*!' cried Dotty. 'Like those
paddling pools you see in municipal parks!'

Albert could not recall ever seeing a paddling pool nor,

for that matter, a municipal park though he supposed she meant something like the playground at Lulling.

'I never meant concrete,' he explained. 'Some nice flat bits of Cotswold stone. Percy Hodge has got no end of odd slabs lying about where his old pigsties was. Settle in nicely round that pond they would.'

'But the plants? I thought of shrubs. Some sort of willow perhaps.'

'You'd be best off standing a few tubs around with some nice bushy fuchsias or lilies. That way you could shift 'em about where you wanted 'em, and them ducks couldn't flatten the plants. Keep the edges dry too. Ducks slop enough water about to drown growing stuff.'

Dotty was silent, envisaging the picture sketched by her companion. It could be the answer. It was practical too.

'Albert,' she said, putting her skinny claw upon his sleeve, 'you are quite right! What a comfort you are!'

Albert smirked. He was seldom praised, and had certainly never been told that he was a comfort to anyone.

He cleared his throat awkwardly. He was as pink with pleasure and embarrassment as a young suitor.

'Well, I don't know – ' he began deprecatingly.

'Well, I do!' replied Dotty. 'Now when can we get hold of Percy to discuss buying the stone?'

Albert straightened his shoulders. He looked as determined as a military commander.

'You leave it to me, miss! You leave it to me!'

9 School House For Sale

THE fact that the school house would be for sale sometime after the departure of the ladies, was soon common knowledge in Thrush Green. Naturally, it was an absorbing item of news. It seemed that the school authorities might be able to sell the property earlier, as private approaches seemed welcome, but it was understood that the present tenants would not be turned out betimes.

Mr Jones of The Two Pheasants reckoned it would be pulled down and an office block erected on the site. He was already envisaging bar lunches of some sophistication for the staff, who would no doubt patronise the nearest establishment.

Percy Hodge said it was a perfectly good solid house, and his great-uncle Sidney had been one of the bricklayers on the job when it was constructed. It would be a crying shame, in Percy's opinion, to pull it down.

Albert Piggott, pint in hand, agreed with him. 'If it was good enough for Miss Watson and Miss Fogerty, let alone all them earlier schoolteachers, then it should be good enough for anyone.'

Muriel Fuller, who was spending one of her half-days of remedial teaching at the school, lamented the fact that the house was not to be maintained as part of the school premises.

'I've always felt,' she said earnestly as the teachers sat in their minute staffroom that playtime, 'that a head teacher needs to be Part of The Community.'

'Why?' said Dorothy Watson, who found that a little of Muriel Fuller went a long way.

Miss Fuller, who was still savouring her last phrase and trusting that it would be impressing her listeners, was somewhat taken aback by Miss Watson's query.

'Well,' she began, 'after all, a head teacher in evidence should be a Good Thing. An Example, I mean, a pattern of Decent Behaviour.'

'What about Ernest Burton?' enquired Dorothy, naming a local recently-dead headmaster who had been requested to leave the profession because of some unacceptable and peculiar habits.

'There are exceptions to every rule,' pronounced Muriel, glad to be let off further justification of her earlier statement.

But Dorothy Watson, as determined as a bull-terrier when she had her teeth into something, was not to be deflected.

'I really can't see why a head teacher worth his salt can't set enough example during school hours, without needing to live on the premises. After all, who is going to see him anyway, on a winter's night? And anyone who wants to get in touch with him need only lift the phone, and get him wherever he lives.'

'That's not quite what – ' began Muriel, but was saved by the whistle. Little Miss Robinson, on playground duty, had just blown a long blast, and the three ladies hastened back to their duties.

Young Miss Robinson's reaction to the news had been one of wistful longing. If only she had enough money, she mourned, she would buy the school house and live happily ever after. Happily, that is, if she could persuade Timothy to marry her. But her present boyfriend seemed remarkably shy about the future, and she had a horrid feeling that the new typist in his office had something to do with it.

So desirous of a home was Miss Robinson, at present in rather dingy digs, that she even sounded out her father one weekend, but got short shrift.

'I might scrape together a thousand,' he told her, 'but you'd want fifty times that, my girl. You save up your pennies while you're in lodgings, and maybe in a year or two you'll be able to think about owning a house.'

Harold and Isobel only hoped that quiet people, who would be unobtrusive neighbours, would take the next-door property when the time came. They were going to miss the two ladies, and Isobel, in particular, felt very sad at Agnes's departure. She determined to keep in touch with her when she moved to Barton.

The news presented Winnie Bailey with a personal problem. She felt that Richard should be told about the coming sale, but did not want him to upset her two old friends by arriving unannounced – a common habit of his – nor did she know if he would consider the house a possibility at all for his needs.

She decided to call at the school house and discuss matters with the ladies before doing anything about informing Richard. To be honest, she felt some qualms about her nephew living at such close quarters. His married life seemed to be remarkably variable and unstable, and Winnie wondered how the sober inhabitants of Thrush Green would view such a bohemian household.

However, she quelled such doubts, for Richard had expressed a desire to find a home nearby, and she had promised to let him know if anything cropped up.

Well, now it had, and she must keep her word. She crossed the green one early evening, timing her visit to fall comfortably between the ladies' teatime and the six o'clock news bulletin from the BBC.

Dorothy answered her knock, and she was soon ensconced in the sitting-room. A fire burned in the grate, and a fine bowl of paper-white narcissi scented the air.

'How snug you are in here!' cried Winnie.

'We like our creature comforts,' said Dorothy. 'We only hope we can find somewhere as agreeable in Barton.'

This gave Winnie her opening, and she explained about Richard's desire to find a home locally.

'It would be lovely to think of Richard living here,' said little Miss Fogerty. 'I remember him so well as a baby – always very forward. And if he now has two children of his own it would be so convenient for them to walk across the playground to school.'

'Only one is Richard's actually,' explained Winnie. 'His wife was married before, and the little boy is hers.'

'Well, by all means let him know about the house,' said Dorothy, 'and if he likes to come and see it we should be very pleased to let him look over it. Out of school hours, naturally.'

'I will impress that on him,' promised Winnie, 'and I shall tell him that he must telephone first to make an appointment. I'm afraid he is terribly absent-minded, and I don't want him to turn up unexpectedly.'

After a few more minutes' conversation, Winnie took her leave, and retraced her steps, planning to ring Richard later that evening, and to make quite sure that the ladies would be consulted about any visit he might make in the future.

She might have saved her breath, for Richard, true to form, was observed by a sharp-eyed infant in Miss Fogerty's class some ten days later.

'Miss,' said the child, 'there's a man walking about in the playground.'

'Probably someone to see Miss Watson, dear,' replied Agnes, who was delving into the cupboard which held, among dozens of other things, some small garments known as 'the emergency knickers'. A tearful little girl, standing close by, was obviously about to receive a pair.

'It ain't a parent,' said the boy. 'I knows all them.'

'Isn't,' corrected Agnes automatically, 'and "I know", not "knows".'

She emerged, shaking out a pair of blue gingham knickers.

'There, dear, just run along and change. Put the others into this polythene bag.'

'And it ain't a policeman, and it ain't the gas man, and it ain't the water man 'cos it ain't got no uniform on.'

'*Isn't*,' repeated Agnes, shutting the cupboard door, and making her way to the window.

'Perhaps it's a loony,' said the boy brightening.

Sure enough, the stranger appeared to be delightfully vague, weaving about the playground, and occasionally bending to study something in the hedge dividing the playground from the Shoosmiths' property next door. Luckily, Agnes recognised their visitor as Richard, opened the window, and called him over.

'Oh, hallo, Miss Fogerty,' said Richard, giving her the winning smile which disarmed so many people who had dealings with the young man, and who had determined to give him 'a piece of their minds' until the smile melted their fury. 'Are you busy?'

'I'm afraid so. You wanted to see the house I expect.'

'What house?' said the boy, who still stood by Agnes's feet.

'Go to your desk,' said Miss Fogerty sternly. 'This has nothing to do with you, Robert.'

'Well, I saw him first,' muttered the child resentfully, making his way towards his desk. Agnes was a little flustered.

'Do call at Miss Watson's classroom,' she said. 'Perhaps we could take you round the house at playtime.'

The class by this time was open-mouthed, and all work had ceased.

'Emily,' said Agnes, choosing a sensible-looking six-year-old, 'take this gentleman to Miss Watson's room, and don't forget to knock on the door first.'

The child bounced out importantly, and Agnes watched her take Richard by the hand to lead him across the playground to the headmistress.

What, she wondered with some apprehension, would Dorothy's reaction be?

Playtime had been somewhat protracted that morning as the ladies took Richard round the house.

Miss Robinson had nobly offered to do playground duty in place of Miss Watson, and watched the departure of her two colleagues and Richard with a sore heart. To think that only lack of money stood between her and a delightful home of her own! She supposed that this Richard, despite his scruffy appearance, had the wherewithal to contemplate buying the school house. Envy filled her youthful heart, but she did her duty resolutely despite an extra ten minutes added to the usual span of playtime.

She watched Richard crossing the green towards his aunt's house. Miss Watson and Miss Fogerty hurried back to their duties.

'Many apologies, my dear,' said her headmistress. 'I shall do your turn myself tomorrow to make up for your kindness. I'm afraid that young man arrived without warning. An expensive education seems to have had no effect on his manners, I'm sorry to say.'

Winnie Bailey was as surprised to see Richard as the two schoolteachers had been.

'Well, I was just passing,' said Richard when rebuked by his aunt, 'and it seemed a pity not to call in. They didn't mind a bit, you know. I don't know why you fuss so.'

'Because you are so selfish,' said Winnie. 'They are busy people, and you obviously didn't think of them at all, but simply pleased yourself.'

'In any case, I don't think it would suit us,' said Richard, ignoring his aunt's criticism of his behaviour. 'The rooms are rather poky, and there really isn't enough room to build on. On the other hand, I might bring Fenella down one day to have a look at it. She's awfully clever at seeing possibilities in a place.'

'Then you think she might contemplate leaving the gallery?'

'I don't know, Aunt Win. All I know is that we ought to get away together before things crack up again.'

He sounded despondent and Winnie's soft heart was touched.

'Well, you must sort things out between you,' she said more gently. 'Now Jenny and I are off to Lulling to do some shopping, so I shall say "Goodbye". Help yourself to coffee if you are staying for a while.'

'No, no. I'm off too. I have to look up something at the Bodleian, and then I thought I'd get a haircut. There's a good chap in the Turl.'

He waved his farewells, and the ladies collected their shopping baskets.

On the way down the hill, Winnie told Jenny about Richard's reactions to the school house.

'Good thing,' said Jenny. 'He'd never do at Thrush Green, and you'd be everlasting minding those children. Or I would!'

'Well, there are only two of them,' pointed out Winnie reasonably.

'So far,' replied Jenny. 'But I bet there'll be more. I always thought Richard looked the sort to have a big family. Profuse, like.'

'Prolific, I think you mean,' said Winnie. 'And I must say, that I hope you are wrong.'

The following Wednesday Thrush Green school broke up for the Easter holidays, much to the relief of the children and staff, and the dismay of some of the parents.

'Can't do nothing with 'im in holiday time,' announced Miss Cooke when she came to collect Nigel on the last afternoon.

'Give him plenty to do,' advised Miss Watson. 'He's an active child.'

'You're telling me,' retorted his mother, 'but he's active the wrong way. Last Christmas the little devil painted my Mum's fireplace with pink enamel paint. Said he was making it nice for Father Christmas. It ponged something awful when we lit the fire.'

Dorothy smiled vaguely and watched her lead the budding decorator away. They were the last to leave the premises, and she and Agnes returned to the school house wearily.

'Only one more term,' sighed Dorothy, 'and frankly it's a great relief to contemplate retirement.'

'I do agree,' said Agnes, easing off her shoes. 'Thank goodness we haven't too many things arranged for this holiday. It will do us good to have a real rest.'

'I must concentrate on my driving lessons though,' said Dorothy. 'Ideally, I'd like to have a day in Barton, just to chivvy the estate agent, and generally have a look round. We could stay the night at our usual place.'

'That would be lovely,' said Agnes. But she sounded half-hearted. Weariness was not all that depressed her. Somehow she had not yet found complete confidence in dear Dorothy's driving.

Besides, who would feed the little cat?

As Agnes was the first to admit, Dorothy had behaved

with outstanding magnanimity over the affair of the cat.
Apologies accepted on both sides, the business of feeding
the animal went ahead, Agnes delighting in the cat's
growing confidence and affection, and Dorothy gallantly
refraining from expressing her disfavour of the whole
affair.

She had even turned a blind eye to the wooden box filled
with straw which appeared in the garden shed, and was
obviously used by the cat at night. Agnes had timidly
expressed the hope that Dorothy did not object to the shed
door being left ajar.

'I can't see anyone stealing our ancient lawn mower and
all our gardening tools are in a deplorable condition. No, it
won't worry me to leave the shed open,' Dorothy had
replied, much to Agnes's relief.

By now, the cat allowed Agnes to stroke its tabby fur,
but leapt away when she tried to lift it in her arms. To
Agnes's pleasure, it purred when she put down its food,
and occasionally rubbed round her legs.

But it always beat a hasty retreat if Dorothy appeared. It
seemed to know that its presence was not welcomed by
that lady.

When she thought about it, Dorothy was still perturbed
at the idea of the animal being left high and dry when they
departed in the summer. However, she told herself, Agnes
had been warned, and there was still time for a good home
to be found for it or, with any luck, it would depart of its
own accord to a cat-lover as fond and foolish as Agnes
herself.

The Easter weekend was as bright and beautiful as it should
be, and St Andrew's church was a bower of daffodils,
narcissi and young leaves.

Round the steps of the font the children had put vases of
primroses from Lulling Woods, and two magnificent pots

of arum lilies from the Youngs' greenhouse flanked the chancel steps.

Mrs Bates from Rectory Cottages had surpassed herself with the cleaning of the church silver and brass, and even Albert Piggott had stirred himself enough to tidy up the porch and the gravel drive.

Everyone agreed, as they gossiped after church, that Easter was one of the loveliest of church festivals, and that St Andrew's had never looked so magnificent.

Young Cooke had mown the grass of the churchyard, and Thrush Green's inhabitants admired its striped neatness. All opposition to the moving of ancient tombstones had now vanished. It was difficult to remember the battle which had raged, some years earlier, about the levelling of the site and the shifting of the gravestones to the outer wall. Poor Charles Henstock had endured many sleepless nights worrying about the hostility of some of his parishioners to the scheme, but time seemed to have healed the wounds very successfully.

As Dorothy and Agnes crossed the green to the school house Ben Curdle appeared trundling a wheelbarrow.

'Ah, Ben!' called Dorothy, hastening towards him. 'Would it be convenient to have a lesson tomorrow evening? I really want to have an intensive course in the next week or so. Would you be free?'

'Any time you like,' said Ben. 'I'll come round about six, shall I?'

'Perfect!' replied Dorothy. 'I always enjoy my driving lessons.'

But she was not to know, when she spoke so enthusiastically, just what was in store for her.

※　　※　　※

Meanwhile, Charles Henstock did his best to assist his friend Anthony to find a suitable post for the young woman, daughter of Mrs Lilly, about whom they had spoken on the telephone.

The manager of the new supermarket about to be opened in Lulling High Street was of no help.

'Sorry, padre,' he said, 'but I've got all the girls I need. Tell you what, I'll write down the young lady's name, and if I get a vacancy she can come for an interview.'

The typist's post at Venables and Venables was satisfactorily filled, and very few people needed, or could afford, domestic help in the house.

'Of course,' said Dimity doubtfully, 'the Lovelocks want help, but they are such hard taskmasters one hesitates to send anyone there.'

'I suppose we could make it clear,' said Charles, 'that she is quite a young woman, and has this small child to care for. You wouldn't care to put the matter to Ada? Suggest that she goes for a trial period, and that not too much is demanded of her?'

'I should dislike the job intensely,' said Dimity with spirit.

Charles sighed. 'Well, we'll go on with our enquiries, dear, but if nothing turns up, I'd better tackle the Lovelock girls myself.'

His woebegone face turned Dimity's heart over, but she did not offer to face the task herself.

Who knows? Something suitable might turn up very soon.

Promptly, at six o'clock, Ben Curdle arrived with his Fiesta at the gate of the school house, and Dorothy hastened to climb in.

It was a warm April evening. The daffodils were nodding in the gardens, and the lilac was already in bud. There was a

stillness in the air, and a gentle radiance, which moved
Dorothy to quote poetry.

' "It is a beauteous evening, calm and free",' said
Dorothy, fastening her seat belt.

'Yes, it is that,' agreed Ben, looking a little startled.
'Beautiful, I mean.'

'Which way?' asked Dorothy, abandoning poetry and
getting down to business.

'I thought we'd take her up the main road, and then
come back by way of Nidden. Then, perhaps, go up the
High Street for a bit of traffic practice.'

'Right,' said his pupil, scanning both mirrors, and letting
the clutch in gently.

She turned down the chestnut avenue in front of Edward
Young's splendid house, and then left along the main
road.

'I really love driving,' said Dorothy. 'Am I doing all
right, Ben?'

'You're doing fine,' said he sturdily. 'But keep the pace
down a bit. Lots of kids on bikes now the evenings are
light.'

They drove in companionable silence for two or three
miles, then turned left into Nidden, and the lane which
would return them to Thrush Green and Lulling.

This was a much quieter road, and involuntarily
Dorothy's pace increased. They were bowling along
between the hedges which bounded Percy Hodge's fields,
when the worst happened.

Out from the farmyard gate burst Percy's young collie
dog, barking furiously. There was a sickening thump as the
near front wheel hit it, and the barking changed to a blood-
curdling squealing.

With commendable speed and control, Dorothy pulled
into the side of the lane, and was out of the car in a flash.

Just as she approached the pathetic black and white

bundle, Percy appeared, rake in hand.

'What you bin and done to my dog?' he yelled menacingly. 'Women drivers!'

He spat in an unlovely fashion, as Ben came up to his pupil's support.

10   The Accident

WITH considerable authority Ben Curdle went into the attack.

'Pity you can't keep your animals under control,' he said. 'There's a couple of cows of yours pushing at the hedge half a mile up the road. And now this!'

He squatted down beside the dog and felt its legs and ribs with expert fingers. Dorothy, much shaken, watched him with admiration, and with thoughts of Ben's indomitable old grandmother, Mrs Curdle, who had met every disaster with the same supreme courage and calm that Ben was now showing.

'We should get the vet,' she said to Percy. 'Can I use your phone?'

She was much alarmed at the condition of the animal. Its eyes were closed, its breathing heavy, but there did not appear to be much blood, except for a cut on its side.

'I'll look after my own dog, thank you,' replied Percy nastily. 'You stay here with Gyp and I'll ring young Bailey.'

He departed, leaving Ben and Dorothy eyeing the dog.

'Do you think we should lift him on to the verge?' asked Dorothy.

'Best not move him. He may have something wrong inside. We'll stay with him till the vet comes.'

'Will he die, Ben?'

Ben looked up at his distraught pupil and gave his slow reassuring smile.

'I'll take my oath, he don't,' he said. 'My guess is he's concussed, just knocked out. This 'ere graze and cut is nothing much. He'll be all right this time next week.'

'I should have seen him.'

'You had no chance. He run into you at the side. Don't you fret, miss. You've nothing to blame yourself for.'

At that moment, Percy reappeared.

'We're lucky. Surgery girl just caught the vet leaving Bill Bottomley's at Nidden. He's coming straight here.'

Dorothy strove to behave calmly. 'I'm extremely sorry to have hurt your dog, Mr Hodge, but it was entirely its fault. Ben here saw exactly what happened.'

'I don't care who saw what or whose fault it was,' declared Percy, now down on his knees beside the recumbent animal, 'but I paid good money for that dog and I'll need compensation and the vet's fees too.'

Dorothy was about to say that she would be pleased to do so, when she caught Ben's eye, saw the almost imperceptible shake of his head, and remained silent.

The dog now gave a little whimper and opened his eyes. At that moment David Bailey's Land Rover arrived on the scene, and the three stood up with relief.

'My old friend Gyp in trouble, eh?' he said, squatting down beside him. The dog began to thump his tail.

The vet ran expert fingers over the animal's body, while the others watched anxiously.

'As far as I can see he's had a bit of concussion, and this cut could do with a couple of stitches and cleaning up. If you give me a hand, Percy, I'll take him back with me to the surgery for a proper check-up. No bones broken luckily.'

'What a relief!' cried Dorothy.

'No thanks to you,' exclaimed Percy, rounding on her. 'Proper careless driving caused this, Mr Bailey. I reckon it's a case for the police.'

'If you take my advice,' said the vet who had heard all this before, 'you won't get involved with the law. The dog's not badly injured, and should have been under control in any event. Now, you lift his legs gently, Percy, and we'll get him into the van.'

'I'm coming too,' said Percy.

'So I should hope,' replied David Bailey shortly. 'Get in the front.'

'I'll telephone in an hour or two,' promised Dorothy, 'to see how he's got on.'

Percy gazed stonily ahead of him, making no reply, as the Land Rover drove slowly away.

'Oh, Ben,' quavered Dorothy, 'what a terrible thing to happen! What shall I do?' There were tears on her cheeks, and Ben's kind heart was stirred.

'You get in the car, and I'll drive us home. Remember you've nothing to blame yourself for, and don't give old Percy Hodge money for nothing. It only puts you in the wrong.'

'Well, I do see that,' admitted Dorothy, busy with her handkerchief, 'but I truthfully would feel so much better if I could have the vet's bill.'

'That's up to you,' said Ben. 'I'd probably do the same. But don't you have no truck with Percy's threats about the law. That dog had no right to be loose like that, and Perce knows it. I bet them cows is all over the road up Nidden by now,' he added with considerable satisfaction. 'Give him something to think about.'

By now they had arrived at the school house, and Dorothy's tears had dried.

'I can't thank you enough, Ben,' she said shakily. 'You were a tower of strength. I was reminded of your grandmother who was such a wonderful woman, I've been told, and a great help in trouble.'

'It was nothing, miss. Don't go worrying about it, and

don't forget I'm coming to take you out again tomorrow evening. You mustn't look upon this as a set-back. It could have happened to anyone. Why, I once ran into one of my gran's fair ponies!'

'Really? What happened?'

'Nothing to the pony. But it dented the front of my motor bike something horrible.'

Charles and Dimity Henstock had no need to brace themselves to approach the Misses Lovelock, for Nelly Piggott had also heard about Doreen Lilly, from Gladys her mother, after a bingo session one evening.

'I know some old ladies who want some help,' said Nelly hesitantly. 'But I'm not sure whether the job would suit her.'

'She can but try,' responded Mrs Lilly. 'She knows she'll have to knuckle down to a bit of hard work to keep herself and the boy. But she's certainly not living with me! For one thing I've no room, and after two days we'd be fighting like Kilkenny cats.'

'I'll do what I can,' promised Nelly, feeling some sympathy for the daughter and her problems.

The Misses Lovelock were duly informed at their next Wednesday lunch at The Fuchsia Bush, and word was sent to Gladys Lilly that they would be pleased to interview Doreen as soon as possible.

'Not that I am altogether happy about the idea of employing an unmarried mother,' observed Ada, when the sisters were back in their cluttered drawing-room.

'Oh, really, Ada,' exclaimed Violet, 'what difference will it make to her housework?' She was struggling with that day's crossword puzzle, and finding an anagram of 'grenadine' particularly elusive.

'It's not her *housework* that is in question, but her *morals*,' pointed out Bertha.

'Well, we can't do much about that,' said Violet flatly. 'It sounds to me as though she has had a hard time. Nelly said the father has vanished completely, and left this poor girl in the lurch.'

'It is very unwise,' pronounced Ada, 'to try and pre-judge the girl, and to let our hearts rule our heads. All we can do is to sum up her abilities when she comes for interview, and to show her what will be required of her. I gather from Nelly that the girl has first to find lodgings, as Mrs Lilly has no room for the daughter and child.'

'What about our top floor?' said Violet. 'There's our old nursery and the maid's bedroom.'

'Out of the question,' said Ada, rolling up her knitting. 'This house is *quite* unsuitable for a young child.'

Violet was about to say that all three of them had been born and reared in this same house, but Ada had on the look which brooked no arguing, and in any case Violet had just realized that 'endearing' fitted her clue, and so busied herself in filling it in.

It was unfortunate that the very morning after Dorothy's accident, Agnes had found the little cat unusually affectionate towards her.

It had allowed her to stroke its ears, and to pat its back very gently near the tail, and in return had patted Agnes's shoe-lace in a remarkably playful manner. Little Miss Fogerty was entranced, and prattled happily at the break-fast table upon such agreeable progress.

Dorothy, still shaken by her ordeal, and awaiting further news from Percy Hodge with some trepidation, found Agnes's enthusiasm hard to bear. Kindly though she was in disposition, on this particular morning Dorothy found the animal kingdom decidedly irritating.

'Don't make too much fuss of it,' she said crossly. 'It will be coming into the house next.'

Agnes curbed her tongue. It was plain that poor
Dorothy was still upset about Percy Hodge's dog, and who
could wonder at that? A truly dreadful experience, and
Percy could be a formidable opponent if it came to warfare.

At that moment the telephone rang and Dorothy hurried
to answer it. Agnes listened anxiously, and for once did not
close the hall door.

'I am greatly relieved to hear it,' said Dorothy.

There was a pause.

'It was good of you to ring so promptly. I have been
very worried.'

There was a second pause. Agnes debated whether to put
a saucer over Dorothy's coffee.

'By all means send Mr Bailey's account to me. I should
like to pay it, although as Ben pointed out, it was really the
dog that was at fault.'

The third pause seemed longer than ever, and Agnes
could hear Dorothy's fingernail tapping on the telephone
rest – a bad sign. It might be as well to put the coffee back
in the saucepan, at this rate.

'Well, we're not going to discuss that now, Mr Hodge,'
said Dorothy, in her most headmistressy voice. 'The main
thing is that Gyp has recovered, and I'm sure you will see
that he is under control in the future.'

She put down the receiver briskly, and returned to the
breakfast table. Apart from unusually flushed cheeks, she
seemed calm.

'Thank heaven that dog is all right,' she sighed. 'Now
Agnes, you were telling me about the cat.'

'Another time will do,' said Agnes with dignity.

The Misses Lovelock interviewed Miss Lilly in their
dining-room. They sat in a row at one side of the immense
mahogany table, and Doreen on the other, facing them.

She was a wispy little thing with fluffy fair hair, and a

permanently open mouth, indicative of adenoids. But she was soberly dressed and was clean and polite.

Miss Violet's kind heart warmed to her. She looked so young to be the mother of a three-year-old.

The girl confessed that she had no written references from her previous post, but said that she knew her employer's name and address and the number of her telephone.

'I was there nearly two years,' she said. 'She'll speak for me, I know. It was after that row with my boyfriend I decided I'd be better off nearer my mum.'

'A row?' queried Bertha.

'That's when he lit off,' explained Doreen.

'Lit off?' said Ada.

'Cleared out,' said Doreen.

'Cleared out?' echoed Bertha.

'Slung his hook,' agreed Doreen.

'Slung – ' began Violet. 'You mean he left you?'

'S'right,' acknowledged the girl.

'And you do not expect to see him again?' asked Ada.

'Hope not. About as much use as a sick headache he is. Better off without him.'

'Well, in that case,' said Ada, 'you had better come and see the kitchen first.'

The three old ladies shepherded the girl all over the house. She made no comment as she was led from the kitchen's archaic grandeur, to the drawing-room, study, and then up the lofty staircase to the over-furnished bedrooms above.

After twenty minutes all four returned to their seats in the dining-room. Violet thought that the girl looked somewhat over-awed at the prospect before her.

Miss Ada produced a paper and pencil. 'Perhaps you would write down the name, address and telephone number of your last employer. That is, of course, if you feel that you want the post.'

'What wages would you be offering, miss?'

Ada told her.

'But I was getting twice that before,' she protested, 'and only half the work as you've got here.'

'My sisters and I will consider an increase, and let you know,' said Ada.

She pushed the paper and pencil towards the girl, and with some hesitation the prospective maid began to write.

'I'm not putting my name to it,' she said, looking bewildered.

'There's no need,' Ada assured her. 'I simply want to speak to this Mrs Miller – or is it Mitter?' She squinted at the paper, holding it at arm's length.

'Mrs Miller.'

'If all is satisfactory, could you start next Monday?'

'Well, I could, I suppose. Nine till twelve, my mum said.'

'That is correct. Three mornings a week. Definitely Mondays, and we can arrange the other mornings to suit you. I think a week's notice either way would be best. If you call again on Friday morning I can let you know what we have decided would be a fair remuneration, and you can give us your decision then.'

The three ladies rose, and ushered Doreen to the door. When she had vanished round the bend of Lulling High Street, the three sisters discussed the affair.

'I do think,' said Violet, suddenly emboldened, 'that you were rather high-handed, Ada. Why couldn't we have had a word together and raised her wages then and there?'

'One doesn't want to rush into these things,' replied Ada. 'I still have to discover from Mrs Miller what sort of person she is.'

'She didn't look very *strong*,' observed Bertha.

'And one must check her *truthfulness*,' continued Ada. 'How do we know that she was getting twice the amount we offered? We'll be in a better position to discuss terms when I have telephoned Mrs Miller this evening. Do the cheap rates start at six or six-thirty? I can never remember.'

It was at the next bingo session that Gladys Lilly told Nelly about the job which Doreen had accepted after a good deal of thought, and some prodding from her mother.

'Well now,' said Nelly, 'she's a brave girl, and I only hope she knows what she's let herself in for. You tell her to pop round to the kitchen at The Fuchsia Bush before she takes up the job on Monday. I can give her a few tips about them old ladies, and the best way to manage 'em. And if she wants my advice, tell her to make sure she never agrees to do the cooking.'

'I'll tell her to look in,' promised Mrs Lilly. 'And she asked me to thank you for finding her the place.'

'Time enough to thank me,' said Nelly darkly, 'when she's had a couple of weeks with them stairs, and that half a ton of silver as needs cleaning once a fortnight. She won't be idle, I can tell you!'

'Hard work,' said Doreen's mother virtuously, 'never hurt no one!'

11 Decisions

IT was during the Easter holidays that Dorothy Watson decided that the time had come to buy her car.

The sitting-room at the school house was littered with glossy brochures from local garages extolling the virtues of innumerable vehicles. Such a plethora of literature bewildered little Miss Fogerty, but Dorothy was made of sterner stuff.

'We know what we want,' she said firmly, when Agnes confessed her perplexity in the face of so much richness. 'The car must be small, so that it will fit into any existing garage, and be easy to park. Also a small car will be more economical to run.'

'Quite right,' approved Agnes.

'Then it must be *new*, so that any defects are dealt with under guarantee. I don't propose to dabble in the second-hand market. We are not knowledgeable enough.'

'Indeed we're not,' agreed Agnes, with feeling.

'And it must be a well-known brand,' continued Dorothy, rather as if she were talking of fish-paste. 'Spares, you know.'

Agnes looked bewildered.

'I gather from Ben and Harold that it is very difficult to get spare parts for some cars. One might have to wait weeks, they tell me, for some vital bit.'

'Oh dear!' commented Agnes. 'But if it were a really new car would it need spare parts?'

'Some cars,' responded Dorothy grimly, 'have been known to be sold with several things missing completely.'

Agnes, already timid about the entire project, felt her spirits quail yet further, but she remained stoically silent.

'So after tea, dear,' said Dorothy, shuffling the jewel-bright brochures into a pile, 'we will pick out three or four possibles, and then get Harold and Ben to give us their expert advice.'

'I'm sure that would be best,' agreed Agnes bravely.

Doreen Lilly began her duties at the Misses Lovelock at nine o'clock on Monday morning.

She arrived punctually, which put all three sisters in a good mood, and Miss Violet undertook to show her the tasks allotted.

'I think it would be best to concentrate on the first-floor bedrooms today,' she said, mounting the stairs before Doreen. Violet's speckled lisle stockings, garments never before seen by the young girl, strode briskly ahead as she opened three bedroom doors to display a daunting amount of heavy mahogany furniture, curtains from floor to ceiling, and a massive washstand in each room, bearing a vast china bowl and matching ewer, soap dish and tooth mug. Such equipment was unknown to Dorren, used as she was to a modern, if scruffy, bathroom at her mother's home.

'We make our own beds,' said Violet kindly, 'so you won't have to bother with those. The curtains will have to come down before long and have a really good shaking in the garden, but today I think a thorough cleaning of the furniture and washing things will keep you busy.'

Not half, thought Doreen, but nodded silently.

'We have a vacuum cleaner for the floors,' said Violet, as one might say: 'We have a helicopter for the shopping.'

'We'd best get it then,' said Doreen.

'Of course,' replied Violet. 'We will get everything together, and I will show you where we keep all the cleaning materials. I'm sure I have no need to tell you that we expect you to use *everything* very economically. No waste in this house!'

They finished the tour of the bedrooms, and returned down the long staircase to the kitchen where Violet displayed the cupboard housing the cleaning aids. They appeared sparse and archaic to Doreen's eye, even by her modest standards.

The brushes and brooms must have been bought many years earlier, and some were almost without bristles. A pile of folded pieces of material, which were obviously squares cut from outworn petticoats and the like, appeared to be the only dusters available. Three long bars of yellow soap and a large bag labelled SODA seemed to constitute the major part of the washing department, but Doreen was relieved to see some canisters of Vim. It was like meeting an old friend amidst ancient aliens.

A mammoth tin of furniture polish, the size which Doreen had once encountered in a hospital, was handed up to her, with two of the deplorable dusters, and then Violet indicated the rest of the store with a vague wave of the hand.

'Well, there you are, Doreen, and if you find you need anything else this morning, just come and find me. You are here until twelve, I believe.'

'That's right, miss,' replied Doreen. 'Well, I'll go and make a start.'

She was half-way up the stairs, struggling with the heavy furniture polish tin, when she remembered the basins and their matching accessories.

'I'd best take up the Vim,' she said to Violet standing below.

'Ah yes! I'll shake a little into a saucer for you,' said Violet, hurrying back to the cupboard.

Doreen deposited her burden on the stairs, cast her eyes to heaven for much-needed help, and followed her new employer into the kitchen.

Percy's dog and its adventure was still a topic of conversation at Thrush Green. Blame for the accident was largely on Percy's shoulders in the bar of The Two Pheasants.

Albert Piggott took great pleasure in recounting this piece of news to Percy while they were busy selecting fragments of Percy's tumble-down wall for future use round Dotty's garden pool.

'A lot of ignorant tittle-tattle,' grunted Percy, heaving a lump of stone into his battered van. 'They wasn't there, was they? Never saw what I see. That Miss Watson was rushing along like a house afire.'

Albert, who was taking care to select pieces of stone less than half the size of his workmate's, tossed his contribution into the van.

'Ben Curdle wouldn't let her go fast. And no one ain't ever seen the old girl do more than twenty-five mile an hour. It was your job to keep old Gyp out of the road. Why, that car might have mounted the bank and tipped over! You might've been had up for murder, mate.'

'Don't talk so daft,' snapped Percy.

He changed the subject abruptly.

'How much more of this stuff do you want? I reckon this little lot will cost the old girl a tenner already.'

Albert eyed his drinking companion with dislike.

'You'll be settlin' with me, Perce, so don't you start any profiteering lark. I'm not goin' to see old Dotty fleeced, that's flat.'

'Have it your own way,' growled Percy. 'But it'll cost you a pint or two.'

Although public opinion was on her side in this much-discussed affair, Dorothy herself was more upset than she would admit.

She had put a brave face upon the matter, and Percy had certainly not gone any further with the threats he had made in the heat of the moment, but she had been shattered by his violence.

As a headmistress of some standing in the village she was unused to enmity and invective. She was also plagued, in the still of the night, by the horrors of the might-have-been, common to all.

Supposing it had been a child? Supposing she had killed not just Percy's Gyp but one of her own pupils? Or, for that matter, an adult, a friend, a neighbour? How devastatingly quick the whole incident had been! How right Ben was to point out that a car could be a weapon as lethal as a gun!

Naturally, as the days passed, her agitation grew less, and reason told her to put aside her fears and enjoy the practical advantages of having a car of her own. She envisaged the pleasure of driving with dear Agnes to various seaside places not far from Barton. There were several beautiful old houses to visit well within driving distance, and shopping could be transported with the minimum of effort.

It had been a sharp lesson, she told herself, and she must learn from it. In future she would keep a wary eye open for such dangers, but she did not intend to spoil the delight of choosing and driving her new car.

Nevertheless, the incident had left one particularly unfortunate scar. It was plain that dogs, cats, birds, and even cattle, could be a hazard, and Agnes's growing pleasure in the visiting cat worried Dorothy greatly. She really wanted nothing to do with animals at the moment, and she certainly did not want to have one permanently in the household.

What would happen, for instance, if she and Agnes decided to go away for a holiday? When they had a car they would be free to go anywhere when they had retired. An animal would be a perfect nuisance, especially a cat which would probably hate to go to a boarding establishment.

Really, thought Dorothy with exasperation, life could be very trying, particularly when one was hoping to simplify it and to make sensible plans for the future.

Well, one thing at a time, she told herself.

She went into the garden to find Agnes, and found her digging up a gigantic dandelion plant.

'Don't forget we're due next door in half an hour,' she said. 'I've collected all the car literature together, and we'll see what Harold thinks of our choice. I shall let you choose the colour, Agnes. I'm afraid you haven't had much say in the rest of the discussions.'

'I really couldn't begin,' confessed Agnes, 'but I should

be delighted to choose the colour. In fact, I rather liked Alpine Snow, or perhaps Moonlight Silver. That is, of course, if you like the idea.'

'I shall like whatever you choose,' said Dorothy handsomely, and they went indoors to get ready.

Winnie Bailey, across the green, observed the two ladies making their way to Harold and Isobel's front door, and guessed correctly that the meeting had something to do with Dorothy's purchase of a car.

The ringing of the telephone interrupted her surmises, and she was pleased to hear Richard's voice.

'Fenella wants to have a look at the school house. We thought we would come down for the weekend.'

'With the children?' asked Winnie, mentally putting up a cot in the spare room, and ordering an extra quart of milk.

'Oh yes! We shall have to bring them. Our help's on holiday. I've rung The Fleece.'

Winnie dismissed the cot and milk with relief. 'And they can put you up?'

'Yes. Friday and Saturday night. Roger is going to call in to feed the animals. The dog can be rather a nuisance in the car. Gets sick.'

'Well, I hope that you will bring Fenella and the children to see me. Tea perhaps, on Saturday?'

'I'll give you a ring when we're in Lulling, after I've sorted out our plans.'

'That will be nice. By the way, you have told Agnes and Dorothy you are coming?'

'Not yet. I was going to give them a call now.'

'Make it later this evening,' advised Winnie. She suddenly recalled the erratic hours kept by her nephew. 'But before nine, dear. They go to bed soon after.'

'*Soon after nine?*' gasped Richard. He sounded shocked.

'Yes, Richard. We keep early hours at Thrush Green. I

shall look forward to seeing you all during the week-end.'

For once, Richard seemed incapable of speech, and Winnie put down the receiver.

The Shoosmiths' sitting-room was littered with Dorothy's brochures. At first sight, it appeared that all was chaos, but in fact much had been accomplished in the first half-hour, and the choice had been whittled down to three suitable vehicles.

'There's not a lot of difference in price and size and performance between the Polo or the Fiesta or the Metro,' Harold assured them. 'It's really a personal matter. Comfort in the seating, for instance, and how you can handle her.'

Agnes, of necessity taking a minor role in this weighty discussion, wondered why cars and ships always seemed to be of the female gender.

'Well, I must say I've enjoyed driving Ben's Fiesta,' said Dorothy, 'but is it *British*?'

'I think so,' said Harold.

'Ben said he thought so too, until he opened the lid –'

'The *bonnet*,' corrected Harold automatically. Agnes thought how fitting it was for a female vehicle to have a bonnet.

'Of course, *bonnet*,' agreed Dorothy, 'and he found it was made in Spain.'

'Really?'

'Not that I have anything against *Spain*,' continued Dorothy magnanimously, 'except the bullfights, but I should like to buy a British car ideally.'

'Then it will have to be the Metro,' said Harold. 'The Polo is German, as you know. Personally, I would plump for the Polo. It's a well-made job, and nicely finished.'

Dorothy looked doubtful, and Isobel rose to refill their drink glasses to refresh all those present. This final decision was obviously going to be taxing.

'That impresses me, Harold. It really does. I value your opinion as you know.'

She sighed heavily, and took a refreshing sip from her glass. 'And of course I have nothing against Germany *now*,' she added, turning over the Polo brochure and studying the bird's eye view of its interior seating arrangements.

'However,' she resumed, putting it aside and reaching for the Metro's contribution to the temporary decor of the sitting-room. 'I still like the idea of a *British* car, supporting home industry and all that.'

'Right,' agreed Harold. 'We'll go down to the garage in Lulling and have a good look at the Metro and a drive around.'

It was a quarter-past ten when the two ladies said goodnight and retired to their bedrooms.

Dorothy was excited but exhausted. It really was dreadfully tiring making such a decision. After all, a great deal of money was involved, and the car would have to last them for several years. Perhaps the Polo would have been the right choice?

She was just removing her stockings when the telephone rang in the hall.

'Now who on earth is ringing at this time of night?' she said testily, making her way downstairs, clad only in her petticoat.

'Richard here.'

'Who? Richard Who?'

'Winnie's nephew Richard.'

'Ah yes! What can I do for you?'

He explained at some length, and Dorothy did her best

to keep her feet warm by rubbing one against the other, with small success.

Filled, as her mind was, with such things as car seats, two- or four-doors, gear-levers and what the trade euphemistically called 'optional extras', Dorothy hardly took in all that Richard was saying, but absorbed the salient point that he and his wife wanted to see the house.

'What about Saturday afternoon? Shall we say at two-thirty?' she said, catching sight of something which looked distressingly like a dead mouse under the nearby radiator. She hitched her cold feet on to the chair rail, in case life still pulsed in that small body.

'Goodbye,' she said civilly, replacing the receiver, and bravely went to investigate.

Luckily, the object was nothing more terrifying than a small ball of wool which must have escaped from Agnes's knitting bag.

Dorothy returned to her bedroom and the comfort of her warm bed.

What a day it had been!

Charles Henstock decided to call at the Misses Lovelocks' house one morning. He was rather anxious about Anthony Bull's protégée, and wondered how she was faring with her new employers.

Prudently, he carried with him a copy of the monthly church magazine, so that he had a legitimate excuse for his morning call.

It was a blustery April morning, and little eddies of dust whirled about the High Street. The striped awning over the window of The Fuchsia Bush flapped in the breeze, and the young leaves of the pollarded limes which lined the street were being tossed this way and that.

Charles took off his hat, and held it in safety with the

church magazine as he waited for the front door to be opened.

It was Doreen herself who performed the operation. She was looking, Charles was relieved to see, quite healthy and well fed.

'Ah, Doreen, I believe? You know my old friend Anthony Bull.'

'Yes. Want to come in?'

Charles entered, somewhat disconcerted by this laconic greeting. He was saved by the arrival of the three sisters from the kitchen quarters. They greeted him with little flutters of excitement, and ushered him into the drawing-room.

'So you've now met Doreen,' said Ada. 'She's settling in very well, considering.'

Charles wondered what doubts were covered by this last word.

'Good. And you find her a real help?'

'Rather slow,' said Bertha.

'And refuses to take on any cooking,' added Violet. 'But works quite hard.'

'Well, of course, it's early days yet,' said Charles soothingly. 'No doubt she will get quicker as she gets used to the work.'

He surveyed the laden occasional tables. Dozens of small silver ornaments gleamed as brightly as ever, and the two massive trumpet-shaped silver vases which occupied each end of the mantelpiece appeared to be equally immaculate. It must make an enormous amount of work, he thought, with a pang of pity for the new maid.

'I have to ring Anthony this evening,' he said, 'about a diocesan matter. I'm sure he will want to know how the girl has settled.'

'Dear Anthony,' sighed Ada.

'What sermons he gave us!' sighed Bertha.

'And always looked so handsome!' sighed Violet.

Not for the first time, poor Charles realised what a lowly figure he cut beside his distinguished predecessor. It was a good thing that he was so devoted to Anthony himself, or common jealousy might have soured his outlook.

'Some coffee, Charles dear?' said Bertha, suddenly recalled from fond memories of Anthony Bull to the duties of a hostess.

'Yes, do,' urged Ada. 'We have some left over from yesterday.'

'Most kind, most kind,' murmured Charles rising, 'but I have one or two things to get for Dimity, so I mustn't delay.'

They accompanied him to the door. Doreen was nowhere in sight, but the sound of a vacuum cleaner hummed from above.

'I meant to ask you about her living arrangements. Is she living here?'

'Good heavens, no!' replied Ada. 'Where would we put her?'

'And the boy,' pointed out Violet.

Charles, knowing full well the plentiful accommodation in the house, refrained from comment.

'It so happens,' explained Bertha, 'that her younger brother has found a job in Shropshire – '

'Somerset,' interjected Violet.

'With an uncle,' went on Bertha, giving her sister a sharp look.

'Cousin,' said Violet.

'So that there is now a spare bedroom at Mrs Lilly's and she has let Doreen and the child stay there.'

'Good. I'm glad to hear it,' said Charles, descending the steps to the pavement. 'I will let Anthony know how things are.'

'And give him our love,' called Violet to Charles's departing figure.

'I think "our love",' said Ada reprovingly, 'is rather forward. "Kind regards" would have been much more suitable for a man of the cloth.'

12 Viewing the School House

AS Winnie Bailey expected, Richard's telephone call came just before noon on the Saturday, when he announced that they would call about three-thirty. Miss Watson had arranged for them to see the house at half-past two.

'Jenny and I will look forward to seeing you,' said Winnie. She wondered if she should offer to have the two children whilst Richard and Fenella paid their visit to the school house, decided that Richard was more than capable of asking this favour, and put down the receiver with some relief.

What was Fenella like? Somehow she envisaged her as a wispy girl, dressed in unbecoming dark garments from an Oxfam shop, and with a vague expression. No doubt she would be entirely subservient to Richard, she decided. Richard, after all, was a very dominant person. It couldn't be much fun being married to someone quite so ruthlessly selfish.

She helped Jenny to set the tea in the dining-room. If Timothy were to be one of the party it was simpler to have him on a chair, at least for part of the meal time. As for Imogen, it was to be hoped that such a young child would be content with a rusk in her pram.

It was striking three by the grandfather clock in the hall when Winnie saw Richard's car parked outside the gates of Thrush Green school. There was no sign of life in or around it, so Winnie surmised that the tour of the house was taking place.

Some twenty minutes later she saw the car driving round the green, beneath the budding chestnut trees, making for her own home. She went out into the spring sunshine to greet them.

Contrary to expectation, Fenella turned out to be a large woman, quite as tall as Richard, and built on statuesque lines. She had a mop of auburn hair which cascaded over her shoulders, and clashed disastrously with the scarlet of her coat.

'Fenella, Aunt Win,' said Richard.

'How do you do? I'm so glad that you decided to have a look at Thrush Green,' said Winnie.

'I know Aunt Win,' said Timothy, appearing from the other side of the car. 'She gave me a banana.'

'What about the baby?' queried Winnie.

'Oh, she's fast asleep on the back seat,' replied her mother, in a deep contralto voice. 'Far better to leave her to it.'

Winnie was a little perturbed at the thought of the child abandoned in the car, but as the rest of the family were making purposefully towards the open front door, Winnie went ahead and ushered them in.

'Well, what did you think of the school house?' asked Winnie, when coats had been removed, and Timothy had departed to see Jenny in the kitchen.

Richard and Fenella exchanged glances.

'Well,' began Richard, 'I like it, of course, although it's really rather small. But then I've always wanted to live at Thrush Green.'

Fenella made an impatient gesture. 'He has this *thing* about Thrush Green. A *fixation*, I suppose you'd call it. Frankly, I prefer town life, but of course one could get to London fairly quickly, I imagine.'

'Would you want to?'

'Naturally. I have the gallery to run.'

Winnie was somewhat nonplussed. She had envisaged a straightforward choice. Either the family moved from town, firstly to remove Fenella from Roger's attentions, and secondly to raise the money for the new abode by the sale of the gallery, or else they did not move at all.

'I think,' said Richard, 'that we might build a large room at the back of the school house, and have a good-sized bedroom above with a bathroom and so on over the new room.'

'It would look clumsy,' said Fenella. 'Far better to knock down that grotty little kitchen, and make a really big living-room there.'

Winnie was glad that neither Dorothy nor Agnes were at hand to hear their immaculate kitchen so summarily dismissed.

'So you think it might be altered?' she said diplomatically. 'I mean, it looks possible for your needs?'

'Richard seems to think so,' said Fenella off-handedly. 'Where he's getting the money from, I really don't know.'

'Fenella,' began Richard, 'you know we've discussed this time and time again! If you sell the gallery – '

'I've no intention of selling my only means of livelihood,' replied Fenella, her voice rising dangerously. 'So you can put that idea out of your mind at once.'

Luckily, Timothy burst into the room at this juncture, and waved a fistful of finely cut bread crusts in his father's face.

'Jenny's making sandwiches for tea. Tomato. She said I was to throw these out for the birds, but I'm not going to. I'm hungry.'

He shook his burden fiercely, scattering crumbs upon the carpet. Richard and Fenella, glowering at each other, appeared to be oblivious of the child's presence, and it was Winnie who took him into the garden, and directed his attention to the bird-table, with some relief.

Whilst the boy deposited some of the crusts there, and three or four into his mouth, Winnie considered the recent conversation. Either Richard had not told her the whole story on his earlier visit, or Fenella had suddenly decided to hold out and remain at the gallery. Without its sale, Winnie had gathered, they could not consider a move, even into something as relatively modest as Thrush Green school house.

Well, it was their affair, she told herself, returning to her duties as hostess.

'Come along, Timothy. We'll ask Jenny to put on the kettle. If you are so hungry we'd better have an early tea.'

Richard was standing by the sitting-room window, gazing across the green, and jingling coins in his trouser pocket. He looked extremely irritable.

Fenella had put her feet up on the couch and was immersed in a copy of *Country Life*. The air was heavy with unspoken acrimony.

'I think we'll have tea early,' said Winnie. 'Timothy seems hungry after his journey, and I'm sure you can both manage a cup.'

Fenella dropped the magazine to the floor, and removed her feet from the couch.

'I never take tea,' she said. 'And, do you know, this is the first house I've been in which takes *Country Life*.'

'I'm having tea,' said Richard.

'So am I,' said Timothy.

'Oh well,' said Fenella, flouncing to her feet. 'I suppose I'd better have some too.'

Winnie would like to have retorted with: 'Don't strain yourself!' but common civility restrained her, and she led the way into the dining-room.

This, she feared, was going to be one of the stickiest tea parties she had ever had to direct.

⁑   ⁑   ⁑

Whilst Winnie and Jenny were entertaining their guests, Albert Piggott and Dotty Harmer were surveying the ornamental pond site.

At the moment it was far from ornamental. The pile of Cotswold stone from Percy's farmyard was stacked to one side, and six inches of slimy water filled the shallow crater which was to be metamorphosed in days to come.

Most people would have found it a depressing sight, but Dotty and Albert, with future beauty in their inner eyes, were beaming upon it as if irises, goldfish, lilies, dragonflies and all the delights of water were already before them.

The ducks were huddled together beneath a nearby gooseberry bush. There was disenchantment in their beady eyes and their only hope, it seemed, was a nice bran mash before darkness set in.

'Won't they just love it,' cried Dotty, pulling her shabby cardigan round her with such force that a button flew into the depths of the pool.

'Ah, they will that!' agreed Albert. 'I've bin thinking. Once we've set these 'ere stones around flat, what about a little stone path for them to walk down into the water?'

'An excellent idea, Albert,' exclaimed Dotty. 'How soon can you start?'

Albert pushed back his cap and scratched his lank locks. Years of procrastination made him cautious when confronted by such a direct request.

'I might manage a couple of days later in the week,' he said grudgingly. 'But I'd need a hand shifting some of these bigger slabs. Too much for you, miss.'

'Never fear,' cried Dotty. 'Kit will help, I know, and I could direct things.'

The prospect of Dotty supervising the laying of the pond's surround, with numerous agitated and contradictory directions, was not one which Albert cared to dwell upon, but having committed himself so far there was nothing much which could be done about it.

He replaced his cap, and sighed. 'Well, see you Wednesday then, if that suits Mr Armitage.'

'He will fit in with you, Albert,' said Dotty firmly.

Poor devil, thought Albert! A rare pang of pity for a fellow-creature stirred his stony heart. There was a good deal of Dotty's rugged old father in her, and a wicked tyrant he had been, as any past pupil of Lulling Grammar School would affirm.

Albert, as a reluctant scholar, had always counted himself lucky to be in the dunces' class at his much more kindly elementary establishment at the other end of Lulling.

'I'll leave all that to you, miss,' he said, shuffling off towards Thrush Green.

Harold Shoosmith took Dorothy and Agnes to view the three cars which they had selected from the brochures, but it was quite apparent to Harold that Dorothy was already determined to have the Metro.

Luckily, there was a demonstration model waiting at the garage, and the manager took out his prospective customer with Harold sitting in the back. Agnes excused herself, saying that she had some Vedonis underwear to collect from the draper's, and four currant-buns from The Fuchsia Bush. She would meet them again at the garage.

Dorothy managed the car very well, and Harold felt very proud of his minor part in her tuition. Ben Curdle had done a good job, and if she had needed to pass a driving test, thought Harold, she would have been perfectly competent.

She coped with the traffic in Lulling's busy High Street, and then drove a few miles out into the Cotswold countryside. Harold was relaxed enough to notice the signs of spring, the lambs in the fields, the warm breeze blowing through the window, and the freshness of young leaves. It was a good time to buy one's first car, he thought, and how much the two friends would enjoy it!

They had certainly earned their leisure after so many years of devoted teaching. He hoped that they had many years of health and retirement before them at Barton.

When they turned into the forecourt of the garage, Agnes was already waiting for them. She looked at Dorothy's face, pink with pleasurable excitement. There was no doubt about it. This was the car she wanted. Left to herself, she would have signed, there and then, any papers put before her by the delighted manager, but Harold felt a few minutes to calm down might be a wise thing.

'I suggest that we have a cup of coffee,' he said, 'and we will let you know after that.'

'Good idea,' said the manager. 'I have one or two telephone calls to make, so I shall be on hand if you need me.'

Harold ushered the two ladies into the café, and ordered a pot of coffee from the languid Rosa who seemed reluctant to leave the job of painting her nails.

'Definitely the right car,' announced Dorothy when Rosa had ambled away. 'What do you think?'

'It will suit you very well,' said Harold. 'The Metro's got a good name, and it is a British car which is what you want. You handled her beautifully, my dear.'

Dorothy flushed with pleasure at such praise.

'But the colour?' faltered Agnes.

'I was coming to that,' said Dorothy. 'You still like the idea of a white one?'

'Well,' said Agnes, 'it's just that I think a *white* car shows up so much better than a dark one. Coming out of turnings, or driving under trees, you know, one always seems to *take notice* of a light-coloured car. But, of course,

Dorothy, if you prefer *another* colour, you know that – '

'White it shall be,' said Dorothy firmly. 'Now, Harold, tell me about any particular points that you think we should consider before we return.'

Over coffee the two discussed such matters as petrol consumption, maintenance, the advisability of having mud flaps fixed, a wiper for the rear window and a host of financial queries, so that Agnes let her mind drift happily on the peculiar names given to car colours. Quite as odd, she thought, as the names on the stockings she had inspected when going to collect her underwear at Lulling's foremost draper's. Who would know what colours to expect from 'Wild Mink', 'Desert Rose', or 'Spring Smoke', if they were ordering by post?

Dorothy and Harold had finished their coffee long before Agnes had got half-way through hers, and as Dorothy had now reverted to her usual sensible self, after her bout of euphoria, she and Harold departed to the garage, leaving Agnes to finish her coffee in peace.

It was while she was savouring the last few drops, that the door of The Fuchsia Bush was pushed open by a young man who was a stranger to little Miss Fogerty.

He was exceptionally tall, with close-cropped auburn hair, and wore one gold ear-ring. He was clad in the usual blue denim trousers and a leather jacket, much decorated with studs and fringe.

Rosa, whose nails were now finished to her satisfaction, sauntered over to this visitor, and exchanged a few words, which Agnes was unable to hear.

Rosa accompanied him to the door, and appeared to be directing him along Lulling High Street towards the church. He vanished from sight for some minutes, and then appeared on the other side of the road, where he stood, partly concealed by one of the High Street's lime trees. He was taking a great interest in one or more of the buildings close to The Fuchsia Bush, and Agnes wondered if he were, perhaps, an architectural student of some sort. Certainly, there were several fine examples of Georgian buildings close by, which many people came to admire.

He was still there when Agnes emerged to make her way to the garage. He was now making a sketch, it seemed, of the front of one of the houses.

Without doubt, a student, thought Agnes kindly, with great plans and ambitions.

If she had known the plans already fermenting in the young man's mind, little Miss Fogerty would have been severely shocked.

The end of the Easter holidays was now approaching and, much to Dorothy's disappointment, the eagerly awaited new car had not arrived.

A *white* Metro, she was told, would have to be ordered. If she would be content to have a blue, a red, a black or a green one then, of course, it could be supplied immediately.

'It really is ridiculous,' fumed Dorothy. 'I'm sure there must be dozens of people asking for a *white* car. So frustrating! I was so looking forward to a trip to Barton during the holidays.'

Agnes was much agitated. 'Oh dear! I feel that it is all my fault, Dorothy, for suggesting that we settled for a white model. Are you sure you wouldn't like to change your mind? You know that I shall be perfectly happy with any colour you choose.'

'I shouldn't dream of it,' said Dorothy firmly. 'White it shall be, even if we wait until the cows come home.'

They spent the rest of the morning tidying the school house garden. The daffodils were now dying, and Agnes felt how sad it was that this would be the last time that she snapped off the dead heads in this much-loved garden.

She said as much to Dorothy who was attacking the

garden bed beneath the kitchen window with a small hand fork.

'And the last time, I hope, although I very much doubt it, when I shall be digging out this fiddling bindweed. These wretched roots travel miles underground, and keep snapping off just when I think I've conquered them.'

She sat back on her heels and pushed the wisps of hair from her perspiring forehead. Agnes was standing, holding the bucket brimming with the golden heads of daffodils. She was gazing intently at the hedge between their garden and the school playground, and very soon Dorothy saw what had caught her attention.

The tabby cat was emerging into the spring sunlight. It paused for a moment, as if to assess any perils in the offing, and then came steadily forward to greet Agnes with little chirruping sounds, half-mew half-purr.

Agnes put down the bucket very gently, and held out her hand. Her face was suffused with pleasure, Dorothy noticed. Without any hesitation the cat came to rub round Agnes's legs and to respond to the rubbing of its striped head.

Dorothy, sitting very quietly, watched this display of mutual affection with mixed feelings. It was touching to see the joy with which Agnes greeted her friend, and certainly the cat was a fine creature, far more handsome now than some months earlier when she had caught sight of the bedraggled animal in the garden. Agnes's succour had certainly been rewarded.

On the other hand, how difficult it was going to be to part these two friends when the time came to leave Thrush Green. Dorothy gave a gusty sigh, and the cat suddenly became aware of her presence.

It darted away to the shelter of the hedge again, and Agnes, still bemused with joy, picked up her bucket.

'Isn't that wonderful?' she cried. 'It's the first time he has come up to me of his own accord! And I haven't even got his saucer with me! It shows how confident he is getting, doesn't it?'

Dorothy scrambled inelegantly to her feet, and sat down on the nearby garden seat with relief. For once, she was speechless.

Much troubled, she watched her friend as she carried her load to the distant compost heap. Agnes was singing quietly to herself. Her step was light. She was a girl again.

Oh dear, oh dear, thought Dorothy! How would it all end?

13 Bingo Gossip

ONE bright morning, Betty Bell burst into Harold Shoosmith's study bearing two dusters and a tin of polish in one hand, and lugging the vacuum cleaner behind her with the other.

'All right to do you now?' she cried.

'Well –' began Harold, folding the newspaper resignedly.

'Good. I always like to get you settled first,' said Betty, dropping the polish, and untangling the flex of the cleaner.

'As a matter of fact – ' said Harold. The whirring of the cleaner drowned his words.

'Where's Mrs Shoosmith then?' shouted Betty, above the racket.

'Shopping.'

'What say? Can't hear a word with this contraption going.'

She switched it off.

'I said that she was shopping.'

'Ah!' Betty bent again as if to switch on, thought better of it, and stood up, hands on hips.

'You seen Dotty's – Miss Harmer's pond?'

'Not yet.'

'It's a real treat. She called me in to see it as I was passing Monday. No – I tell a lie! It must have been Tuesday, because it was Bright Hour, Monday. Or was it Tuesday now?'

'Does it matter?'

'What, Bright Hour?' cried Betty indignantly. 'Of course it matters! Why, we have lovely talks about what to do after being in prison or hospital – *after-care* it's called – and how to keep your husband off the booze, and that!'

'I'm sorry,' said Harold humbly. 'I meant, does it matter if you saw the pond on Monday or Tuesday?'

Betty looked baffled. 'Well, I never saw it *both* days. Now I come to think of it, it was definitely Tuesday because my book come.'

The book, as Harold knew, was her weekly magazine. Occasionally she had pressed a copy upon him, recommending one of the stories whose illustrations had been enough to quell any desire to read the text. However, he had kept it for a day or two, out of politeness, before returning it.

'So, go on,' he said.

'What about?'

By now Betty was on her knees retrieving the tin of polish which had rolled under a chair.

'The pond.'

She sat back on her haunches.

'It looks a bit of all right. Percy Hodge took the stones there, out of one of his old buildings what fell down. I bet he charged poor old Dot – Miss Harmer – more'n he should. He's that sharp, is Perce, must have been born in the knife drawer.'

She stood up, puffing heavily.

'And Albert Piggott and Mr Kit laid 'em round. Mind you, Miss Harmer stood by and told 'em how she wanted it, but between them all it looks lovely.'

Harold could well envisage the operation, and particularly the part of overseer played by the redoubtable Dotty.

'Well, can't stop here all day chatting to you,' said Betty cheerfully. 'Best get on.'

She switched on the cleaner again, and Harold made good his escape into the peace of the garden.

Here all was cool and calm. The schoolchildren were safely in their classrooms. The playground lay empty in the sunlight, and Betty's activities were muted by distance to a low humming noise.

Harold seated himself on the garden bench, and looked about him with approval.

The tulips were making a brave show, stretching up to meet the budding lilac. The gnarled old red hawthorn was breaking into rosy bloom, and the irises were in bud close by. There was no doubt about it, Thrush Green was the right place to live!

He thought of the years he had spent abroad, of the dust, the heat, the appalling smells of tropical lands where he had been obliged to spend his working life, and he sighed with pleasure at his present surroundings. He still came across old friends who had shared his life abroad, who bemoaned the fact that they had so little help with their domestic duties, who bewailed the fact that it was they who now had to shop and cook, to clean and mend, where once the ubiquitous 'boys' obliged.

Harold had no time for such self-pity. Left alone, he had managed pretty well and enjoyed the change of occupation. His happy marriage had added to his well-being, and the advent of the boisterous Betty into the household had certainly helped with the everyday chores. He was a lucky man!

He could hear her now, voice uplifted in song.

> *'See what the boys*
> *In the back room will have,*
> *And tell them*
> *I'm having the same!'*

carolled Betty. Her fresh country voice was in complete contrast to the husky tones of Marlene Dietrich's rendering which Harold recalled from years ago.

'I bet she didn't learn that at the Bright Hour,' observed

Harold to a gaggle of chaffinches nearby, and went in to find his newspaper.

Dotty's pond was now a topic of discussion generally at Thrush Green. Albert Piggott was flattered to find several people congratulating him on his efforts. In such a beneficent atmosphere he almost smiled, and certainly Nelly found him a relatively cheerful companion when she returned from her labours at The Fuchsia Bush.

'It's the exercise,' she told him, as she sizzled liver and bacon for their supper. 'That's what you need. You're always on about your diet, but good food never hurt no one, and I don't care what Doctor Lovell says. A good bustle about in the fresh air is all you need.'

'In moderation! In moderation!' growled Albert who did not want to abandon his role as a martyred invalid too readily. It came in useful when unwelcome jobs such as tidying the church cropped up. 'That's what my old dad always said,' he continued. 'So don't think you can go on everlasting with that frying pan, just because me ulcer's a bit better.'

Nelly snorted, and slapped a heaped plate before her husband. It gave her some satisfaction to see that it was cleared in ten minutes.

'It's my bingo tonight,' she informed him. 'So don't go swilling beer next door while I'm out.'

She cleared the table, bustling briskly about the kitchen despite her bulk, and was ready within half an hour to accompany her friend Mrs Jenner to the Corn Exchange at Lulling, for her weekly treat.

Half-way through the evening's proceedings there was always a welcome break for coffee and biscuits. On this occasion, Nelly found herself sharing a small table with Gladys Lilly, and asked how Doreen was faring at the Lovelocks.

'It's pretty hard going,' admitted Mrs Lilly, 'as you said it would be, but I tell her she's lucky to have a job at all.'

'That's right,' agreed Nelly comfortably.

'But between ourselves,' continued Gladys, lowering her voice, 'she's proper unsettled. Keeps wanting to go out of an evening instead of stopping in with the baby. After all, I have him all day. It's only fair she takes over when she's home.'

'Well, she's young, of course,' said Nelly indulgently. 'Probably misses her husband.'

'He never was her husband,' said Gladys shortly.

'Sorry. I never thought.'

'To tell you the truth, that's another worry.'

'What is?'

'That chap of hers. I don't mind telling you, because I know it won't go any further – '

'Of *course* not,' said Nelly, now agog.

'But he was sent down for a twelvemonth for stealing, and I reckon he's just about out now.'

'In prison?' breathed Nelly.

'It wasn't all his fault,' said Gladys. 'Mind you, I'm not making excuses for him. I'm chapel and proud of it, and stealing's stealing, no matter what these social workers tell you. But all I'm saying is that the lad got into bad company soon after he left school, and they led him on. You know how it is. A bit of threatening, and a bit of jeering, and some of these tough boys can get the weaker ones to do the dirty work.'

'Well, I never!' gasped Nelly, suitably impressed with these disclosures. 'So where is he now, do you think?'

'That's what I don't know, but I hope he doesn't come worrying our Doreen to go back to him. She's that soft, she might well give in.'

'Surely not, if he left her in the first place?'

'Well, I hope not, but girls these days are soppier than

we were, for all their dressing tough in denims and that. I
blame this pill for a lot of it. In my young days we just said
"No", and that was that.'

'You're quite right,' agreed Nelly virtuously.

At this moment the master of ceremonies called the
company to the second half of the proceedings.

'Mind, not a word to anybody,' warned Mrs Lilly, as the
two made their way back to their seats.

'Trust me,' Nelly assured her.

Of course, she told Mrs Jenner this delicious morsel of
gossip as they returned home after bingo, and her friend
was suitably impressed.

'I don't like to speak ill of anybody,' said Mrs Jenner,
who was obviously about to do just that, with every
appearance of enjoyment, 'but Doreen Lilly was always a
fast hussy, and Gladys Lilly was too soft with her by half.'

'Is that so?'

'There was talk of a baby on the way when she was in
her last year at school. I never knew the rights of the affair,
but there's no smoke without fire, I always say.'

'Very true. Some of these young girls get very head-
strong, I must say.'

'They bring their troubles sometimes,' agreed Mrs
Jenner. 'And I'm always so thankful that my Jane never
gave us cause for concern. A thoroughly good girl she
always was.'

'Properly brought up, that's why,' said Nelly, as they
puffed up the hill to Thrush Green.

'Well, maybe that had *something* to do with it,' conceded
her friend.

They said goodnight with affection, and made for their
own abodes with the comfort of this new nugget of news
to warm them.

✻   ✻   ✻

Within a week or so, as might be expected, it was generally known that the father of Doreen Lilly's child had been in prison.

Probably the only two people unaware of this interesting fact were Dorothy Watson and Agnes Fogerty. They had more than enough to do to cope with their own affairs at the moment.

This last term at Thrush Green school seemed to be packed with out-of-classroom activities. Already the ladies had been asked to keep the final afternoon of the school term free, for what Charles Henstock called 'a little celebration'.

He was considerably agitated when Dimity pointed out that 'a tribute' might have been a better way of putting things.

' "A celebration" might sound as though you are celebrating their departure,' explained Dimity.

'Well, we are,' protested Charles.

'Yes, but you are not *pleased* that they are going! It's like those notices in the "Deaths" column about a service of thanksgiving. If only people would fork out the extra money to add: "For the life and work of etc.," all would be clear, but it does look sometimes as if the bereaved were thankful to see the back of the dear departed.'

'Really,' exclaimed Charles, 'you horrify me! I had *never* in all my life, looked at it that way!'

'That's because you are a thoroughly good man,' said Dimity affectionately. 'Now stop worrying about it.'

The two teachers had also been asked to 'a meeting (venue to be arranged)' on the last Sunday of term, and to the July meeting of the Parent–Teacher association when 'a presentation to two well-loved ladies' was planned.

The engagement diary, kept beside the telephone in the school house, was getting uncommonly full although it was only May, and already Dorothy and Agnes were beginning to feel somewhat harried.

'I know it is all meant so *kindly*,' said Dorothy after school one day, when the two were restoring themselves with a cup of tea in the sitting-room, 'but I must say I shall be quite relieved when it is all over.'

'I feel exactly the same,' confessed Agnes.

The telephone rang, and Dorothy padded out in her stockinged feet to answer it.

She was some time in the hall, and Agnes sipped her tea and studied Dorothy's abandoned shoes lying askew on the carpet.

'Not another party?' she asked when her friend returned.

'Worse,' said Dorothy. 'Ray and Kathleen are calling in on their way back from Dorset next week.'

'How nice!' exclaimed Agnes. Dorothy's brother Ray and his wife were always more welcome to Agnes than to Dorothy who had little time for Ray and even less for his self-pitying hypochondriac of a wife.

'Well, at least they won't stop long,' said Dorothy, thrusting her feet into the shoes. 'They're stopping for tea before they get here, so a glass of something should foot the bill, and make less washing up.'

'Do you think they will bring their dog? What's-his-name?'

'Harrison? Heaven forbid!' Dorothy shuddered at the remembrance of the havoc caused by the exuberant animal in the house.

But Agnes was anxious about the well-being of her dear little cat, who might be scared away from the garden by the boisterous visitor. With commendable restraint she forbore from mentioning her fears to Dorothy, but she hoped that Ray and Kathleen would have the sense to leave their pet safely in the car.

One of the first people to visit and admire Dotty's new plaything was Winnie Bailey, who took advantage of a fine

May afternoon to cross the green and take the footpath to Dotty's cottage.

The air was soft and balmy. Rooks wheeled above the lime trees in the gardens behind The Two Pheasants, bearing food for their vociferous nestlings.

In the Youngs' garden a sea of forget-me-nots surged around some splendid pink tulips lined up against the Cotswold stone of the fine house. A waft of warm air brought the scent of a bed of wallflowers, hidden from Winnie's sight by a mellow wall, and already the chestnut trees were showing embryo flower spikes.

Nothing, thought Winnie, could touch the month of May for sheer natural beauty. There were many devotees of autumn, praising the blazing trees, the joys of harvest and the like, but May was a time of hope, of youth, of splendours to come. It renewed her strength every year with its promise of summer joys.

She found her old friend in the chicken run, clutching an armful of wet weeds to her cardigan.

'Ah, Winnie!' cried Dotty. 'How nice to see you! Just let me scatter this nourishing salad for the girls, and I'll be with you. Such richness! Chickweed, hogweed, dandelions, shepherd's purse, groundsel, and lots more – all *teeming* with natural goodness. I can't persuade Connie to use such things for us unfortunately, but I suppose we get the nourishment, at second-hand as it were, in the hens' eggs.'

She cast her burden from her among the cackling birds, wiped her muddy hands down her skirt, and emerged from the run. Her bedraggled appearance somewhat shocked Winnie.

'Don't you think you should change your cardigan, Dotty? It's soaking wet, and you know how easily you catch cold.'

'Nonsense!' said Dotty, slapping her skinny chest. 'It'll soon dry. You're as bad as Connie.'

Winnie did not like to point out that it was Connie who had to do any nursing of this rebellious patient, and she followed Dotty across the garden to the new pond.

It certainly looked a fine piece of work, although still rather raw in appearance. No doubt, thought Winnie, once the stones had weathered and Dotty's tubs of plants were in place, it would be very attractive. The ducks seemed to be enjoying themselves, half of them diving with their feet waving happily, and the rest preening themselves on the surrounding stones in the sunshine.

'Dear things,' said Dotty fondly. 'It's such a treat for them, and I've had four eggs already.'

She waved her friend towards a garden seat, and they took their ease.

'And you are keeping well?' asked Winnie, trying to ignore Dotty's damp bosom.

'Just a touch of the jim-jams in my back, but Connie's taking me to see Tom Porter tomorrow, and he'll put me right.'

'You still go to him?'

Tom Porter was the local osteopath, used by a great many Lulling people, but Winnie had never had need, or desire, to take advantage of his gifts. Donald had never countenanced osteopathy and Winnie remained loyal to his beliefs.

'I never liked to tell your dear Donald,' said Dotty, as if she could read Winnie's thoughts. 'I know he didn't approve, but I always felt that Tom had such a sound working knowledge of the *skeleton*!'

'So have doctors,' replied Winnie defensively.

'Not to the same extent. I'm sure that Donald was very good on muscles and skin and the fleshy bits. And, of course, all those inner tubes – so alarmingly complicated – but the *framework* seems to be somewhat ignored by general practitioners.'

'Well, I shan't argue with you,' said Winnie. 'But what does he do?'

'He makes me lie flat on his rather hard couch, and crosses one leg over the other for a start.'

Here Dotty thrust out her skinny legs in their wrinkled lisle stockings for Winnie's approval.

'Then he presses on one knee, *quite gently*, and keeps measuring the lengths.'

'Of your knees?'

'No, no, dear! My legs! One seems to get shorter than the other which makes my back hurt.'

Winnie was about to say that surely the displacement of the back did the leg-shortening, but Dotty's grasshopper mind had already leapt to other topics.

'Tell me about Dorothy and Agnes. Have they got their car yet? And have they found a house at Barton? I hear from Betty Bell that Ray and Kathleen Watson are going to visit them soon. I wonder if they might take the school house eventually? Ray must be almost at retirement age, and I'm sure that country air would be good for Kathleen's health.'

'I don't know much about Ray and Kathleen's plans,' began Winnie, 'but I know that Dorothy is still waiting for a *white* car, and I don't know if a house at Barton has cropped up yet.'

She paused, while Dotty

leapt to her feet, entered the nearby garden shed and reappeared with a hunk of stale bread which she began to tear into pieces and throw to the ducks.

A frenzied quacking and splashing ensued, while Dotty beamed upon her charges and scattered her largesse.

She really grows scattier every month, thought Winnie, but when it came to keeping an eye and ear open to local gossip then Dotty was as sharp as the rest of Thrush Green.

Part Three

Journey's End

14   Trying Times

AFFAIRS at Thrush Green school seemed to grow more hectic as the weeks passed. As well as the interminable tidying up, wondering what to reject completely, what to pass on to Miss Robinson for future school use, and what to keep 'just in case', the two retiring ladies had had several visits from would-be future teachers at the school.

To give them their due, these aspirants were careful to make an appointment and were sensible enough to make their visits brief, but nevertheless Dorothy found the interruptions to routine excessively wearing.

'I suppose it is only right that they should want to see where they might be spending the rest of their lives,' said Dorothy, 'and these are all on the short list.'

'I wonder how many have been invited?' pondered Agnes.

'Five or six for each post, I presume,' replied Dorothy. 'I imagine they'll appoint to both posts on the same day. What do you think?'

'I've no idea,' said Agnes, secretly hoping that none of them would be as nervous as she had been when she applied for her present post so many years ago.

'Quite a few men among the applicants, I noticed,' went on Dorothy. 'For the headship, of course. Naturally, a woman will take on your place.'

'I don't see why a nice man couldn't do the job,' said Agnes, with some spirit. 'I particularly liked that young fellow in the National Trust tie you brought in.'

'I can't see him coping with young children,' said Dorothy grimly. 'He talked of nothing but racing cars and rugby football.'

'No news, I suppose, from Better and Better?' asked Agnes, steering the conversation into different, if not less controversial, waters.

'A small house and two flats,' replied Dorothy, fishing in her handbag. 'I meant to show you at breakfast but you were out feeding that cat.'

'Any hope?' said Agnes, ignoring the slight on her pet.

'The small house,' said Dorothy, adjusting her glasses, 'is reached "by a long drive". That means we'd have to keep it up, dear, unless it's a cart track, in which case it would probably be impassable for part of the year.'

'And the flats?'

'In the same garden, and four miles from Barton.'

'So we are no nearer?'

'As you say. Sometimes I think our estate agent should be called "Worse and Worse". If only we had the car, we could run down and visit the estate agent and try and get some sense out of him.'

'Perhaps another letter – '

'I sometimes wonder if they ever read letters,' replied Dorothy with despair. 'Ah well! There's the bell. Better get back to our classrooms.'

Some of the applicants had asked to see the school house, although they knew that it did not now automatically go with the post, and Dorothy and Agnes had readily invited them to view the property in case they wished to buy.

Otherwise, only Richard and Fenella, and a local couple who had heard about the future disposal of the building, had visited the ladies, and for this Dorothy was grateful.

She admitted to herself that these last few months were a great strain. After so many years of well-organised living she found the unknown a little daunting. Impatient by nature, she suffered far more from the frustration of waiting for the new car and from the interminable delay of finding suitable living places in the Barton area, than did Agnes.

Agnes, however, was equally agitated about the change of circumstances. Devoted as she was to Dorothy, would it be difficult to live for the whole of the day, every day, with her partner? She had found her extremely short-tempered of late, and although she knew only too well that they were both living under extra pressure, she was secretly hurt by one or two wounding remarks, and had had to curb her own tongue.

Then too, she was beginning to get very anxious about the cat. It was now remarkably tame and affectionate, and Agnes felt quite sure that it could be introduced into the school house, and later transported to Barton, without much trouble.

Alone, of course, there would have been no difficulty, but Dorothy still appeared adamant, and showed no sign of relenting, or even being willing to discuss the matter. With so much else to occupy their minds, Agnes had shelved the problem, and simply enjoyed the growing companionship of her new friend.

She was the one, she realised, who would miss severely the children and all their old friends in Thrush Green. Dorothy was more out-going and would soon make friends at Barton. Agnes, less bold, knew full well that it would take her longer.

However, there was not much one could do about it at this stage, and apart from deciding to keep up with such dear neighbours as Isobel and Harold, Winnie Bailey, Muriel Fuller and the like, by letter writing, or the occasional telephone call, Agnes pursued her gentle way from day to day, and dealt with the problems as they turned up.

It was about this time that Isobel received a letter from her old friend in Sussex. It was several pages long, and seemed to engross Isobel all through breakfast time.

'Your post seems more interesting than mine,' observed Harold. 'I've only got one offering me a loan, another asking me to support a family in Africa, and a demand for the rates.'

'This is from Ursula,' said Isobel.

'The one who gave you splendid picnics on the way to see some aged relative? Strawberries and cream, wasn't it?'

'And cold asparagus wrapped in brown bread,' agreed Isobel, smiling at him. 'How greedy you are!'

'What does she want?'

'Nothing. Just the other way about in fact. She has a rather splendid tea set to give me.'

'How's that?'

'The aunt at Barton has evidently left it to me. Ursula said I admired it, and her aunt made a note of it. Very sweet of the old lady, I must say. I remember it well – Wedgwood, white with a gold band, very elegant. We must keep it "for best", Harold.'

'Does she want us to fetch it?'

'That's the idea. She's at Barton clearing up the place. I imagine she will live there eventually.'

'Well, it won't take us long to run down. Does she give her telephone number?'

'She does indeed. I will ring this evening. Isn't it a lovely surprise?'

'A much nicer one than my rates demand,' agreed Harold.

*   *   *

Ray and Kathleen's visit coincided with a particularly trying day at Thrush Green school.

For a start, one of Agnes's children fell in the playground before school began. The boy grazed both knees, and understandably yelled the place down, which upset Agnes considerably. Furthermore, he resisted any attempts at first aid with such violence that Agnes was obliged to scribble a note to his mother, luckily at home nearby, and dispatch note and child in the care of the oldest and most responsible girl in Miss Watson's class.

In her classroom, after assembly, Dorothy noticed a girl weeping. Her face was flushed, her forehead afire, and on examination Miss Watson discovered a fine bright rash on the girl's chest, which she readily recognised as chicken-pox.

As the child had twin sisters in Miss Robinson's class, it seemed sensible to send all three home, but both parents were at work, and there seemed to be no obliging aunts, grannies or neighbours to take charge.

Dorothy took them over to the school house, put the sufferer on to the spare bed with a doll and two books, and ensconced the twins in the kitchen with lemonade and drawing paper.

At playtime it was discovered that all the milk was decidedly off-colour, and none of the children would touch it. The staff's coffee had to be black which none of them liked.

By midday, the mother of the three invalids had arrived in answer to the message sent to her place of work. She seemed to blame Miss Watson for allowing her child to catch chicken-pox, and gave no word of thanks for the care which the children had been given.

School dinner consisted of fatty minced meat and boiled potatoes with the eyes left in. Jam tart, normally greeted ecstatically, was burnt round the edges and refused by a number of pupils.

The nurse who came to look at heads arrived un-announced in the middle of the afternoon, and when Dorothy, interrupted in her reading of *Tom's Midnight Garden*, remonstrated, nurse told her that she knew for a fact that notice had been sent a fortnight before, and it was probably that Willie Marchant's fault for not delivering it.

It did not improve Dorothy's temper to discover the letter later, unopened, tucked inside a stern missive from the office about 'Economy and School Stationery'.

After school, Agnes had felt obliged to call at her wounded boy's home to see how he was faring, and found him, catapult in hand, doing his best to hit a nearby sparrow, luckily without success. His mother was per-functory in her thanks, and Agnes tottered back to the school house ready for tea.

'I could well do without a visitation from Ray and Kathleen,' commented Dorothy, as they cleared away their teacups, 'but there it is. I only hope they don't stay long. What a day it has been!'

The ladies went upstairs to change from their workaday clothes, and Agnes was just trying to decide whether the occasion warranted the addition of her seed pearls to the general ensemble, when the car arrived.

Dorothy admitted her brother, his wife and the bois-terous Labrador dog Harrison who, luckily, was on a lead.

'Is he going to stay indoors?' queried Dorothy, in a far from welcoming tone.

'He'll soon calm down,' Ray was assuring her as Agnes entered the sitting-room. 'He's very obedient these days.'

Harrison leapt upon Agnes and nearly felled her to the Axminster carpet. She sat down abruptly on the couch.

'Down, sir!' shouted Ray in a voice which set the glasses tinkling. 'D'you hear me? Down, I say!'

Dorothy put her hands over her ears, Kathleen bridled, and Agnes attempted a polite smile.

'It's just that he's excited,' bawled Ray, tugging at the lead. 'So pleased to see everyone. Awfully affectionate animal!'

The affectionate animal now attempted to clamber on to Agnes's lap. As it was twice her size and weight, she was immediately engulfed.

'Take him out!' screamed Kathleen. 'He's obviously upset. He's extremely highly-strung,' she explained fortissimo, to the dishevelled Agnes.

Reluctantly, Ray tugged the dog outside, and to the relief of the two hostesses Harrison was deposited in the car.

'Well!' exclaimed Dorothy. 'I should think you could do with a restorative after all that. A drink, Kathleen?'

'Thank you, but no,' said Kathleen primly. 'I have to keep off all alcohol, my doctor says.'

'Tomato juice, orange juice?'

'Too acid, dear.'

'Perrier?'

'I simply can't digest it,' said Kathleen, with great satisfaction.

'A cup of tea? Or coffee?'

Dorothy was starting to sound desperate, and Agnes noticed that her neck was beginning to flush.

'If I might have a little milk,' said Kathleen, 'I should be grateful.'

'I will fetch it,' said Agnes, anxious to have a moment's peace in the kitchen.

It would be today, she thought, examining the dubious milk, that Kathleen wanted this commodity. For safety's sake she took the precaution of pouring the liquid through the strainer into a glass, and hoped for the best.

Without Harrison the sitting-room was comparatively tranquil. There was general conversation about the Dorset holiday, the state of their respective gardens, Ray's health, soon disposed of, and Kathleen's, which threatened to dominate the conversation for at least two hours, if not checked.

Over the years, Dorothy had developed considerable expertise in cutting short the recital of her sister-in-law's complaints and their treatment. At times, Agnes had felt that she was perhaps a shade ruthless in her methods, but today, exhausted as she was with the vicissitudes it had brought, she was glad to have the conversation turned in the direction of their own future plans.

'It surprises me,' said Kathleen, 'to know that you haven't found a house yet.'

'It surprises us too,' replied Dorothy tartly. 'It's not for want of trying, I can assure you.'

'Time's getting on,' observed Ray. 'You ought to make up your mind. Prices seem to rise every week.'

Agnes trembled in case Dorothy responded with a typical outburst, but for once her friend remained silent.

'Once we have the car,' Agnes said timidly, 'Dorothy and I intend to have a thorough look at houses.'

'I imagine that you will be getting rid of a good deal of furniture,' remarked Kathleen. 'What do you propose to do about it?'

'Nothing, until we've seen what we need in the new place,' said Dorothy.

Kathleen drew in her breath. Agnes noticed that she cast a quick glance at her husband.

'I only ask,' she continued, 'because we wondered if we could help at all by taking it off your hands.'

'What had you in mind?' enquired Dorothy, with dangerous calm.

'Well, this nest of tables, for instance,' said Kathleen, putting down the glass of milk, 'and dear mother's kitchen dresser, and any china which might be too much for the new home.'

'Anything else?' asked Dorothy, her neck now scarlet.

Ray, ill at ease, had now gone to the window, removing himself, man-fashion, from all source of trouble.

'There were one or two items that Ray was always so fond of,' said Kathleen, looking somewhat sharply at her husband's back. 'He often talks of that silver rosebowl his mother always cherished, and her silver dressing-table set.'

'I cherish those too,' said Dorothy.

'And I don't suppose that any of the carpets or curtains will fit the new place,' continued Kathleen happily. 'So do bear us in mind if you are throwing anything away.'

At this point, a desperate howling from Harrison pierced the air, and Ray leapt at the excuse to hurry outside.

'He's probably seen a cat,' said Kathleen. 'Hateful creatures!'

Agnes, full of fears, betook herself to the window. There certainly was a cat in sight, but to her relief it was only Albert Piggott's, an animal which could well take care of itself, and was now sitting smugly on the garden wall, gloating over its imprisoned enemy.

'We must be on our way,' announced Kathleen. She drained her glass, much to Agnes's relief, and began to fidget with her gloves and handbag. 'Who would have thought it was half-past six?'

Ray returned, and seemed glad to see preparations for departure.

'Is he all right?' asked Kathleen anxiously. 'We don't want him unsettled with a journey before him.'

'Just a cat,' replied Ray, in what Agnes felt was an extremely callous manner. Just a cat, indeed!

'It was good of you to break your journey,' said Dorothy, her feelings now under control. 'We'll keep you in touch with our plans. I can't see us moving from here much before the late summer.'

'But won't the new head want it?' queried Ray.

Dorothy explained about the sale of the house.

'I wonder,' began Kathleen, making her way to the front door, 'if it would suit us, Ray?'

'We are quite happy where we are, dear,' Ray said firmly. 'Besides, it would be a terrible upheaval for Harrison. He's so used to his present daily walkies, and no one could be better with him than our local vet.'

'Of course,' said Dorothy, as she kissed them in farewell, 'it would save us taking up the carpets and curtains if you took over, and we might even come to some arrangement about the kitchen dresser. Mother's silver, of course, means too much to me to part with.'

Deafening barking put a stop to all further conversation, and the two drove off with much waving and hooting.

'Well,' said Dorothy, with infinite satisfaction, 'I think I had the last word there!'

Half an hour later, the two ladies were sitting with their feet up, going over all the problems of the day.

'One thing after another,' said Dorothy, 'and then Ray and Kathleen on top of everything. Really, it's as much as I can do to be civil to her. If I weren't so devoted to Ray, I could say a great deal more than I do.'

'She is rather trying,' agreed Agnes. 'I suppose it's partly because she is delicate.'

Dorothy snorted. 'Delicate my foot! She's as strong as an ox, and always was. A great pity they didn't have half a dozen children to take her mind off herself. As it is, they make a fool of that awful animal.'

'Not a very tractable dog,' said Agnes, with considerable understatement.

The telephone rang, and Dorothy padded out to answer it.

'Probably some irate parent,' she commented on her way out. 'Just to add the final straw to the camel's back.'

Agnes could not hear much of Dorothy's side of the conversation, but at least she sounded pleased. Agnes closed her eyes, and promised herself an early night after the hazards of the day.

'The car's arrived!' cried Dorothy, returning. Her eyes sparkled, her cheeks glowed.

'How splendid!' said Agnes, sitting up.

'I can fetch it tomorrow after school,' went on Dorothy. 'Isn't it marvellous? And it's a *white* one!'

Agnes did not like to dampen her friend's high spirits by pointing out that it was exactly why they had waited so long, but smiled kindly at her.

'I think I shall ask Harold to accompany me,' said Dorothy. 'Do you mind if I slip round now and have a word?'

'Of course not,' said Agnes, deciding that this would be just the time to feed the little cat. 'And don't be surprised if I have gone up to bed. I'm terribly tired.'

'No wonder,' said Dorothy. 'Me too, but this last bit of news has made up for all the day's annoyances. Now we can really start to make plans.'

And the two ladies parted to pursue their errands.

15   Agnes Is Upset

THE choice of presents for the departing teachers was now becoming a pressing problem for those responsible.

Miss Robinson's task was probably the simplest. The tenpenny pieces came in apace, and were stored in a small biscuit tin which was decorated with illustrations from *The Country Diary of an Edwardian Lady*. So often had it been opened that the hinge had given way, but it still shut firmly, and Miss Robinson was proud of the number of coins it enclosed.

The children much enjoyed the secrecy surrounding this project, and had all sorts of suggestions ranging from a puppy to keep them company, to two electric blankets. Miss Robinson still thought that two bouquets and two boxes of chocolates would fit the bill far better, as the rector had suggested.

Charles Henstock, as chairman of the governors, had been surprised to find how determined his fellows were to present the ladies with a clock.

'Always have given a clock,' said the oldest member of the governors. 'Useful too.'

'Excellent idea,' said another.

The good Charles, remembering Harold and Isobel's suggestions, was somewhat taken aback by this solid attack.

'I wondered if a piece of china or glass might be acceptable.'

'Such as?'

'Well, a nice decanter, say.'

There was a sharp indrawing of breath from the only teetotaller on the committee.

'Or a fruit bowl,' added the rector hastily.

'I still think a clock would be best,' said the first speaker. 'What do the PTA people suggest?'

Charles remembered, with relief, that the Parent–Teacher association were combining with the governors in this matter, and put in a word.

'We must consult them, of course. Now I have your suggestions here, and have noted that the general feeling is that a clock of some kind would be your choice.'

'A decent-sized one,' said the oldest member firmly. 'None of those fiddle-faddling things you can't see without your glasses. Something with a good big face. We're none of us getting any younger.'

Hearty agreement broke out, leading to discussions of arthritis, the afflictions of themselves and aged relatives, and general denigration of the National Health Service.

'Well, ladies and gentlemen,' said Charles, patting his papers together. 'I think we've done very well for this evening, and with your permission I will get in touch with Mrs Gibbons and then report back to you.'

The meeting dispersed slowly, and as the rector crossed the green to his car, he overheard the oldest governor explaining to his companion about the efficacious properties of a potato, carried in the pocket, for warding off the pains of rheumatism.

'Better than the Health Service any day!' he assured his friend.

Mrs Gibbons, on behalf of the PTA, had already gone ahead with her plans to get a suitable picture of the school for the unsuspecting teachers.

She had first approached Ella Bembridge, who had lived

at Thrush Green for many years, and was recognised as the most artistic resident there.

But Ella was not much in favour of the idea, and said so in her usual gruff way.

'I was quite taken aback,' said Mrs Gibbons, reporting on the interview to the Gauleiter that evening. 'She said she gave up "finicking about" with water-colours thirty years ago. She's now besotted with stitched rugs evidently.'

'I should get a decent photograph,' advised her husband, whose practical approach to all problems had led him to his present position of eminence. 'That chap at Lulling, by the butcher's, seems to know his stuff. He did a good job at the Rotary Club dinner.'

'I suppose that would be best,' said his wife doubtfully. 'Not very *imaginative*, of course.'

'The two ladies won't want anything *imaginative*. A nicely-composed photo, by a local chap, should be very acceptable.'

'I'll put it in hand straightaway,' promised Mrs Gibbons, and did so.

There were times when she found the Gauleiter's down-to-earth advice a great comfort.

It was about this time that Dorothy and Agnes heard about their successors.

To Agnes's delight the young man with the National Trust tie had been appointed as headmaster.

'Such a cheerful young fellow,' she said, 'with short hair too.'

'Short hair is back in fashion,' Dorothy told her.

Agnes suddenly remembered the cropped red hair of the stranger who had been so interested in the architecture of Lulling High Street. Who could he have been, she wondered?

'And I think the young woman who will take your

place,' went on Dorothy, 'should do very well. Mind you, *no one* can really take your place, Agnes.'

'And *no one*,' Agnes replied loyally, 'can take yours.'

They smiled fondly at each other.

'Ah well,' said Dorothy, 'we've had a good run for our money, as they say, and now it's time for a change. What about a little spin in the car, as the evening is so lovely?'

'A good idea,' replied Agnes, trying to look enthusiastic. 'Somewhere quiet, I think, don't you? What about the road to Nod and Nidden?'

'As long as Percy Hodge has his dog under control,' said Dorothy. That disastrous encounter still rankled, but there was no point in raking up old memories, she told herself, as she collected the car keys.

It so happened that Isobel Shoosmith made the journey to Barton alone, as the only day that fitted in with Ursula's plans was the day which Harold had fixed with a local tree-feller to take down an ancient plum tree at the end of the garden.

This hoary monster had produced no plums for years, but still had enough life in it to send out dozens of healthy plum suckers which sprang up from the grass for yards around.

It was a cloudless morning towards the end of May, and Isobel enjoyed her journey. The New Forest was fluttering with young leaves, the roaming ponies and cattle were as endearing as ever, and Isobel's spirits were high.

She had always been fond of Ursula, and secretly missed her company now that she lived at Thrush Green. One thing, she told herself as she peered at a signpost, Ursula would be much more accessible at Barton than at her old home in Sussex, and the New Forest was a joy at any time of the year. Next time she would bring Harold down to meet her old friend.

She remembered the aunt's road as soon as she saw it, and the white bungalow seemed little changed outside. Ursula was at the gate to meet her, and they embraced warmly.

'So little changed,' said Isobel, eyeing the house.

'Wait till you come inside,' warned Ursula, and sure enough chaos greeted the eye.

There were tea-chests everywhere, the dining-room chairs were upturned on the table, and the sitting-room was shrouded in dust sheets. A man in a boiler suit, spanner in hand, was doing something to the pipes in the kitchen, and Ursula led the way into the garden at the back.

Here there was a seat in the sun, and the two friends found a little peace.

They went out to a nearby pub for lunch, and Isobel gratefully packed her inheritance in the boot of the car, well-wrapped up in a car rug. Both women were hoarse with exchanging news.

'I shall ring you about half-past six,' she told Ursula. 'It's been a lovely day, and I'll tell you more then.'

She had plenty to think about as she drove home. There the plum tree was down, the tree-feller had vanished, and Harold was ready for all the news.

'She's selling the place, and I really think it might suit Agnes and Dorothy. To be honest, I don't know why she doesn't settle there herself. It's so convenient and easily managed.'

'Probably prefers her own home,' responded Harold. 'People do, you know.'

'I think she likes being near the daughters and the grandchildren,' said Isobel, 'and I must say moving is the most appalling upheaval.'

'So did you say anything about our neighbours?'

'Rather tentatively, but I did say that they were looking

for something that way. Now I'm beginning to wonder if I should have done. Perhaps I shouldn't interfere?'

'Nonsense!' said Harold robustly. 'You pop round and have a word with the girls, before you ring Ursula.'

'I feel like Meddlesome Mattie,' she said, setting off reluctantly next door.

She found the two friends busy weeding.

'Must try and keep the place decent,' cried Dorothy, removing her gardening gloves. 'I see the plum tree has gone.'

'Well, it was more of a nuisance than anything else,' said Isobel apologetically, 'and not a plum to be seen.'

'Harold told us you had gone to see a friend,' said Agnes, coming up.

'Yes, at Barton, strangely enough,' replied Isobel and launched into her tale. The ladies listened attentively.

'And you say that she has just put it into the hands of Better and Better?'

'I think that was the name. She said it was an excellent firm.'

Agnes waited for Dorothy's snort, but none came.

'You don't think me too interfering, I hope,' pleaded Isobel. 'It just seemed a marvellous possibility, and of course you need not take it – or even go and see it.' She was horrified to hear her voice babbling on apologetically.

Dorothy cut her short. 'It was a great kindness, and Agnes and I would love to drive down to see it whenever your friend – '

'Ursula.'

'Ursula can show us round. Or of course, the estate agent can do his duty at last.'

Isobel explained about the telephone call she was about to make, thanked the two for being so understanding, received thanks for being so thoughtful, and returned to her own home in a state of extreme agitation.

'What you need,' said Harold looking at her kindly, 'is a nice little something before you ring Barton.'

And he went to pour out two glasses.

Naturally, before the week was out, it was common knowledge in Thrush Green and Lulling that Miss Watson and Miss Fogerty had found a home at Barton.

Some said an aunt of Isobel's had left her the property. Others maintained that it was a relative of Harold's who was selling the house. One or two actually got it right, and said that a friend of Isobel's was the vendor. All trusted that the good ladies would be very happy in their new abode.

'And we haven't even seen it yet,' cried Dorothy, when she heard the gossip. 'Really, one despairs of trying to keep anything private in this place.'

'It is aggravating,' agreed Agnes.

Both ladies were tired after a day at school. Dorothy's legs were aching, and Agnes's head throbbed. It was at times like this that they longed for the end of term, to have the various leaving parties behind them, and to set off to a quiet life of retirement. Would it ever come?

At that moment, Agnes's sharp ears heard a small mewing sound. She hurried to the french window and saw the tabby cat looking hopefully at her.

'Ah! The dear thing's here,' she cried, turning sharply to go and fetch its early supper. She caught her foot in the hearth rug and fell sprawling.

'Oh, Agnes!' cried Dorothy. 'Are you hurt?'

Agnes struggled up.

'No, no,' she said, somewhat shakily. 'How clumsy of me.'

'You shouldn't rush about so after that animal,' exclaimed Dorothy, her anxiety on Agnes's behalf showing as irritation. 'It's a perfect pest. And anyway, how do you think it will manage when you have abandoned it?'

At these appalling words Agnes felt her eyes fill with tears, and hurried from the room. In the privacy of the scullery she prepared the cat's food, and a few salt drops mingled with the tinned meat in the enamel dish.

It was that word 'abandoned' which hurt most. There was something so cruel and callous about it, and of course Agnes had tortured herself quite enough already thinking about the cat's future. And to call her tabby friend 'a perfect pest'! It was more than flesh and blood could endure.

She put the plate outside in its usual position, and the cat came trustingly towards it. But this evening Agnes could not bring herself to stand and watch this normally happy sight. Conscious of her tear-stained face, and complete inability to control her emotion, she rushed down the garden, and betook herself to the privacy of the field beyond.

Here she sat down on the grass behind the hawthorn hedge, and abandoned herself to the grief which engulfed her. It was insufferable of Dorothy to behave in this way! For two pins she would tell her that the idea of sharing a retirement home was now absolutely repugnant to her. A vista of long grey years giving in to Dorothy's bullying suddenly assailed her mind's eye. Could she bear it?

Why should she part from her dear new friend? If she stayed at Thrush Green she could keep it. After all, she had lived very happily for many years in digs at Mrs White's. There must be other lodgings where a well-behaved cat would be welcome.

Agnes's sobs grew more violent as she grew more rebellious. Her small handkerchief was drenched, and her head throbbed more painfully than ever.

It was at this stage that Isobel, who had been depositing vegetable peelings on her compost heap, came through the wicket gate at the end of the garden to see what the strange noise was about.

She was appalled to see her old friend in such a state of despair, and dropped to the grass beside her.

'But what is it? What has happened?'

She put her arm around Agnes, and felt hot tears dampening her shoulder. The colander, which had held the peelings, rolled away unnoticed, as Agnes's distress increased in the face of her friend's sympathy.

From an incoherent jumble of sobs, hiccups and comments about Dorothy's remarks and the cat's pathos, Isobel began to understand the real nature of Agnes's anguish, and was seriously perturbed.

It was even more alarming to hear Agnes's ramblings about her future, and the possibility of refusing to leave Thrush Green if it meant parting from the cat.

'If only Mrs White were here,' cried Agnes, shoulders still heaving. 'I know she would take me back again, and the cat too. She adored cats.'

At the thought of Mrs White's affection for the feline world, Agnes's tears broke out afresh.

There was little that Isobel could do apart from patting her friend's back and uttering words of comfort.

At last, the paroxysm passed, and Agnes was able to mop her eyes and control her breathing again.

'Oh, Isobel!' she wailed. 'What a comfort you are! What am I going to do?'

'You are coming home with me,' Isobel told her. 'And you are going to have a rest until you feel better. Does Dorothy know you are out?'

A look of panic crossed Agnes's tear-stained face. 'No, I'm sure she doesn't. Oh, please don't say anything to her! I shouldn't want to upset her.'

'Don't worry,' said Isobel. 'The first thing to do is to get you to my house for a little drink.'

'But Harold – ' quavered Agnes.

'Out at a meeting,' replied Isobel. 'We shall be quite alone.'

The two friends made their way through the evening sunshine to the house next door.

There, feet up on the sofa, and a restorative cup of coffee to hand, Agnes recovered her composure, regretted her outburst, and thought, yet again, how much she loved Isobel.

Dorothy meanwhile, ignorant of all the upset her words had produced, was engrossed in a television programme about education.

Those taking part were obviously more theorists than practitioners, and Dorothy's disgusted snorts accompanied many of the panel's remarks.

The programme which followed was about birds, and Dorothy found this equally absorbing and far less irritating. It did occur to her, half-way through, when a humming-bird was extracting honey from a trumpet-shaped exotic bloom, how much Agnes would enjoy it, and where could she be, but she guessed – correctly, as it happened – that she was probably next door visiting Isobel.

So that when the sitting-room door opened a chink, and Agnes said that she proposed to have an early night as her head ached, Dorothy replied that it was a sensible idea and she would come up later, and kept her eyes glued to the television screen, quite unconscious of all that had devastated her friend's evening.

True to her word, at ten o'clock she switched off the set, and made her way upstairs.

She knocked gently on Agnes's door, but there was no response. She eased it open and listened. There was no sound at all. Presumably, Agnes was asleep, and she closed the door, with infinite care, and crept across to her own room.

She was asleep within half an hour, but next door Agnes lay awake, too agitated to settle, until she fell asleep at five o'clock completely exhausted.

When Harold Shoosmith returned from his meeting, Isobel told him what had happened.

'Poor old dear,' was his response, 'but not much we can do about it. After all, this cat business is their affair.'

'I agree. But I feel rather responsible for Agnes.'

'Good heavens! Why?'

'She has no family. She talked wildly of staying on at Thrush Green in digs – somewhere where she could have the cat.'

'You mean she's thinking of ditching Dorothy, and Barton, and all the rest of it?'

'At one stage this evening, she certainly was. And how would she manage? Her pension won't be much. She'll be horribly lonely. I'm quite willing to have her here for a few weeks until she finds lodgings, if that's what she really wants, but the long-term outlook is so dismal.'

'She can't possibly intend to leave Dorothy!'

'No, I don't think she will when it comes to it. But it does show how desperate she is. I don't think Dorothy has any idea how much she wants that cat. I think I shall have to tell her.'

Harold sighed.

'Well, watch your step, my dear. It's really such a storm in a teacup.'

'Not to Agnes. I've never seen her like this, and I'm appalled to think she may be jettisoning her future – and Dorothy's too, for that matter. If I get the chance, I shall let Dorothy know how things are, and what's more I shall try and persuade her to accept the cat into the household.'

'You're a brave woman,' said Harold.

16 A Trip to Barton-on-Sea

WHILE little Miss Fogerty was weeping in the shelter of the hedge, attended by Isobel, two more old friends were enjoying each other's company on the other side of Thrush Green.

Dimity had called to see Ella Bembridge. She looked with affection at the cottage which they had shared for several happy years before Charles had proposed and she had gone to live at the bleak rectory across the road.

A fire had razed that home to the ground, and now some very pleasant homes for old people were on the site, called Rectory Cottages in remembrance of the former building.

Ella appeared to be wrapped in a brightly stitched garment reminiscent of those worn by Peruvian peasants. Actually, it was one of the stitched rugs which so engrossed her at the moment, and after she had disengaged herself from its folds, she showed her work to Dimity with some pride.

'It's wonderfully colourful,' said Dimity politely. Secretly she thought it downright garish and quite unsuitable for the cottage. A nice plain beige Wilton now, thought Dimity, would look tasteful anywhere.

'It's a runner for the hall,' explained Ella, looking fondly at her handiwork. 'Nice cheerful welcome it'll make, won't it?'

'Very colourful,' repeated Dimity, trying to be truthful without giving offence, a common predicament among well-mannered people.

'Let's have a cup of something,' suggested Ella, 'or a glass. Which, Dim?'

'Nothing for me,' said Dimity.

'Well, I must have a gasper. I'm cutting down but it's killing work, I can tell you.'

She rooted among the clutter of bright wools, magazines, ashtrays and two apples on the table, and found the battered tin which constituted her cigarette-making factory.

As she rolled a very thin, and very untidy, cigarette, she asked Dimity about any news from Lulling.

'Charles is getting rather agitated about the Lilly girl at the Lovelocks.'

'What's the trouble? Slave driving?'

'Pretty well. They are adamant about how little they ask of her, but I gather she's already talking of giving in her notice. Gladys Lilly is pretty cross about it.'

'So why does Charles worry?'

'He feels he's letting down Anthony, you see. It was his idea to see if the Lovelocks would take on the girl. I don't think he realises how demanding they are.'

'Tell him from me to forget it. Half the time these things

blow over. In any case, he acted in good faith and if things have gone wrong I don't see that it's any fault of his.'

Dimity took some comfort from these stout words.

'And now your news. I heard about the house at Barton. Have they seen it yet?'

'Next weekend, I believe. I hope something comes of it. This hanging about would drive me up the wall.'

Patience, Dimity knew, was not one of her old friend's strongest virtues, and was not surprised when she changed the subject to Muriel Fuller who had evidently called earlier in the day.

'What's known as "an excellent woman",' said Ella, shaking ash in the vague direction of the ashtray. 'She came here at eleven o'clock just when I was counting twenty-five holes on my canvas, and stayed until twenty-past twelve.'

'Was she collecting for something?'

'Yes, she always is. Something to do with an African mission. I gave her fifty pence and hoped she'd go, but I had to listen to the history, customs, marriage rites – and very unpleasant they were, I can tell you – not to mention how much they needed my money. She really is the most outstanding bore.'

'Oh, come!' protested gentle Dimity. 'She's only trying to do good.'

'All I can say,' said Ella forthrightly, 'is that doing good always seems to bring out the worst in people.'

Charles Henstock's concern about Doreen Lilly's position at the Misses Lovelock was shared by the ladies themselves.

They certainly expected too much of the girl, and Violet at least recognised this.

All three sisters had been used to first-class resident help until the last ten or twelve years. They still expected the house to look immaculate, the meals punctually on the table, the laundry snowy and the prodigious array of silver in sparkling condition.

While their parents were alive, a cook, a general maid and a parlour maid had occupied the two attic bedrooms, and served the family devotedly from seven-thirty in the morning until ten-thirty at night.

It was hardly surprising that, with the sketchy domestic help now available, the house and its contents had lost their pristine look, and that the mingled fragrance of beeswax polish and home-baked bread had been superseded by a general fustiness.

The three old ladies did their best in the circumstances, but they were untrained in the art of housekeeping themselves, and had no knowledge of the effort needed to keep such an establishment as theirs in perfect order. They found Doreen's ministrations deplorably inadequate, and became more and more querulous.

'Surely she knows that the *bedroom* furniture needs polish on it,' protested Ada. 'Why just do the dining-table?'

'Because she sees it gets marked,' explained Violet. 'So she gets out the polish and tackles it.'

'And she hoovers for hours,' added Bertha, 'but never thinks to dust the skirting boards.'

'I have told her,' said Violet, 'but I don't think she takes in anything very readily.'

'And she's getting a little impertinent,' added Ada. 'Tossed her head at me when I pointed out the smears on the landing window, and said she had no head for heights. Why, dear old Hannah thought nothing of balancing a plank across the stairwell when she did the high parts of the landing and stairs.'

'Dear old Hannahs have gone,' said Violet shortly.

There was a heavy silence, broken at last by Ada. 'Well, what's to be done? Do we give her notice or not?'

'Who could we get in her place?' queried Bertha. 'You know how difficult it was to find Doreen.'

'Carry on as we are,' advised Violet. 'It wouldn't surprise me to find that *we* get given notice, not Doreen.'

And so the unsatisfactory state of affairs was left.

Gladys Lilly was equally worried about her daughter.

She confided her fears to Nelly Piggott one evening before the bingo session began.

'She's proper unsettled. Back to biting her nails, like she used to do as a little mite. Always was secretive. I tell you, I'm real worried about her.'

'I can't say I'm surprised,' said Nelly. 'That house of the Lovelock ladies would get anybody down. Can't she find some other place?'

'I doubt it. And to tell the truth, I'm not so sure the work is the real trouble.'

She looked around the hall, dropped her voice, and spoke conspiratorially to Nelly. 'I think she's fretting for that useless chap of hers. He's out again, we do know that. One of his pals told us. I've told Doreen time and time again to keep clear of him, but you know what girls are!'

Nelly and Gladys sighed heavily together over the shortcomings of susceptible females.

'Things were different in our young days,' agreed Nelly. 'We took heed of what our parents said. And I was always told to bring home any young man who was being attentive.'

'Quite right,' approved Gladys.

But there were quite a few attentive young men in the youthful past of both ladies who had certainly not been presented to their parents. And these they dwelt on, secretly and fondly, as they settled down to bingo.

✲   ✲   ✲

Isobel had been busy on her neighbours' behalf and had arranged for the ladies to visit Ursula's house at the weekend.

She had offered to take them down in her car, but Dorothy was looking forward to her first long drive in the Metro, and turned down Isobel's invitation politely but firmly.

However, on Friday evening she spoke to Isobel over the hedge. She sounded somewhat agitated.

'Oh, Isobel! So glad to catch you. Poor Agnes is not too fit. In fact, she's been very much off-colour all this week, and I'm afraid she won't be able to face the journey tomorrow.'

'Oh dear! Well, shall I take you? I think we ought to go as Ursula has planned everything.'

'No, no! But if you don't mind coming with me, I should be most grateful. I feel quite competent about the *driving*, but should anything happen to the *engine*, I must admit total ignorance, although Ben did explain how it worked.'

'Well, I shan't be much better,' confessed Isobel, 'but I could always go for help. And of course I should love to keep you company, and introduce you to Ursula.'

It was Harold who pointed out later that this was the heaven-sent opportunity to broach the delicate subject of the tabby cat.

'I suppose so,' said Isobel doubtfully. 'On a straight piece of road where she won't get too agitated.'

And so, soon after ten o'clock on a glorious June morning the two ladies set out, leaving Agnes to enjoy the peace of the school house and a possible visit from the cat.

It was true that she had been remarkably quiet, even by her standards, since her outburst. The headache had never really departed. She was sleeping badly, and occasionally found herself trembling violently.

She did not intend to bother Doctor John Lovell with these minor ailments, recognising only too well that they were the result of all the worry over the cat, the future, the extra labours involved in clearing out the debris of many years' teaching, and general anxiety about her relationship with Dorothy, as retirement drew ever closer.

But she was relieved not to have to make the journey. She was quite sure that Dorothy was a good driver, but then there were so many people on the roads who were not. She did not mind admitting that she was most unhappy in the passenger seat, and foresaw all sorts of appalling situations involving hospitals, firemen cutting one out of the wreckage, bodies and blood strewn over the road, followed by interminable court cases about two years later, when one could not reasonably be expected to remember a thing, not to mention permanent injury with possibly one or more limbs missing.

While Agnes was quietly pottering about with the duster, hoping for a few minutes with the cat, Dorothy and Isobel were enjoying the countryside on their way south, and the latter was trying to pluck up courage to approach the subject of Agnes's unhappiness.

Luckily, it was Dorothy who brought up the matter.

'She's too conscientious,' said Dorothy. 'Everything has to be done perfectly, and of course she gets over-tired. I shall be mightily glad when we've finished at the school. Of course, we shall find it all a great change, and I think Agnes worries more than I do about missing the children. She needs something to love. More than I do, I must admit.'

Isobel took a deep breath. The road was straight, and there was very little traffic.

'That's why she is so devoted to the stray cat,' she began.

'I know she is fond of it – ' said Dorothy.

'But I don't think you realise *how* fond,' broke in Isobel, and began to tell her about the sad scene she had encountered behind the garden hedge.

Dorothy listened in silence, and then drew in quietly at the next lay-by.

'Tell me more,' she said, her expression very grave. She shifted sideways in her seat so that she could study Isobel's face as she unfolded the tale.

Isobel, taking the bull by the horns, spared her nothing, even recounting Agnes's anguished doubts about their future happiness together.

'It's so little to ask,' went on Isobel, 'and there is so much to lose. She would be most unhappy if she really took this idiotic step of staying behind. From the practical point of view, I don't think she could manage financially. And then she would be so lonely.'

'And so would I,' said Dorothy. 'I can't imagine why I have been so dense, and so thoughtless. I honestly had no idea that she felt like this. It makes me want to turn round straightaway, drive back, and apologise.'

'Well, we can't do that now,' said Isobel practically, 'as Ursula is expecting us. But I felt that you should know how Agnes is feeling. I love her dearly, and have for years. I should hate her to throw away her future with you.'

'And so should I. I've always enjoyed her companionship enormously. The cat will be invited in tonight, and made welcome.'

Isobel gave a great sigh.

'You know,' said Dorothy, looking at her steadily, 'you must have dreaded telling me all this. What a brave woman you are!'

'It's true,' admitted Isobel, 'and I've still to face Agnes's dismay when she finds what I've done. But I can truthfully say I'm glad it's all in the open now.'

'I shall never forgive myself,' said Dorothy, starting the

car, and continuing the journey. 'To have been so *cruel* to my most loyal friend!'

'As long as you make it plain that you are truthfully happy to include the cat in the household,' said Isobel, 'I think everything will sort itself out splendidly. And there's no need to abase yourself too much with Agnes. Least said soonest mended. It would only upset her, and if she realises that you have simply had a change of heart about the cat, all should be well.'

'I shall get Ben Curdle to make a cat flap in the back door,' said Dorothy, adjusting to this new situation with her usual common sense. 'And I propose to buy Agnes a splendid cat basket in Barton, and take it back with us this evening. What about that?'

'You couldn't make a more generous gesture,' Isobel assured her.

Meanwhile, at Thrush Green, Winnie Bailey had just welcomed her nephew Richard, who had arrived, as was usual, quite unannounced.

'I had to return some books to Aubrey Hengist-Williams,' he explained. 'He rang up last night and said that he wanted them urgently. Getting some lecture notes ready for next term.'

'Isn't that the great Professor? I think I've had a glimpse of him on Open University on television when I've been trying to get the right time.'

'Well, he's on television, I know, but that hardly makes him great,' replied Richard. 'Actually, I've always thought him a very silly fellow, and I never have been able to subscribe to his theory on the side-effects of nuclear fission. Have you?'

Winnie smiled patiently. 'Richard dear, I am completely ignorant of nuclear fission, let alone its side-effects, but tell me all about the family.'

She did not like to add that both Richard and Fenella had left in a black mood on the last occasion, but hoped that things were now amicably settled.

'Oh, they are fine,' said Richard vaguely. 'Fenella seems happier now that Roger has gone.'

'Roger? Gone? Where?'

'Spain, I think. He and his wife have made it up, and gone to live abroad permanently. I think I helped in the decision.'

'I must say it seems all for the best,' agreed Winnie. 'Did you persuade him?'

'I punched him on the nose,' said Richard, with evident satisfaction. 'I went into the gallery to get some drawing pins, and he was kissing Fenella's left ear. I didn't like it, so I punched him.'

'Then what?'

'Oh, he bled rather a lot. And all over the gallery carpet which was a nuisance, but Fenella and I sponged it with cold water after he'd gone, and it's not too noticeable.'

'But what did Fenella say?'

'She said we could stand a stool over it, and no one would notice.'

'No. I mean about Roger going?'

'She hasn't said anything about it. I think she was getting rather fed up with him drooping about in the gallery all the time. He was an awful drip, you know. I should have punched him years ago.'

'Yes, well, I can see your point,' said Winnie reasonably, 'but has this made any difference to your future plans? No chance, I suppose, of persuading Fenella to come to Thrush Green to live?'

'Fenella,' replied Richard, 'does not respond to persuasion. I do not propose to punch my wife on the nose, but sometimes I think it would be the only way to make her change her mind.'

'So the school house won't be seeing you as its new owners?'

'I'm afraid not. The fact is, Aunt Win, the gallery is Fenella's life, and I'm away such a lot that it would be foolish and silly to deprive her of it. As far as I can see we shall be staying where we are until I retire. And then too, I expect,' he added resignedly.

'I'm sorry, but not surprised,' said Winnie. 'It was obvious that she did not want to come here, and she would have been resentful about leaving the gallery anyway. I'm sure things have worked out for the best, and now that Roger has gone she may settle down more happily.'

'At the moment she's busy getting an exhibition of abstract art in the seventies and eighties ready for next month.'

He began to fish in his pockets. 'She gave me an invitation for you, but I expect I left it with Aubrey's stuff by mistake. I'll send you one by post.'

'Don't trouble, dear. I find a trip to town rather too much these days, and my knowledge of abstract art, of any date, is on a par with my grasp of nuclear fission. So just give her my thanks and love.'

'I must be getting back,' said Richard, standing up.

'Won't you stop for lunch? Take pot luck?'

'No. I promised to take Timothy to the zoo this afternoon. He's fallen in love with a baby giraffe there.'

'That sounds harmless enough,' observed Winnie.

They went to the front gate together, and Richard paused for a moment to look across the green at the school house.

'It would have been fun,' he commented wistfully. 'But not worth losing a wife for, I suppose.'

'Definitely not,' said Winnie. 'You take care of what you've got, my boy. And don't get too pugnacious. One day you might get punched back!'

'If I started on Fenella,' replied Richard, 'I certainly should!'

He climbed into the car, grinned cheerfully, and drove away.

It was half-past nine when the two ladies arrived back from Barton-on-Sea. Dorothy had insisted on taking Isobel to have a remarkably delicious dinner on the way home, after telephoning Agnes to explain the delay, and over it they had discussed the pros and cons of putting in an offer for Ursula's property.

'Do come in,' pressed Dorothy. 'I know Agnes would love to see you.'

But Isobel declined, saying that Harold would be expecting her, and secretly feeling that she would like to have a night's sleep before facing any recriminations which might come from gentle Agnes after her own exposures.

Agnes heard the garage doors slam, and hastened to the window.

She saw her friend coming up the path, and carrying an awkward circular object. It appeared to be made of wicker-work, and was giving Dorothy some difficulty, tucked as it was under one arm.

Agnes hurried to open the door for her, and met her on the threshold.

Dorothy smiled and held out the basket in silence.

'For me?' quavered Agnes, deeply perplexed.

'For our cat,' said Dorothy.

17 Summer Heat

JULY brought a spell of welcome sunshine. The first week was greeted by all in Lulling and Thrush Green with immense pleasure.

The flower borders burst into colour. Oriental poppies, pink and red, flaunted their papery petals above marigolds, godetia, penstemon and pansies, vying only in height with the pink and purple spires of lupins and larkspur.

In less than a week, it seemed, summer had arrived in full splendour. Deckchairs were brought out from sheds and garages, rustic seats were brushed clean, bird-baths needed filling daily, and cats stretched themselves luxuriously in the heat.

Prudent housewives took the opportunity of washing winter woollens, blankets, bedspreads and curtains. Window cleaning was much in evidence, cars were hosed clean of past dirt and lawn mowers whirred.

Out in the meadows around Thrush Green the cattle gathered under clumps of trees, welcoming the benison of cool shade. Their tails twitched tirelessly against the constant torment of flies.

In the sparse shade thrown by the dry-stone walls, sheep rested, flanks heaving rhythmically, in the heat of the day. Butterflies hovered above the nettles and thistles, or alighted on the warm stones to flaunt the beauty of their wings. The air was murmurous with insects of all kinds, and bumble bees crawled languorously from one meadow flower to the next.

In the distance, Lulling Woods shimmered in the heat

haze. The little river Pleshey moved even more sluggishly than usual, only the trailing willow branches, it seemed, disturbing the glassy mirror of its placid surface.

At Thrush Green the inhabitants of Rectory Cottages either took to the shade of the chestnut trees or drew their curtains and lay on their sofas. Tom and Polly were among the former seekers after coolness, and sat contentedly surveying the peaceful scene before them. Both man and dog relished the warmth which comforted their old bones, and Tom hoped that this spell of splendid weather would last a long, long time. He intended to stay there, his head in the shade, and his thin shanks stretched out into the sunshine, until the children came out from school and then he would think about returning slowly to make himself a cup of tea at his home. It was a good life, he reflected, and much better than he had found it when he lived by the water in the Pleshey valley. He had been happy enough while he was still active, but looking back he realised that the damp cottage had been partly to blame for his increasing rheumatism. Since the move to higher ground and to the warmth of the new house he had felt very much better, and knew that the care he received there from the kindly wardens contributed to his well-being. Any aches and pains now were due, he knew ruefully, to advancing age, and there was little one could do to fight against that.

Meanwhile, he drowsed in the heat, one gnarled hand resting on the glossy head of his beloved Polly beside him.

At the school the children looked expectantly at the wall clock. Would it never be time to go home, to be free, to grab bathing things and rush down to the shallow pool in an arm of the river Pleshey?

The backs of their thighs stuck to their wooden seats. Their sunburnt arms smelt of fresh-cooked biscuits, and sweat moistened their brows.

In Agnes's terrapin classroom it was hotter than ever. The door was propped open with one of the diminutive wooden armchairs, giving a view of the shimmering playground and the Shoosmiths' hedge beyond, but little relief from the heat.

Agnes, clad in a blue checked gingham frock and Clarks sandals worn over lightweight summer stockings, read *The Tale of Jeremy Fisher*, hoping that its background of rain and ponds and water-lilies would give some refreshment on this afternoon of searing heat, but she too was relieved when the hands of the clock reached three-thirty and she could let her young charges go free.

It was very peaceful when at last she was left alone. She locked her desk and the cupboards, brought in the little armchair, and closed the door. She stood there for a moment, looking at the well-loved view towards Lulling Woods in the blue distance.

In this brief pause between activities, she suddenly became conscious of living completely in the present. It came but rarely. One was either looking back anxiously wondering which duties had been left undone, or forward to those duties which lay before one.

Now, in temporary limbo, she felt the sun on her arms, heard a frenzied bee tapping on the window for escape, smelt the dark red roses which stood on the desk, and saw, with unusual clarity, the iridescent feathers of the wood pigeon pecking in the playground. All her senses seemed sharpened. It was a moment of great intensity, never to be forgotten.

The spell was broken by a child opening the classroom door.

'Forgot me book,' he said, retrieving it from the top of the cupboard, and then vanishing.

Little Miss Fogerty sighed. She was going to miss Thrush Green school sorely. She wondered if Dorothy had any real misgivings about the ending of a long and successful career. They had, of course, talked of such things in a general way, but latterly so many day-to-day problems had beset them that little had been said of the deeper emotions.

It was only natural, Agnes supposed. They were both women who abhorred emotional outbursts, and kept their private feelings well under control. Maybe it was a good thing that they had so much to think about from the practical point of view. Time enough to be sentimental when term was over, Agnes told herself robustly.

Meanwhile, she would hurry across to the school house and put on the kettle. Perhaps a few tomato sandwiches would be pleasant? They could have tea in the shade of the apple tree, and look out for the dear little cat, still to be named.

'*Our* cat,' said Agnes aloud, with infinite satisfaction.

She left the classroom and made her way home, happy in remembering Dorothy's generosity of spirit, and looking forward to the future.

To Agnes's delight, the tabby cat pushed its way through the Shoosmiths' hedge and approached the two ladies cautiously, as they sat in the shade relishing their rest and the tomato sandwiches.

When it was within a few yards of the garden seat, it sat down, very upright, very dignified, its eyes fixed upon Agnes.

'It really is a handsome cat,' commented Dorothy in a low voice. The cat was still wary of her, which was understandable, but it was rather hard, she thought, to be so steadily ignored, when Agnes could now call her new friend to her side without much effort.

'It's only to be expected,' said Agnes, reading Dorothy's thoughts. 'After all, I have been feeding it for some time

now. Before long, it will come to you just as readily. I feel sure.'

The cat yawned, displaying a healthy pink tongue and sharp teeth.

'It's time it had a name,' said Dorothy. 'What do you think? It's obviously male. We had a very sweet white cat once called Butch.'

Agnes looked pained. 'I don't think this one looks like a Butch. I rather thought of Tim, after Tiger Tim, you know – he was striped like this one.'

Dorothy nodded approval. 'What pleasure we had from that comic! I was a great devotee of Mrs Bruin. Perhaps that's why I took up teaching?'

'Possibly,' agreed Agnes. She poured some milk into her saucer and put it down gently beside her Clarks sandals.

'Tim! Tim!' she called softly.

Dorothy held her breath.

The cat came fearlessly to the saucer and began to lap quickly.

'Poor thing,' said Dorothy in a whisper. 'This heat has made it terribly thirsty.'

'You see,' said Agnes happily, 'it really did answer to its name.'

'I think,' said Dorothy, with a hint of malice, 'that it would have come if you had simply said: "Milk! Milk!" '

'Possibly,' said Agnes equably. 'And I think we ought to call it *him* now, don't you?'

'Without a doubt,' agreed Dorothy, helping herself to another sandwich.

Later that evening, as the evening air cooled, the two ladies discussed their future housing plans.

Things had now got to the interesting stage of dealing with something that they both wanted.

Agnes had found herself charmed by Ursula's aunt's property when Dorothy had taken her to see it one weekend. She liked its sunny aspect, its small neat garden, the mature shrubs, and the fact that there were no exhausting hills in the neighbourhood. She had not admitted to anyone that she was beginning to find the steep hill from Lulling rather more than she could cope with now that her arthritis was taking hold.

Inside, the house was light and warm. There were two good-sized bedrooms, a large sitting-room and kitchen, and what was called by Ursula's estate agent 'a morning room'. This, it was agreed, should be Dorothy's study, though what she intended to study was not stated.

'But it would be handy to keep my desk in there,' said Dorothy, 'with the bills and things. Besides, if someone should call particularly to speak to just one of us, it would be somewhere to take them if the television happened to be on.'

'An excellent idea,' agreed Agnes.

The big kitchen, they decided, was where they would eat.

'At our age,' said Dorothy, 'we don't need a dining-room anyway. Any visitors will be invited to a cup of tea, or a glass of something. If we are *retired people*, then we have retired from cooking large meals as well as from school-teaching.

Agnes admired such masterly forethought.

'But what about Ray and Kathleen?' she ventured.

'We take them out to one of the excellent hotels nearby,' said Dorothy firmly.

They had gone ahead. A Lulling estate agent, used by both Harold and Isobel in their earlier househunting, was engaged to make a survey of the property, to negotiate an acceptable price, and young Mr Venables, now well into his seventies, had agreed to deal with the conveyancing and any other legal matters.

'And now,' Dorothy had said, 'they can all get on with it while we concentrate on the end of term. I want to leave everything ship-shape for the next head. The poor young man has never had a headship before. I only hope that he realises what he is taking on.'

From the way she spoke, one would have thought that the new headmaster was about to undertake the running of the United Nations single-handed, instead of a small and efficient country school, but Agnes observed a prudent silence, knowing from experience that Dorothy occasionally enjoyed seeing herself as an unsung heroine overcoming fearful odds.

The date of the move was something which gave the two ladies some concern. There seemed to be so many ifs and buts about the timing. If the survey proved satisfactory. If the legal arrangements went forward smoothly. If the alterations to the new house were finished. If they could stay where they were until everything was ready for the move. All these matters gave the ladies much worry, but two facts also gave them comfort.

The education authority was obliging about the timing of their departure, simply stating that as soon as the house was on the open market would be soon enough, and implying that this contingency was not expected to occur until late in the year.

The other factor was the attitude of the incoming headmaster, who made it clear that he would be making the journey from his present home, some twenty miles away, while he looked for a house in Lulling or Thrush Green, at his leisure.

The two ladies had hoped that he might put in an offer for the school house, but this did not happen. Whether he, or perhaps his wife, just disliked their much-loved abode, no one knew. Perhaps, Agnes surmised, he did not like 'living over the shop'?

'Always been good enough for us!' Dorothy had snorted.

But she agreed that it was a great relief to know that they would not be thrown out, on the last day of term, like orphans in a storm.

The sunny spell of weather continued unabated, and the first rapturous welcome to the heat began to turn to disenchantment. The flaunting poppies dropped their silky petals. The lupin spires turned rusty. Brown patches appeared on lawns, and cracks grew wider on well-trodden earth.

Stern notices appeared in the local press about the use of hoses and sprinklers in the gardens, with dire threats of the fines to be imposed on malefactors.

The river Pleshey dwindled visibly, exposing fast-drying mud banks, and giving forth unpleasant odours in those stretches where the river weed dried in the heat. The cattle took to standing in the water, tails ever-twitching, and heads tossing to scare away the clouds of flies.

Dotty's new plants languished by the pool, and gave her great concern. Albert, when appealed to, took a strong line.

'We got plenty of rain-water in them butts,' he told her, 'and we be going to use it.'

'But when that has gone, Albert?'

'We use tap.'

'But Albert, you know it is forbidden.'

'Only them hoses and sprinklers the paper say. It don't say nothin' about watering cans.'

'But it is just as wrong, surely?'

'I'll slip down after dark. What the eye don't see, the heart don't grieve over.'

Dotty, brought up on the stern precepts of her father, looked unhappy.

'Think of them poor plants,' urged Albert. 'Ain't hardly got to know theirselves before this hits 'em. It's cruel to let 'em die for a drop of water.'

'I do see that,' agreed Dotty doubtfully. 'But I still dislike breaking the law.'

'That ain't the law, that old stuff from the local. Just some jumped-up know-nothin' like Councillor Figgins! You leave it to me.'

'Well, I only hope it rains before the rain-water butts dry up,' said Dotty, seeing that Albert was adamant. 'Otherwise, I can see us both in court.'

In Lulling High Street the sun awnings gave a gay continental look to the Cotswold scene. People kept to the shady side of the road. Cars were too hot to touch. The trees were beginning to turn yellow, and dust eddied in the gutters and veiled the window-sills.

At The Fuchsia Bush a brisk trade in ices and lemonade took the place of the usual tea and coffee, and Nelly Piggott found that the demand for cakes at teatime had much decreased.

'Too hot to eat,' she told her friend Gladys Lilly who had called in for a vanilla ice-cream after her shopping.

'Too hot to sleep too,' said Gladys. 'I don't get off until about two these nights. In fact, I usually go for a walk, just before it gets dark, to cool off.'

'Well, walk up our way sometime,' suggested Nelly. 'It's quite fresh sitting out on the green once the sun's gone down.'

'Thank you, dear. I might do that. Not tonight though, I've got a heap of ironing to do. Doreen is everlasting changing that child's clothes, but don't offer to do the ironing of 'em.'

'She settled down now?'

'Far from it. Seems proper restless, but it's no good my questioning her. She shuts up like a clam. Funny girl, though she is me own flesh and blood.'

She scooped up the last melted spoonful, and stood up. 'Probably pop up tomorrow night, all being well. About nine, say?'

'Suits me,' said Nelly, and the two friends returned to their separate duties.

Ben Curdle had made a neat square hole in the back door of the school house, and had fitted a new cat flap for the convenience of Tim. Needless to say, the cat completely ignored this innovation, and continued to wait near the french windows or by the dustbin.

'He doesn't seem to understand it,' said Agnes, much bewildered. 'Ben has been so patient, propping up the flap with a cork in the join so that Tim can see through, but he still won't venture in.'

'He's bound to be over-cautious,' Dorothy said re-assuringly, 'having had to look after himself for so long, and exposed to all sorts of dangers.'

'That's true,' agreed Agnes.

'And he's not likely to come in during this heat wave. He seems to prefer that cool patch under the holly bush.'

'Yes. I do see that. It's just that I did so hope to get him used to indoor life before we go away.'

'At the rate we're going,' replied Dorothy grimly, 'he'll have until Christmas to get used to that cat flap. Sometimes I think lawyers and estate agents could do with a squib behind them.'

'They do seem a trifle dilatory,' agreed Agnes, expressing the understatement of the year.

St Andrew's clock was striking nine when Gladys Lilly emerged from her front gate and turned left.

The house stood in a cul-de-sac not far from the hill up to Thrush Green. At one end of the short road were some allotments, the gateway being overshadowed by a large elder tree.

Gladys could smell the sharp scent of its great flat blossoms which glimmered like a hundred moons in the gloaming. She noticed too, a shabby van drawn up in the shadow of the tree, but took little heed of it, imagining that one of the allotment holders might have brought some bulky article such as wire-netting or a sack of manure to his site.

She strode briskly away, and was at Nelly's within ten minutes. Nelly welcomed her with a cup of tea, and the two ladies agreed that it was amazing how refreshing tea was whatever the weather.

'And how's Albert?' enquired Gladys politely.

'Fair enough,' said Nelly. 'He's next door, so he's all right.'

She rose to collect the cups and saucers, and stacked them neatly on the draining board.

'Well, let's have a bit of air, shall we?' she said, leading the way.

They settled themselves on a nearby bench, and admired the remains of a spectacular sunset. Bands of lemon and pink glowed above Lulling Woods, and nearer at hand the lamps shone from the windows of The Two Pheasants and the school house. Across the green, Mrs Bailey's light winked, and nearby the lamplight shone from Ella Bembridge's cottage windows.

It was all very peaceful. There was no one else about. The children's swings hung motionless in the still air. A pigeon roosted on Nathaniel Patten's shoulder, and only a tiny scuffling sound from the nearby churchyard told of some small nocturnal animal about its business.

The scent from a fine bank of tobacco plants in Harold Shoosmith's garden added to the contentment of the two friends who sat in companionable silence, enjoying the rest from their work and the welcome freshness of the cool air, after the heat of the day.

The evening star appeared on the horizon. Gladys gave a satisfied sigh, as St Andrew's clock began to strike ten.

'Well, I suppose it's time I was going, Nelly. I've thoroughly enjoyed it here. Perhaps I could come up again sometimes, while this heat's on?'

'Any time,' said Nelly. 'It's good to have a bit of company. As you can see, our Albert don't give me much of an evening.'

'Ah well!' said Gladys diplomatically. 'We all knows what the men are like, and in any case I hear he's doing a good job down at Miss Harmer's. I expect he needs a break after that.'

She rose to her feet, and Nelly walked with her to the brow of the hill. The lights of Lulling winked below, and the air was beginning to stir with a light breeze.

'Goodnight, my dear,' said Gladys. 'It's been lovely. Now, you pop in and see me one evening. Promise?'

'I'll do that,' said Nelly.

It was during Gladys's hour of absence, as dusk was falling, that Doreen Lilly emerged cautiously from her mother's house.

She stood in the shelter of the front porch looking about her, but all was quiet. The neighbours were by their television sets. The allotment holders had finished their labours, locked their tools in the little sheds dotted about their plots, and had gone home.

Doreen sped across to the shabby van, now hardly discernible in the near-darkness. The scent of the elder flowers, mingling with the cloying sweetness of the privet blooms nearby, was over-powering.

A tall young man emerged from the driver's seat, and the two embraced. They both got into the van, Doreen looking anxiously up to a bedroom window where a nightlight was giving a glow-worm illumination for the comfort of her young child.

All was as quiet as the grave. No one was in sight, and after ten minutes Doreen emerged, and returned to the shelter of the porch.

The van turned and drove off, and Doreen was busy at the kitchen sink, washing her hair, when Gladys Lilly returned.

'Nice to see friends, isn't it?' she said conversationally.

'I suppose so,' said Doreen, groping for a towel. 'By the way, I'm off to London tomorrow to see Jane.'

'Well, you might have said!' protested her mother.

'I forgot. Be back Sunday night anyway. It means

catching the nine-thirty tomorrow, but as it's Saturday I
don't have to go to them Lovelocks.'

'Maybe it'll do you good,' said her mother. 'You've
seemed a bit peaky lately.'

'And so would you if you had to work with them old
slave-drivers.'

There was a note of vindictiveness in her daughter's tone
which distressed Gladys.

'Well, you'd best get your bit of packing done tonight,'
she said. 'Want a hand up to the station tomorrow?'

'No. I've got the pushchair, and I shan't take much.'

'Be nice to see Jane again,' continued Gladys. 'She was
good to you when you first went to work with the
Reverend Bull. If you should see him, give him my
respectful regards. He's a good man, even if he is Church,'
said Gladys with commendable magnanimity.

But Doreen made no reply.

18   An Intruder

GLADYS Lilly was not the only one to have difficulty in sleeping during the heat wave.

Violet Lovelock, always the lightest sleeper of the three sisters, found herself listening for the chimes of St John's church throughout most of the night.

At two o'clock, on that same night which had seen Gladys Lilly's visit to Thrush Green, Violet became conscious of unusual sounds below. Could she have left the door ajar? But then, on such a still night, would the door have moved?

She crept to the window and looked out. Lulling High Street was deserted except for a white dog, ghostly in the darkness, which was padding by the closed shops on the other side of the road, intent on its own affairs.

The lime tree nearby was already beginning to flower, and through the open window its heady fragrance drifted.

There was another bump from below, and Violet froze into rigidity. Could there possibly be a burglar in the house?

Already the Lovelock ladies had experienced this upsetting occurrence. On that occasion they had been in the garden, picking gooseberries, when some opportunist thief had tried the front door, found it open, and whisked much of the silver so generously displayed into a bag, and vanished. Little of that haul had been recovered, but the beautiful rose bowl presented to their father had been replaced on the dining-room sideboard on its return.

It would certainly prove a temptation to any dishonest

intruder, thought Violet. And there was so much else in the house. The drawing-room occasional tables were laden with the silver knick-knacks collected over the years, and the Queen Anne coffee set was permanently on display on its exquisite silver tray on the table just outside her door on the landing.

At this horrid thought Violet became thoroughly alarmed. Should she rouse her sisters? They would not be best pleased if there were no real cause for such stern measures. Violet, despite the brave front she put on things when dealing with Ada and Bertha, was secretly still in awe of her older sisters, and hesitated to incur their wrath.

She put on her dressing gown and slippers, listening for every untoward sound, and crept to the door. The trayful of silver on the landing table still glimmered comfortingly, she was relieved to see.

With extreme caution, Violet began to descend the stairs. The fourth one from the top was liable to creak, as she well knew, and she stepped delicately upon it. At the same time, there was a metallic clanging sound from the dining-room, and Violet froze into stillness.

It was suddenly very quiet. Should she go on, or go back, or wake Bertha and Ada after all? If only there were an upstairs telephone she would dial 999 and let the police come, even if it turned out to be a groundless scare.

But, of course, one telephone in the house had seemed gross extravagance to the Lovelocks, and that was kept in the hall where everyone could hear at least half of the conversation, whilst enduring the cross-draught from the front door and the dining-room. There was no help there, thought poor Violet.

After a few minutes, which seemed like hours to Violet, immobile on the stairs, the noises began again, though more quietly.

Violet, who was no coward, descended firmly, intent on

confronting the intruder. She traversed the hall, heard an almighty crash, and flung open the dining-room door.

She was just in time to see a figure forcing its way through the kitchen window beyond the dining-room. Within seconds there was the sound of metal jangling, receding footsteps, and a minute or two later, the sound of a car engine revving furiously.

Violet found herself shaking violently. She went into the dining-room, and found the silver on the sideboard had gone, and the two drawers containing the heavy silver cutlery, upturned and empty on the floor. The kitchen window still swung gently to and fro from the violent exit of the marauder.

Violet, with commendable control, remembered the earlier burglary, and forbore to touch anything. Instead, she went to the telephone, and was about to dial for help, when her two sisters appeared at the head of the stairs. Their skimpy locks were plaited into thin grey braids, and both wrinkled faces looked extremely vexed.

'What on earth, Violet, are you doing at this hour?' said Bertha.

'Are you ill, dear?' enquired Ada. 'You woke us up, you know.'

'We've been burgled,' said Violet flatly. 'I'm just about to ring the police.'

'*Burgled*? Not again!' cried Ada.

'But will there be anyone at the police station at this hour?' cried Bertha.

Violet, telephone to ear, twirled the dial forcefully.

'Yes, *again*,' she replied. 'And naturally the police should be informed immediately, and *of course* there will be someone on duty, Bertha!'

The two old ladies descended the stairs and stood one on each side of Violet.

'Yes,' she was saying. 'Miss Violet Lovelock speaking. I

want to inform you of a burglary here. About ten minutes ago. The thief made his getaway in a car or van.'

'I don't like that word "getaway",' complained Ada. 'It sounds American.'

'We shall expect an officer here immediately,' said Violet. 'No, of course nothing has been touched. We know the correct procedure in cases like this.'

She put down the telephone.

'Really, Violet dear,' said Bertha admiringly, 'you coped with that very competently. Shall I make us a hot drink?'

'Better not,' said Violet, much mollified by Bertha's appreciation of her actions. 'Let's wait until the police arrive. But it might be as well to get dressed,' she added. 'It's going to be a long night, I fear.'

Another cloudless day dawned, and the country awoke to banner headlines in the press telling it that THE DROUGHT IS NOW OFFICIAL and that penalties for wasting water would be severe.

It also had some distressing pictures of dried-up water-beds with stranded fish, sheep and cattle dying of thirst, wilted crops and various other horrid sights guaranteed to curdle the blood of breakfast-time readers.

'I can never understand,' remarked Ella Bembridge to Winnie Bailey, when they met on Thrush Green, 'why a nation which is fanatically absorbed with its weather conditions is so bad at organising them.'

'How do you mean?'

'Well, take last spring. There we were, up to our hocks in puddles, the Pleshey water-meadows brimming over, all our water-butts overflowing, and a few months later, here we are, being told we'll be clapped in irons for watering the lettuces.'

'I think it's all right to water lettuces with *used* water,' Winnie began, but was swept aside by Ella's eloquence.

'And look at snow!' declaimed Ella unrealistically. 'The Canadians and Americans, and the Swiss for that matter, get yards of the stuff overnight, and their trains continue to run, and the children get to school, and the milk's delivered. And what happens here?'

'You tell me,' said Winnie equably, knowing that she would anyway.

'Two inches and the country's paralysed! No buses, no trains, no deliveries! Chaos!'

'I thought everyone coped very well last winter,' said Winnie. 'I know we never went short of milk, and the postman never missed once.'

'You've a much nicer nature than I have,' said Ella. 'You look on the bright side. I don't. Sometimes I think I'll write to the papers.'

And with this dark threat she stumped off homewards.

On Sunday evening Gladys Lilly was a little annoyed at the non-appearance of her daughter and grandson. A piece of smoked haddock was simmering gently, awaiting poached eggs on top for the two travellers, but at nine-thirty Gladys ate the fish herself, and became resigned to the fact that Doreen would probably turn up the next morning in time for work.

Nothing happened. Now becoming agitated, Gladys called at the Misses Lovelocks' house to find out more. The gossip about the burglary had not reached Gladys.

She found the ladies in frosty mood, far from pleased at Doreen's dereliction of duties.

'We have had a most upsetting weekend,' Ada told her. 'And we were relying on Doreen to help us clear up after a burglary on Friday night.'

'Oh, my lor', m'm,' gasped Gladys. 'I'm real sorry about that! Did they take much?'

'Far too much,' said Bertha.

'And what's more,' added Ada, 'the police think that *someone* helped the intruder by leaving the kitchen window ajar.'

The full impact of this last remark did not dawn on poor Gladys until she was next door at The Fuchsia Bush, steadying her nerves with a cup of Darjeeling tea.

Nelly Piggott spared a few minutes from her labours in the kitchen to offer consolation.

'Don't take no notice of them old tabbies,' she told her friend. 'How could your Doreen have been mixed up in it? She was washing her hair when you got home, and then you know she went up to bed. You'll be her alibi, if they make accusations against her.'

'Well, I've no wish to be whatever it is, but I can certainly say she was home when Miss Violet saw that chap.'

'That's right,' agreed Nelly, secretly relishing this drama.

'But where on earth has the girl got to today?' wailed Gladys, setting down her cup. 'Why ain't she turned up? Should I tell the police?'

'I wouldn't get the law in yet,' replied Nelly prudently. 'You wait and see if she turns up today. If she's not home by this evening I'd telephone this Jane friend of hers. Perhaps she's been took bad.'

'In *hospital*, d'you reckon?'

Poor Mrs Lilly went white at the thought of her daughter in one of those dreaded institutions.

'Not necessarily,' said Nelly, feeling she may have gone too far. 'Perhaps just a bilious attack.'

'But I don't know Jane's telephone number, nor where she lives, come to that. She just worked nearby where our Doreen did. For the Reverend Bull, you know.'

'Well, he'd know Jane's address.'

Gladys Lilly was now near to tears, and Nelly's heart was touched.

'Look here, I must get back to the kitchen. Them new girls are making a proper pig's breakfast of the flaky pastry. But if she ain't turned up by closing time, you come in here and I'll get the Reverend's number from our Mr Henstock. Then we'll go on from there. All right?'

She patted her friend's shoulder encouragingly. Gladys mopped up her tears, and tried to smile.

'That's what I'll do, Nelly. And thank you for being a true friend.'

Still sniffing, she went to pay her bill. Rosa, one of the two haughty waitresses, was consumed with curiosity, as Gladys departed.

'What's up then?' she enquired of her colleague who was engrossed in filing her scarlet fingernails rather too close to a tray of meringues.

'Search me,' was the answer. 'But we do see a bit of life here, don't we?'

It was six o'clock before Nelly and Gladys met again. The owner of The Fuchsia Bush, Mrs Peters, had gone home early in the afternoon to totter to bed with a blinding migraine.

The rest of the staff had also gone, leaving Nelly to lock up the premises, and this she was doing when a tearful Mrs Lilly appeared.

'No sign of her,' she cried. 'D'you think I could ring Mr Henstock?'

'You come in and sit down,' said Nelly, unlocking the door, 'and I'll get the number.'

Charles Henstock was much perturbed to hear of Doreen's disappearance. He supplied Anthony Bull's telephone number, and expressed the hope that all would be well.

'I feel quite guilty about all this,' he told Dimity. 'I know that Anthony would never blame me for any trouble that has cropped up, but I wish I hadn't suggested her to the Lovelock girls. I fear that they may have overworked her.'

'You did what you thought was right at the time,' Dimity comforted him. 'After all, you were not to know how matters would turn out.'

Meanwhile, Gladys Lilly rang Anthony Bull, who said that he would go down the road immediately to make enquiries of his neighbour, and would ring back.

The two friends sat in the empty restaurant awaiting the call.

'I must pay for these telephone calls,' said Gladys. 'I'd feel better about it, if I could. And what about Albert's tea? You ought to be getting off home by rights. What a nuisance I am!'

Nelly did her best to allay Gladys's fears. By now, she too was imagining the worst – abduction, seduction, incarceration, even murder!

'They say,' said Gladys, 'that Miss Violet said the chap was exceptionally tall and had cropped hair. Head like a bullet, she said, though she never saw much else.'

'Which way did he go, I wonder?'

'Ran off down the garden to that lane as runs along the back of these places here. That's when she had a glimpse of him. Must have left his car out there, I suppose.'

'Well, he'd need a car or something to carry all that stuff from the Lovelocks! Never see so much silver under one roof in all the time I was in service,' said Nelly. 'I used to dread silver-cleaning days in that place, I can tell you.'

At this moment, the telephone rang, and Gladys leapt to answer it.

Nelly watched her face crumple as she listened to the voice at the other end of the line.

'Oh dear, sir! What a terrible thing. Now I really don't know which way to turn.'

There were soothing sounds coming from the other end, while tears began to course down poor Gladys's face.

'Yes, sir. I'm sure you're right. It's just that I'm that upset that she told me a lie.'

She mopped her face with a handkerchief. The other hand quivered as it held the telephone. Nelly's kind heart was touched at this display of motherly concern.

'Well, thank you, sir, for all your help,' sniffed Gladys. 'You've been real kind, and I shan't forget it. I'll do what you say. I'm sure you're right.'

There were a few more murmurs from the other end, and Gladys put down the receiver.

'She never went to Jane's at all,' sobbed Gladys. 'Nothing better than a liar. Me own daughter – and brought up chapel too!'

Nelly gave what comfort she could, but Gladys was almost too distracted to take in Nelly's kind words.

Eventually, Nelly accompanied Gladys to her home, in the hope that the truant had returned, but the house was empty.

'Mr Bull said I was to go to the police,' she said. 'What d'you think, Nelly?'

'I think,' said that sensible woman, 'that you need a cup of tea. I'll put the kettle on, pop up and see to Albert, and be back with you within half an hour. Then we'll walk up to the police station together.'

'Oh, Nelly!' cried Gladys, tears starting afresh at such kindness. 'How I ever got on before I met you, I can't think!'

'Well, I'm glad to be of help,' said Nelly, making her departure.

Gladys came with her to the door. The kettle was beginning to sing, promising comfort.

'What I truly fears now,' admitted Gladys, 'is that them Lovelocks was right. I bet our Doreen left that window open, and I bet it was that chap of hers that done it. I wonder if I ought to tell the police?'

'Find the girl first,' advised Nelly, 'and what follows will have to be faced when the time comes. See you in half an hour.'

She set off to puff up the steep hill to Thrush Green.

What a day it had been, one way and another! And not over yet, thought Nelly.

19 The Drought Breaks

NATURALLY, the news of the Lovelocks' burglary was common knowledge, within twenty-four hours, in Lulling and Thrush Green.

Comment on the incident varied considerably. It was felt at The Two Pheasants that 'them old girls asked for it, showing all that stuff openly for any passer-by to covet'.

Winnie Bailey, and other Thrush Green friends, were profoundly shocked that such a thing should have occurred, and that the three sisters had been robbed again.

Young Cooke, who did most of the caretaking work now at St Andrew's, said that in his view 'nobody should own all that valuable stuff, and the chap as took it was only evening out wealth, like, and good luck to him.'

At this, Albert gave him a hefty swipe on the shin with the broom which had been supporting him, and a string of curses, of Anglo-Saxon derivation, which surprised even young Cooke.

It was sometime later that the possibility of Doreen Lilly being mixed up in the affair was being mooted abroad with great relish.

Nelly Piggott, unable to keep such richness to herself, mentioned it to little Miss Fogerty when they happened to meet on the green.

'Her mum's real upset,' said Nelly, with evident satisfaction. 'That Doreen'll do anything that fellow tells her, despite the way he's treated her. So Mrs Lilly tells me. She reckons he's behind this, and one or two people have said they've seen this Gordon around here recently.'

'What does he look like?'

'Tall chap. Red hair, what there is of it. He's a skin head, or was. Then he was in jail, you know, so his hair would still be short. Rosa, down The Fuchsia Bush, reckons he came in earlier this summer.'

Agnes remembered the young man screened by the trunk of a lime tree in Lulling High Street. Perhaps not an architectural student after all? Perhaps something far worse?

'He left her with that baby, you know,' continued Nelly. 'Treated her awful, but it never made no difference to Her Love. When he called her back, she just come. There's nothing so wonderful as Love, is there, Miss Fogerty?'

Agnes tried to recall who it was who had said that she felt that a sound bank balance and good teeth were really more important, but refrained from uttering these sensible sentiments, in the face of Nelly's maudlin expression.

She bade her farewell as calmly as she could, but hurried back to Dorothy, seriously perturbed.

'But, Agnes dear, I really see no need to rush to the police,' said Dorothy. 'Should this young man *happen* to be the burglar, and Rosa's tale needs corroboration, then perhaps your evidence – very slight evidence too – might be needed. After all, he didn't look particularly felonious, you say?'

'No, indeed,' replied Agnes, although she did not like to tell Dorothy that somehow she still imagined criminals with shaven heads, attired in suits with broad arrows all over them, and shackles round their ankles attached to heavy weights. Perhaps a subconscious memory from her comic-reading days?

'In fact,' volunteered Agnes, beginning to feel calmer, 'he looked rather like a student of some sort. Rather scruffy, of course, but most young men do these days, don't they?'

'They do indeed,' agreed Dorothy. 'Now we must get on. We have the PTA meeting tomorrow night, and we must look respectable for the presentation. I shall go up and wash my hair.'

She made her way towards the door, checked by the window, and said, 'There's dear little Tim, waiting for his supper. Shall I give him something, or will you?'

'I'll do that,' said Agnes, bustling towards the kitchen. 'You carry on with your hairwash.'

She went, humming happily, to cut up Tim's supper, all fears of suppressing vital evidence now forgotten.

The hot spell of weather began to show signs of ending. During the next day clouds began to gather in the west, and little breezes shivered the leaves.

By the time Agnes and Dorothy were dressing in their best for the great occasion, there were distant rumbles of thunder to be heard.

'It seems much cooler,' commented Agnes, as she followed Dorothy down the stairs. 'I wonder if I should bring my cardigan.'

'You look so nice as you are,' said Dorothy, 'that a cardigan dragged over it would quite spoil the effect.'

Grateful though Agnes was to be told that she looked nice, she was a trifle put out at the suggestion that her cardigans were usually 'dragged on'. However, this was no time to take offence at such a small matter, and she gave Dorothy a smile.

'Well, I must admit my new cardigan doesn't quite go with this blue dress. I try to tell myself it *tones*, but I know really that it *clashes*.'

'Blue is always difficult to match,' said Dorothy. 'Now how do I look?'

She turned around slowly on the front door mat.

'Superb!' announced Agnes. 'Every inch a headmistress!'

'Then in that case,' said Dorothy, head held high, 'we will go over.'

The partition had been pushed back, throwing Miss Robinson's and Dorothy's room into one. Already the place was crowded and to the ladies' discomfiture a round of clapping greeted their entrance.

The rector ushered them to the seats of honour, beside himself and Mrs Gibbons, facing the throng. Gauleiter Gibbons, looking very spruce in a Prince of Wales check suit, was flanked by the other members of the PTA committee, the school governors and Mrs Cooke, the formidable matriarch of the Cooke family, who had joined the party uninvited and whom nobody dared to move away.

Agnes, much embarrassed by all this publicity, tried to shut her ears to the eulogies which Mrs Gibbons and the rector poured forth.

Dorothy, on the other hand, appeared to be relishing the list of her virtues which was now being given to an attentive audience. Agnes envied her aplomb. She herself was trembling with fright, and praying that she did not burst into tears at the crucial moment.

'And we hope,' concluded Mrs Gibbons, proffering a large and obviously heavy parcel, 'that you will both think of us when you use it.'

Dorothy rose, and gave a small jerk of the head, summoning Agnes to join her, and the two ladies held the package between them.

'Undo it now!' hissed Mrs Gibbons. 'Everyone wants to see it.'

Obediently, Dorothy put it on her own desk, now in command of Mrs Gibbons, and began to unwrap the clouds of tissue paper. Agnes stood at one side, excited at the sight.

There was a murmur in the hall, as the final swathings were unfolded, and a cut glass fruit bowl was displayed.

'Ah!' sighed the audience rapturously. Dorothy held the beautiful object aloft, and Agnes gave a genuine smile of delight.

'Madam Chairman, Mr Henstock, ladies and gentlemen,' began Dorothy, swinging gracefully into her prepared speech. 'What can I say? Except to give you our heartfelt thanks.'

She continued, mentioning the happy years both had spent at the school, the kindness and generosity of the parents and governors, and the wrench that it would be for both of them to leave Thrush Green.

The rector looked a little bewildered, as well he might, for it had been planned that he should hand over the governors' present of a clock as soon as the fruit bowl had been unwrapped.

However, Dorothy's prompt, and somewhat lengthy, reply had taken him by surprise, and short of halting her peroration which would have been uncivil, and anyway pretty well impossible, the rector was obliged to await the lady's conclusion with as much grace as he could muster in the face of his fellow-governors' agitation in the front row.

At last, Dorothy came to the end of her speech of thanks amidst polite applause. The rector arose and lifted the governors' package from beside his feet.

'And I have the great privilege,' he said, bowing politely to the two ladies, 'to present you with a small token of esteem and thanks from the governors of Thrush Green school.'

He held out the parcel, not sure which lady should take it. But Dorothy, now realising that she had leapt in rather too prematurely with her thanks, motioned to Agnes to accept the second present.

Agnes went forward diffidently, and a storm of clapping and some cheers broke out, completely dumbfounding that modest lady.

There was no doubting the affection which prompted this spontaneous tribute, and Agnes's eyes filled with tears. Dorothy too, joined in the clapping, obviously delighted on her friend's behalf.

'Speech!' yelled someone at the back, and little Miss Fogerty raised a trembling hand for silence.

'Ladies and gentlemen,' she quavered. 'Dorothy has said all I want to say, but I am just going to add a heartfelt "thank you" for many happy years, and to let you see me unwrap this exciting parcel.'

The applause grew again, accompanied by some energetic stamping at the back by old pupils, as Agnes undid the paper and held up a charming brass carriage clock for all to see.

Taking heart from the obvious show of affection, Agnes added, 'This lovely present from the governors will be a memento of our friends at Thrush Green for many years.'

At which, she sat down, smiled across at Dorothy, and thanked heaven that her tears had not actually run down her cheeks throughout her ordeal.

'You were absolutely splendid,' Dorothy told her later

that evening, when they had regained the peace of the school house.

'And so were you,' Agnes said loyally. 'I could never have made such a wonderful speech.'

'I didn't find it easy,' admitted Dorothy. 'Thank goodness it's over. But you know what I shall always remember?'

'Mrs Cooke among the governors?'

'No, dear. The well-deserved tribute to you that came from every heart.'

Before midnight, as Dorothy and Agnes were seeking sleep, the storm broke.

The thunder had become louder as the evening had worn on, but it was past eleven o'clock before the rain began.

It fell in a heavy deluge. Great drops spun like silver coins as they hit the parched earth. Within minutes, it seemed, little rivulets gushed along the gutters and down the steep hill to Lulling.

Agnes stood by her bedroom window to watch the transformation. The roofs of Thrush Green glistened. Rain dripped from Nathaniel Patten's shoulders, and from the heavy foliage of the chestnut avenue.

The playground was already awash, and the tombstones ranged round St Andrew's churchyard stood wet and shiny like so many old men in mackintoshes.

There was little wind, just this ferocious cascade from the heavens, and Agnes felt the overpowering relief which the plants and trees, and the thirsty earth itself, must be experiencing.

The scent of water on stone, grass and soil, filled her with joy. The hot weeks, so warmly welcomed at first, had held Thrush Green, men, animals, trees and all living things, in a relentless grip of drought for too long.

Now release had come. Agnes held out her hands to catch the raindrops, patted them on to her hot forehead, and went contentedly to bed.

The Misses Lovelock were still without their silver, and still without help in the house.

They took these reverses remarkably well, and looked out a canteen of cutlery of somewhat inferior calibre, which had been in use by the domestic staff in the old days, and trusted that their usual tableware would reappear before long.

The police gave them little hope as the days passed. There was a rapid and well-organised turnover of such objects, the Lovelock ladies were told. The young man probably passed on his haul within an hour or two of collecting it, and there was no sign of his whereabouts.

The only development was a grubby postcard from Doreen to her mother. The postmark was so faint and smudged that it was quite illegible, but the message was clear:

Me and the boy are all right. Don't worry. I will write again.
Love,
　Doreen

'You see,' said Gladys to Nelly, 'there's not a word about this Gordon, or about coming back. But she's with him all right. I don't doubt that, and I suppose I'd better take this card to the police.'

Nelly agreed that it would be the proper thing to do. She felt very sorry for Gladys, and for the Lovelock sisters, blaming herself partly for furthering the introduction of the truant to the three old ladies.

Charles Henstock was equally concerned, and had rung his friend Anthony Bull several times to ask if he had heard anything at his end. But nothing occurred to give him comfort. Wherever Gordon, Doreen and the child were, was a mystery, and all that could be done was to wait and hope.

The thunderstorm which had ended the drought, also seemed to have ended the summer as well, for it was followed by a period of cool rainy weather during which Agnes had recourse to her cardigan again.

Most of the residents of Thrush Green greeted this return to semi-winter philosophically, grateful for the refreshment of their gardens, and freed from the bondage of those exhorting them to save water.

Albert Piggott and Dotty Harmer took pleasure in the new pool, admiring their handiwork. Dotty wondered if another six or so ducks would give added glory, but Albert was less enthusiastic.

'They makes a mort of mess,' he observed dourly, watching a dozen webbed feet transferring water, pond-weed and general slime from the pool to the freshly-laid stones.

'No, no, Albert!' protested Dotty. 'They are simply behaving naturally. You can see the dear things are really happy. I should like to give a few more ducks the chance to enjoy it. There must be a lot of *deprived* ducks about.'

Albert thought of the few weedy specimens kept in a pen at Perce Hodge's farm, but forbore to tell Dotty of their plight. She'd have them down before you could turn round, he thought, surveying the muddy stones around the pool. His labours were already being spoilt. No point in hastening the process.

Winnie Bailey was another person who was busy in her garden now that it was cooler.

She was pulling up groundsel and some obstinate weeds from the flower border, whilst picking a summer nosegay

for the house, when Jenny hailed her from the kitchen window.

'Telephone, Mrs Bailey! It's Richard.'

Winnie hurried indoors, and sank thankfully into the chair by the telephone.

'May I call to see you tomorrow morning?'

'Of course. Can you stay to lunch?'

'I'd love to.'

'And Fenella?'

'Afraid not. She's not up to travelling. Rather poorly at the moment.'

At once, Winnie saw Fenella in hospital, probably in the intensive care department, with some fatal disease which would leave Richard without a wife, and the two children motherless. She was already trying to decide on a boarding-school, a reliable housekeeper, or possibly a second wife for Richard, when she heard herself say, quite calmly, 'I do hope it's not serious, Richard?'

'No, no! Just that she's feeling rotten first thing now. Morning sickness, you know. We're having a baby after Christmas.'

'Well, I'm delighted,' cried Winnie, much relieved. 'What good news! Now, would she like me to do some knitting for her, or does she bring her babies up in those gro-bag things?'

'I'll ask her,' said Richard. 'Yes, we are very pleased. Puts the kybosh on Roger, I hope.'

Richard sounded unpleasantly smug, Winnie felt, and slangy with it. However, she was so pleased to hear the news, that she forgave her nephew, said that she looked forward to seeing him, and then went to break the news to Jenny.

'Good thing we had that chicken from Perce,' said Jenny. 'With plenty of stuffing and a pound of chipolatas, it should do us a treat.'

With great plans of knitting and cooking to engage them, the two friends resumed their tasks.

'It's high time,' said Dorothy one evening, 'that Tim came in to sleep. What about bringing his basket into the kitchen tonight, and shutting the shed door?'

'But it's so wet everywhere,' protested Agnes. 'And it seems to rain every night.'

'Exactly. If he can't get into the shed, he'll look for his basket elsewhere. Let's put the cat flap wide open, and put his basket just inside where he can see it. I'm sure it would work.'

Agnes looked unhappy. Already she had a vision of her beloved cat, shivering in a rain storm, coat spiky with wetness, eyes half-closed in anguish.

'Perhaps we could leave a folded sack in the shed as well,' she suggested, 'and leave the door ajar as usual. Then he has the choice.'

'We don't want to give him any choice,' said Dorothy firmly. 'Let him find his basket and use it.'

There was no gainsaying Dorothy in this headmistressy mood, and Agnes gave in.

She went up to bed in a very unhappy state. A steady

rain pattered against the windows and cars swished through the puddles bordering Thrush Green.

The cat flap had been propped open to its widest extent, with a cork firmly wedged at the top of the join, and Tim's basket, with its blanket plumply folded, stood just inside.

Dorothy had left these little arrangements to Agnes, and had volunteered to go down the garden to shut the shed door. She was half-afraid that Agnes would be tempted to leave it ajar as usual, and Dorothy was intent on cat-discipline tonight.

She fell asleep within ten minutes of climbing into bed, but poor Agnes next door lay listening to the rain and grieving for her pet.

At about two o'clock she could bear it no longer, and sliding out of bed, she crept downstairs.

The house was still and quiet. Only the whispering of the rain outside stirred the silence. Agnes tip-toed to the kitchen door, and gently turned the handle.

There was no flurried movement of a cat making his escape, or the creaking of a wicker cat basket.

Timidly, fearing the worst, Agnes pushed the door farther open, so that she had a clear view of the cat basket.

There, curled up in deep sleep, one paw protectively over his nose, lay Tim, oblivious to all about him.

A great surge of happiness engulfed little Miss Fogerty. He had come in of his own accord! He had used the cat flap, and found his old familiar bed! There was no doubt about it. He was a highly intelligent cat.

And what was more, thought Agnes, creeping back to bed, he now looked upon this house as his rightful home.

She slept as soundly as the cat below.

20 Last Days

THE last day of term was as cool and damp as those which had preceded it, but for young Miss Robinson, in a bustle of responsibility over the presentation of two bouquets and two boxes of chocolates, the atmosphere seemed feverishly hot.

Directions to the Lulling florist had been explicit and much repeated. The flowers were to be delivered *not later than two-thirty* to Miss Robinson herself, who would be waiting in the lobby to receive and then secrete them.

One small girl had been coached *ad nauseam* to present Dorothy's bouquet, and another who was in charge of Agnes's, was equally well primed.

Two little boys, with extra clean hands, and comparatively polite manners, had been detailed to present a box of chocolates apiece. It all sounded simple, but as any teacher will know, such apparently spontaneous gestures need a week or two of anxious preparation, and then they can easily go wrong. Poor Miss Robinson suffered.

It was open house at Thrush Green school that afternoon, so that parents, governors, representatives from the local education authority, friends, neighbours crowded into the classroom in a much more informal manner than at the PTA presentations earlier.

Dorothy and Agnes knew exactly what was going on for a number of children had informed them of the proposed tributes, adding for good measure, the sum which they themselves had contributed to the general largesse. It was a good thing that Miss Robinson, in her innocence, knew nothing of this.

It was a happy party, and the children did their duties admirably. Dorothy and Agnes expressed their surprised delight, and thanked everyone – particularly Miss Robinson – for such beautiful flowers and delicious chocolates.

There were no other speeches, but Dorothy informed the throng that cups of tea were available in Miss Fogerty's terrapin, as Mrs Betty Bell and Mrs Isobel Shoosmith had kindly arranged this. At this juncture, Agnes whispered in her ear, and she added that the Thrush Green Women's Institute had most kindly lent their cups and saucers, and this courtesy was very much appreciated.

In the mêlée that followed, she and Agnes mingled with the guests, accepting good wishes and sometimes a personal present, and it was past four o'clock before the school emptied and the two ladies bore their tributes to the school house. The flowers were deposited in a bucket of water to await later arrangement, and the friends sank thankfully into their armchairs.

'It all went beautifully, didn't it? Do you know,' confessed Dorothy, 'I wondered if I should find this parting too much for me. But it was such a jolly afternoon, wasn't it? I shall telephone Miss Robinson this evening to thank her particularly. I think she's going to be a tower of strength to the new head.'

Agnes agreed, still amazed that Dorothy should admit to the frailties from which she herself suffered. Somehow it made the bond between them even stronger. She too had dreaded the last afternoon, and had been relieved to find it a wholly cheerful occasion.

'And of course,' continued Dorothy, 'we shan't really be saying goodbye for some time yet. It's a comforting thought.'

'Anyway,' added Agnes, 'we can always come back to visit Thrush Green from Barton.'

Dorothy began to tear away the cellophane from her box of chocolates.

'I don't see why we shouldn't celebrate, Agnes. The square ones are hard, I warn you.'

Nelly Piggott had kept her word and accompanied Gladys Lilly to Lulling police station with the postcard from the errant Doreen.

'Well, thanks very much,' said the sergeant on duty. 'You did right to bring this in, Mrs Lilly. I'll pass it on to the officer in charge of the enquiries. Might be a Vital Clue.'

The ladies departed feeling much comforted by this encounter, and Gladys was already making plans to welcome her daughter and grandchild to her home again.

Nelly was not so sanguine, but said little about her doubts to the hopeful mother.

However, later that day she met her good friend Mrs Jenner who was walking across the green to see her daughter Jane, the warden at Rectory Cottages.

To her, she admitted her reservations about bringing the culprit to justice, and Mrs Jenner nodded her head in agreement.

'If you ask me,' said that lady, 'poor Gladys won't see her Doreen, nor Gordon and the boy, for a very long time. And the Lovelock ladies won't ever set eyes on their missing silver either.'

And Mrs Jenner was quite right.

It had been Dorothy's idea that they should spend a few

days at Barton, staying at their favourite guesthouse, as soon as they broke up.

'Now that the business side is settled,' said Dorothy, 'we can chivvy the electrician and decorator if we are down there.'

Dorothy, thought Agnes, seemed to think that her presence would hasten the completion of the work in hand, and maybe she was right. In any case, Agnes looked forward to a few days by the sea, and to visiting the new house again.

They set off on the Saturday morning, planning to stop for a pub lunch near Andover. Isobel had been given minute instructions about the feeding and general care of Tim the cat.

'It's such a relief to know that you are looking after him,' said Agnes. 'He half-knows you already, and he won't be scared away if he sees you about. I'm so anxious that he keeps up the habit of sleeping indoors, and gets thoroughly used to the cat flap.'

Isobel assured her that she would undertake her duties with every care, secretly rather amused at Agnes's earnestness.

'Good thing,' was Harold's comment, when she related this matter to him. 'All the devotion she's put into looking after scores of infants is going to be funnelled into that lucky cat's welfare. I hope the animal knows when it's well off!'

One of the first things that Agnes wanted to see to was the installation of a similar cat flap at the Barton house. Dorothy was more concerned with measuring for carpets and curtains. As always, it seemed, not one pair of the latter could be transferred to Barton, a common disappointment to all who move house.

They arrived at the guesthouse soon after two, and then set out on foot to visit their new home. As it was a

Saturday, no one was at work there, and the house was very still. Their footsteps echoed on the bare boards as they went from room to room.

The biggest job to be done was the rewiring of the whole place, and as this was a messy job, involving cutting channels in the walls, Dorothy had decided that the decorating might just as well follow this upheaval.

'One thing I have insisted on,' said Dorothy, surveying the work, 'is that the plugs should be half-way up the wall. I don't see why we should grovel about bent double to find switches on the skirting board. They can site them just behind the curtains. Perfectly simple when you think about it.'

Agnes, mindful of her arthritis, applauded this sensible suggestion.

'And we'll have a telephone extension beside each bed,' went on Dorothy, 'and good rails by the bath. I'm afraid we shall have to replace the present bath sometime. It's got badly stained. But we will have time to choose something really pretty.'

They wandered into the garden, but rain began to fall, and they left the few late roses and clematis, the tussocky lawn and weedy borders, and returned to the shelter of the house.

'What a pity we didn't bring a couple of deckchairs with us,' said Agnes. 'I could do with a rest.'

Dorothy surveyed the empty kitchen.

'Nothing simpler,' she announced. She went to the kitchen sink, and pulled out two of the drawers below it. Turning them over, she put them near the wall. 'Try that, my dear,' she said, with understandable pride.

Agnes lowered herself cautiously and rested her back against the wall. Dorothy sat on the other upturned drawer beside her. There was a protesting squeak from the wood, but the temporary seating held well.

'How very clever!' commented Agnes.

The two friends sat side by side, legs stretched out above the dusty kitchen floor, and saw in their minds' eye a fully-furnished, warm and comfortable haven.

To Agnes suddenly came comfort. Her thoughts had been sad ones when she had had time to consider them. She hated change, and her natural timidity made her apprehensive of the unknown. She grieved at leaving her friends, her home and the loved surroundings of Thrush Green.

But, for the first time, sitting inelegantly on the kitchen floor, she began to look ahead with stirring excitement. This was going to be her home! Here she would have the company of Dorothy and dear little Tim. There would be new friends in her life, new interests, new countryside to explore.

'And we can always go back,' she said, thinking aloud.

Dorothy seemed to know what was in her mind.

'Of course we can,' she said cheerfully, 'and the Thrush Green people will come and see us here. We're certainly not losing friends by this move, Agnes, but simply finding a lot of new ones.'

Agnes sighed happily. Dorothy consulted her watch.

'Well, I think we should be getting back. If you could manage to stand up first, I should appreciate what the children used to term "a good lug-up".'

And little Miss Fogerty, much refreshed in body and spirit, obliged.

Back at Thrush Green, the future of the two ladies was a prime point of conversation, and the fate of the school house one of pleasurable speculation.

Betty Bell told the Shoosmiths that she had received an official letter asking her to continue to look after the school until further notice.

'And that's a real relief, I can tell you,' she informed Isobel and Harold. 'I mean the money's regular, which is more than you can say about some.'

She must have noticed the bewilderment on her hearers' faces for she added hastily, 'Not but what you do pay me pronto – always ready done up in a clean envelope as soon as the work's done. But poor old Dotty – Miss Harmer, I should say – she don't know if she's coming or going, and sometimes it's weeks before she remembers.'

'But, Betty,' protested Isobel, much shocked by this disclosure, 'surely Mrs Armitage sees to that?'

'Well, no. You see, Dotty wanted to do it, and of course Mrs Armitage thinks she does, but she don't, if you follow me.'

'Then you must mention it to her,' advised Isobel, mentally making a note to do it herself as well. 'Things can't go on like that.'

'Lor' bless you,' laughed Betty, 'they've been going on like that for years down Dotty's!'

Albert Piggott was doing his best to persuade Mr Jones of The Two Pheasants that he should put in a bid for the school house and turn it into a small hotel.

'And where would I get the cash for that?' appealed the landlord. 'Don't get very fat on your and Percy's half-pints of bitter, I can tell you.'

Even Ella Bembridge, across the green, flirted with the idea of changing her residence for one short afternoon.

Dimity was horrified. 'You aren't serious? You've been quite happy in the cottage, haven't you?'

'Well, yes, of course I have,' replied Ella, blowing a cloud of acrid cigarette smoke towards the ceiling. 'But it would make a change. Besides there are twice the number of cupboards over there, and mine are uncomfortably full.'

'Then have a good clear-out for the next Jumble Sale,' advised Dimity, 'and go on enjoying this place.'

The folk at Rectory Cottages were perhaps the most keenly interested in the future of the school house. One school of thought was positive that it would be razed to the ground, and eight or ten houses would be built on the site. Tom Hardy maintained that it would be turned into offices, and Muriel Fuller surmised that the education authority would incorporate it into the school itself, possibly as a store and school kitchen.

'Well, at least,' said Winnie Bailey, summing up the general feeling, 'that's all in the future. We shall have Agnes and Dorothy with us for some time yet, thank heaven.'

The two schoolmistresses returned from their break feeling that much had been accomplished. Dorothy had enjoyed urging the electrician and decorator to brisker efforts, and had purchased some particularly attractive cretonne, at sale prices, for curtains and chair covers.

Agnes had given a local handyman minute instructions about the cat flap. They had attended the local church and met the vicar of whom they both approved. The post-mistress seemed welcoming and helpful, and the owner of the guest-house had recommended a jobbing gardener. All in all, the ladies were well content.

They were now in a relaxed enough frame of mind to enjoy the spate of informal invitations which came along from old friends and well-wishers. It was a joy to be free during the day to accept coffee in the morning with Ella and Dimity, or afternoon tea with Isobel and Harold next door. With no worries about the term ahead to daunt them, life took on a wonderfully relaxed air, and Agnes and Dorothy blossomed in these first early days of their retirement.

The cat, by this time, now kept them company, though always showing a preference for Agnes, rubbing round her legs, purring loudly, and even jumping on to her meagre

lap, much to her delight. Dorothy was large-hearted
enough to approve, and only hoped that she too, in time,
would be so honoured.

The relaxation of her responsibilities seemed to mellow
Dorothy. She even offered the school house curtains and
carpets to Ray and Kathleen, when they moved to Barton,
and for good measure threw in the nest of coffee tables,
much coveted by her sister-in-law, as there was really
nowhere to put them in the new house.

'I only hope,' said Isobel to Harold, 'that this general
goodwill prevails. They are so happy at the moment. I
wonder if they will start having pangs when term begins? I
wouldn't put it past Dorothy to drop in on the new head to
tell him where he is going wrong.'

'Never fear,' said her husband. 'The sound of infant
voices raised in battle in the playground will simply bring
home to them how marvellous it is not to have to cope.
Anyone with any sense welcomes retirement, and those
two have plenty of that between them.'

And time proved that Harold Shoosmith was right.

Term began at the end of August, and the two ladies were
far too engrossed by then in plans for the move to take
much interest in the activity so close to them.

But they did invite the three staff to tea during the first
week of term and were much impressed by the good sense
and deference of the new headmaster. He was a pastmaster
in diplomacy, and congratulated Dorothy on the ship-
shape way everything had been left, and the ex-headmistress
beamed with pleasure.

As always the jobs at the Barton house took twice as
long as estimated, and two days after term began Dorothy
issued her ultimatum.

'We shall be moving in,' she told the estate agent, the
electrician, the plumber and the decorator, 'in a fortnight's

time. The removal men have been engaged this end, and we expect to be in and settled before nightfall on Tuesday, September the sixteenth.'

All protestations, explanations and excuses were swept aside, and Agnes, yet again, was filled with awe and admiration at Dorothy's command of the situation.

Promptly at eight-thirty the removal van arrived and loading began.

In between supervising the bestowal of their household belongings, Dorothy prepared a substantial picnic lunch, and Agnes superintended the arrangements of Tim's travelling basket.

The greatest worry, of course, was the strong possibility that he would keep well away from all the unaccustomed activity, and Agnes had opened a tin of sardines as a particular bribe.

Amazingly, it worked, and Agnes secured the cat in the basket just as the removal men were about to move off.

The two ladies were to follow in the car, and to meet the van at Barton at two-thirty. The time now had come to say goodbye to Isobel and Harold who had been helping them.

But not only Isobel and Harold, it seemed, for although the children of Thrush Green school were supposed to be at school dinner, they were instead all at the railings of the playground, with the three staff standing behind them, smiling and waving.

'What a wonderful send-off!' said Agnes, as they drove off towards Lulling. 'What a nice idea of the headmaster's!'

'Yes, a kindly thought,' agreed Dorothy, negotiating the traffic in Lulling High Street. 'I think the school should do *quite well* under him.'

Greatly content, the two friends drove southward to their future.

CHRISTIAN HERALD
People Making A Difference

Christian Herald is a family of dedicated, Christ-centered ministries that reaches out to deprived children in need, and to homeless men who are lost in alcoholism and drug addiction. Christian Herald also offers the finest in family and evangelical literature through its book clubs and publishes a popular, dynamic magazine for today's Christians.

Our Ministries

Family Bookshelf and **Christian Bookshelf** provide a wide selection of inspirational reading and Christian literature written by best-selling authors. All books are recommended by an Advisory Board of distinguished writers and editors.

Christian Herald magazine is contemporary, a dynamic publication that addresses the vital concerns of today's Christian. Each monthly issue contains a sharing of true personal stories written by people who have found in Christ the strength to make a difference in the world around them.

Christian Herald Children. The door of God's grace opens wide to give impoverished youngsters a breath of fresh air, away from the evils of the streets. Every summer, hundreds of youngsters are welcomed at the Christian Herald Mont Lawn Camp located in the Poconos at Bushkill, Pennsylvania. Year-round assistance is also provided, including teen programs, tutoring in reading and writing, family counseling, career guidance and college scholarship programs.

The Bowery Mission. Located in New York City, the Bowery Mission offers hope and Gospel strength to the downtrodden and homeless. Here, the men of Skid Row are fed, clothed, ministered to. Many voluntarily enter a 6-month discipleship program of spiritual guidance, nutrition therapy and Bible study.

Our Father's House. Located in rural Pennsylvania, Our Father's House is a discipleship and job training center. Alcoholics and drug addicts are given an opportunity to recover, away from the temptations of city streets.

Christian Herald ministries, founded in 1878, are supported by the voluntary contributions of individuals and by legacies and bequests. Contributions are tax deductible. Checks should be made out to Christian Herald Children, The Bowery Mission, or to Christian Herald Association.

Administrative Office: 40 Overlook Drive, Chappaqua, New York 10514
Telephone: (914) 769-9000

 Fully-accredited Member
of the Evangelical Council
for Financial Accountability